To the Hermans,

Enjoy the hunt!

Lindsay

Schaffer

THE ADVENTURES OF KELTIN MOORE

The Beast Hunter
Into the North

ALSO FROM LINDSAY SCHOPFER

Lost Under Two Moons
Magic, Mystery and Mirth

The Beast Hunter

A Keltin Moore Adventure

LINDSAY SCHOPFER

to Steve Charak
who taught me how to "just get it down"

ACKNOWLEDGMENTS

First, I want to thank all my loyal fans who have followed *The Beast Hunter* online serial. Your encouragement and faith have meant so much to me throughout this process.

Chris Barrows, Bob Manion, Chad Knapp, and many others for their instruction and advice on both firearms and hunting.

Aaron Volner, for being a great fan, an invaluable source of information, and a good friend.

All my beta readers for their hard work and dedication to the story.

My friends and family for their faith and prayers on my behalf.

And, most of all, my wife Elicia, my eternal companion and best friend.

PROLOGUE – A HUNTER AT WORK

Keltin Moore deftly stepped over a twig, stirring the smoky mist with the toe of his boot. The full moon filled the night with a pale glow between the black trunks of the trees, bathing the forest in ethereal light. Keltin moved slowly through the gray haze, sometimes taking a minute between footfalls. He needed no speed, only stealth. His quarry would not be moving after it had eaten. He knew it would be sleeping.

An hour stretched into three and still Keltin crept forward. The bracken thickened, forcing him to circle the denser pockets of brambles. He held his rifle vertically, angling the long steel barrel towards the sheltered sky to avoid tangling his most prized object in the bushes. The oak stock felt solid and reassuring in his grip, the cool of the metal trigger guard seeping through his gloves.

A rustle in the bracken froze him in mid-step. A long moment passed and Keltin let his hovering foot gently lower to the ground. The faint odor of ammonia drifted through the trees to his nostrils. The beast was before him. Shifting his weight gradually, Keltin inched forward until a shaft of moonlight gave soft definition to the monster lying barely a dozen yards from him.

Its forearms were over-large and muscular, wrapped around

its massive head and serrated horns. The broad shoulders and thick chest flowed into two coiling tails, each tipped with a poisonous barb. The bristles and fur covering its back were blacker than the night around them. Keltin judged the total size of the beast as somewhere between a bull and a gray bear.

His quarry found, Keltin now began the studied examination of his prey. The muscular forearms wrapped around its head made a neck-shot impossible, and the broad shoulders suggested muscles thick enough to halt his bullets before they could find internal organs. Instead, Keltin decided upon a place on the beast's side under one of the extended forearms, where the skin pulled tight just under the joint. He moved a few yards to the left, allowing the angle of his shot the best chance of piercing deep into the beast's chest. Satisfied with his position, Keltin crouched down to finish his final preparations.

The five chambers in his rifle were loaded with Reltac Spinners, designed for deep penetration. Keltin gauged the short distance between himself and the beast and decided to replace the final three bullets with Alpenion rounds filled with the metallic acid belferin. At this range, he knew that if the beast did not fall on the first two shots he'd need it distracted by as much pain as possible to allow him a chance to finish it with the Ripper. He placed this final weapon within easy reach before him. The wicked-looking stabbing point and wide-edged ax blades barely reflected the light of the moon on their tempered surfaces.

Thus prepared, Keltin lifted his rifle to his shoulder and took aim. With practiced ease and steady hands, he aligned the sights with the shadow just below the beast's forearm. He breathed out, breathed in, held it, and fired.

The report of his rifle shattered the still night. The body of the beast shuddered and lurched. The creature rolled and screamed, smashing the brambles around it even as the second shot roared. The beast's howl was like the whine of a teakettle. Despite the two bullets deep in its body the beast stood and straightened, its vivid orange eyes unerringly turning to Keltin's hiding place. It launched itself forward with a gurgling scream, using its coiling double tails and powerful forearms to gallop directly towards him.

Keltin watched the bellowing beast approach and aimed his final shots carefully. One shot to the space between the shoulder and neck, one in the stomach, and one in the elbow. Each shot rocked the massive beast, but still it charged forward. Keltin dropped his rifle and snatched up the Ripper. He stood, taking a defensive stance as the beast continued to bear down on him. For a moment, Keltin's blood chilled in the face of that furious advance. Had all his shots missed their marks?

With only a few yards between them, the beast's wounded elbow gave way, damaged beyond use by the spreading belferin acid. The beast collapsed to the ground and Keltin sprinted forward, swinging the wide blade of the Ripper down onto the beast's uninjured forearm. The blade cut deep, and Keltin leapt back again, barely dodging a flailing swipe from the beast's now useless second limb.

Keltin went back into a defensive stance, but the beast did not rise up again. Thrashing and rolling, the creature floundered in the bracken, unable to attack as the internal damage caused by the Reltac Spinners quickly bled away its life. Keltin stood at a safe distance, watching for signs of a final charge until he was satisfied the beast was mortally wounded. Minutes passed. The creature lay panting and whining on the forest floor as the belferin acid seeped throughout its body. Keltin allowed himself the time to reload and fire two more Spinners into the beast's neck. At last, the forest was silent once again. The beast was slain.

Keltin sank to the ground. He offered a silent prayer of thanks for protection and success before backtracking to his traveling pack. Returning, he knelt next to the still beast and began cutting off its serrated horns with a small saw. The saw was sharp and the work went quickly as he whistled tunelessly to himself.

A fifty jeva bounty for both horns had been the mayor's

offer. He calculated. Five to the church, fifteen sent to his mother and sister. Another ten to replace his ammunition and supplies, and fifteen more to Mrs. Galloway for another month's room and board. That left him a profit of five jeva for himself. He tucked the two horns under one arm, rested his rifle on his other shoulder, and began the trek back to town. As he walked, he smiled and continued whistling, musing to himself what he might spend his extra bounty money on.

CHAPTER 1 – A NEW OPPORTUNITY

Keltin entered the courier's office to the jingling sound of the bell above the door. Mr. Jastin glanced up from a ledger he was totaling.

"Ah, Keltin," he said, pushing his wire-frame spectacles down his nose to look at him. "Are you sending out or picking up today?"

"Sending out. I need fifteen jeva sent to Maplewood," said Keltin, removing the appropriate bank notes from his pocket.

"Of course," said the clerk. "Your mother's address I assume?"

"Yes."

Mr. Jastin gave him a sly smile as he took the jeva notes from him. "This wouldn't be part of the bounty Mayor Cumbly posted over in Brakerville, would it?"

"It would. Just in time too. My rent was coming due this week."

Jastin 'tsked' as he filled out the order of transfer. "I've said it before, son. I'll be the first to hire you for the courier line. I can't think of a better shot or a clearer head to guard the moneybox on the Jackson stagecoach. It's leaving in the morning, and you can make it a one-way trip if you're going somewhere."

Keltin smiled and shook his head. "If I can't find another bounty in time for next month's rent I may take you up on that, but I'd like to stay off that buckboard if I can. Too much jostling and noise for me."

Jastin heaved a sigh and handed Keltin his receipt. "Have it your own way, but you know where to come if you ever need the work."

"I'll remember that."

"Good. Oh, hold on."

Jastin disappeared into the backroom for a moment and returned with a small envelope.

"It arrived on the stage this morning. I was going to send it along to Mrs. Galloway's, but I thought you might want it now."

Keltin eagerly took the letter. He didn't have to read the sending address. He knew the handwriting from ten paces.

"Thank you, Mr. Jastin."

"Take care, lad."

Keltin resisted the urge to tear open the envelope until he was outside. The letter was written in a delicate script, and he devoured every word.

Dear Keltin,

Good luck finding the Brakerville Beast, though knowing you, you've already claimed the bounty and are reading this by Mrs. Galloway's fireplace. I know that I have no reason to fear for you, so I refuse to. Mostly. I'm sure you'll forgive your sister some small amount of worry.

Mother is well. The school year has begun, and she is busy with teaching. I wish the same could be said of me, but unfortunately the Middletons have given me notice and I will no longer be able to work for them. Please don't worry about us however. We will be fine. The money you sent last week was most welcome, and I know that Mother appreciated it too, though she would never say any such thing. You know how she is.

The rest of the letter was mostly gossip involving people

Keltin had never met, but he read it all anyway. Mary ended her letter hoping that Mrs. Galloway was well and that he was safe. Keltin folded the letter and carefully placed it in his pocket to read again later that night.

Dusk was falling, and the lantern lights were beginning to glow in the small town of Gillentown as he began to make his way home. Keltin found himself worrying about his sister's letter, and the news of the loss of her employment. He thought of the fifteen jeva he had just sent to Mary and his mother. Would it be enough? Maplewood was an expensive city, and with Mary out of work, it would be even more difficult for them. He wished that he still had the five-note he'd set aside for himself instead of replacing his worn-out boots in Polockha before coming back to Gillentown.

The tinkling sound of a piano drifted out into the street from the Azure, one of Gillentown's seedier dancehalls. Keltin walked past without even glancing inside. He turned a corner on South Hampton Street and finally saw the welcome glow of Mrs. Galloway's stately boarding house. The rich smells of a home-cooked meal greeted him as he let himself in through the front gate and opened the stout mahogany door.

"It's me, Mrs. Galloway," he called to the kitchen.

"Keltin?"

Mrs. Galloway hurried into the entryway, her face as red as her hair from working over a hot stove. She gave him a fierce hug even as she scolded him.

"How long have you been back in town?"

"I got back just this afternoon. I had to send something at the courier's office before coming back."

She held him at arm's length and tried to glare angrily up at him, though the twinkle in her eyes lessened the effect.

"Well, you might have at least stopped in to let me know you were back and safe. Where were you this time?"

"Brakerville."

"That's right. And did you have any luck there?"

"Yes. I have the rent money right here."

"Oh, well that's good."

Mrs. Galloway took the jeva notes and quickly tucked them away in her apron as if embarrassed to have to take them at all.

"I'm sorry I'm a little late again with the payment," said Keltin. "I got caught in that rainstorm between Polockha and here."

"Did the stagecoach get stuck?"

"No. I didn't take the stage here."

Mrs. Galloway's eyes went wide. "You walked all the way from Polockha?"

"It's not that far, and I wanted to break in my new boots."

"Well, you don't have to worry about the rent. You're all paid up for the rest of the month."

"All right, and I'll do my best to be on time next month."

Mrs. Galloway nodded without meeting his eyes. "I understand that it's difficult for you, but if you could I'd greatly appreciate it." She looked up. "Will you be having dinner here tonight?"

"I wouldn't miss it for the world."

The good woman beamed at him. "Good, it's nearly done. Oh, Keltin, there's a man that's stayed here for two nights now waiting for your return. He's been wanting to speak with you."

"He wants to talk with me? Do you know what about?"

"He hasn't said. Perhaps it's more work for you?"

"Maybe. Do you know which town he came from?"

"Can't say I do, but he seems to be a distinguished gentleman. I think he may be sitting in the parlor just now."

"I'd better go see him then."

"All right. Supper will be ready soon."

She bustled her way back to the kitchen as Keltin went to what Mrs. Galloway insisted on calling her parlor. In reality it was little more than a sitting room, with more dishes than books in the shelves and not a single painting that had felt the brush of the original artist. Still, its polished wood chairs and corner tables were kept scrupulously clean and a welcome fire was always burning in the ample fireplace.

Keltin entered the parlor to find a long, slender man sitting in a low-backed chair reading one of Mrs. Galloway's classical romances. He was well-groomed and sat comfortably in a three-piece charcoal suit. His blonde hair was cut in a conservative style favored by eastern business men and he sported a thick, well-manicured mustache which he stroked absently as he read. Keltin cleared his throat and the man glanced up to give him a polite smile.

"Good evening," he said.

"Good evening. I heard that you wanted to speak with me?"

"Oh, are you Keltin Moore?"

"I am."

"Splendid," said the man, quickly laying aside the novel and standing. "I'm glad to have finally found you."

"I'm sorry I was difficult to find, Mr.-"

"Paulsen," he supplied along with a soft, dry handshake. "Don't trouble yourself over the wait. I was unexpected after all. I have a matter of business that I need to discuss with you."

"All right."

Mr. Paulsen returned to his seat while Keltin sat in the overstuffed chair across from him.

"What do you need?"

"I'll do my best to be brief, Mr. Moore, but there's a certain amount of background information that you should know. First, I am not the one who intends to pay for your services, nor do I work for him in any direct sense. I am an employee of the Bachman Turnstein Bank."

Keltin frowned. "I've never heard of it."

"Really? It's one of the largest banking houses in Krendaria, and has branches in nearly every country on the continent. I am an employee at the Collinsworth branch here in Riltvin. However, the matter I wish to discuss with you comes from our headquarters in Krendaria. A group of some of the bank's most important clients is in need of assistance. From what I understand, they are a partnership of some of the leading nobility in the capital city of Carvalen." Paulsen paused. "Incidentally, have you kept abreast of the civil unrest in that country?"

Keltin shook his head. "The local paper has little in the way of world events. Is there some kind of trouble going on there?"

"Trouble?" Paulsen gave a delicate snort. "Turmoil would be more accurate. The common people claim they are tired of oppression at the hands of the aristocracy, and the nation has never truly recovered after the economic upheaval caused by the Heterack Empowerment in nearby Malpin. Add to that an unpopular distant war with Selvia along with an infant monarch on the throne, and Krendaria's Parliament is in a desperate struggle just to keep the kingdom functioning. Law and order in the capital is tenuous at best, and many think that revolution is not far off, especially if the beast attacks in the north are not stopped. That's why I've come to speak with you."

"I don't understand. What do beast attacks have to do with the threat of a revolution?"

"I'm coming to that. You see, the beasts are appearing in Dhalma Province, just to the north of Carvalen. The region provides most of the crops used in the capital and surrounding provinces. It also experiences seasonal outbreaks of beasts coming down from the largely undeveloped territories to the north, though these are usually contained by the local hunters. However, the influx of beasts this year seems to be much worse than it has been in the recent past. Dhalma farmers have been flooding the capital city for weeks now, adding to the already swelling population and stirring the locals into a near-hysteria with their stories of a horde of ravenous beasts driving them from their homes and crops."

Keltin sat forward in his chair.

"What kind of beasts were the farmers describing?"

"I asked the same thing when I received this assignment, but the man I spoke to said that none of the farmers could agree on a description of the creatures. Some said that they were local predators gone mad, while others swore that they had seen monsters in the fields, and still others claimed that the creatures were made of nothing but smoke and shadow. But whatever they are, these monsters couldn't have come at a worse time.

"The fields will be ready to harvest next month, and that food will be desperately needed. If the Dhalman crops aren't brought in, people could begin starving in the very streets of Carvalen. If that happens, there'll be no stopping a revolution that spills every drop of noble blood in the capital city."

"Why hasn't the military responded?"

"Most of the Krendarian Regulars are locked in trench wars with Selvia in the far south. Even if the troops received redeployment orders today, they wouldn't be able to reach the northern provinces of their homeland until next spring."

"So what's being done?"

"An independent organization of concerned nobility led by Carvalen's Duke Gregson has pooled their resources and offered bounties for each beast that is killed."

"And have the local hunters had much success?"

"It doesn't seem so, and the situation is growing more desperate. Duke Gregson and his partners have taken out a considerable loan from the Bachman Turnstein Bank to double all the bounties. I'm not sure why the bank would agree to a loan like that. Too risky, I'd say, but I suppose they stand to lose just as much in a revolution as the nobility. Bankers may look too much like barons to a murderous mob for their liking."

"And that's why they've sent out employees like you looking for more hunters."

Paulsen nodded. "The bank has seen fit to protect its investment by charging all of its branches with the task of finding capable hunters to assist in the rescue of Dhalma Province and its crops."

Paulsen gave a short sigh and stared into the fire as he continued. "I was given the assignment from my employers at the Collinsworth branch, though I know little of beast hunting and care to know even less. But I have been given a charge, and I gave my word that I would see it through. I made inquiries in Collinsworth, but it seems there's little demand for exotic hunters in that part of Riltvin. I then inquired at the offices of the Collinsworth Gazette and its sister papers, which is where I found the story of how you single-handedly killed the Copperton beast. I thought I'd come out to see if you were all that the local papers made you out to be."

Paulsen looked at Keltin and raised an eyebrow. "Incidentally, was it true that the Copperton beast had two heads?"

Keltin gave a slight smile and shook his head. "I'm afraid the paper that you read felt the need to embellish. The creature only had one head, which was still quite enough for me."

Mr. Paulsen smiled politely and nodded, but made no comment. Keltin sat back in his chair and considered all that the banker had told him. Krendaria had only ever been a name to him, a great presence somewhere off in the world beyond Riltvin. How far away was Dhalma Province from Gillentown? Whatever the distance in miles may be, he knew it would be farther than he'd ever traveled for a beast bounty before.

"How much is the current bounty for each beast?" he asked.

"Forty drechs, though it may have changed since I was given my assignment."

"And how much would that be in Riltvin jeva?"

Paulsen glanced at the ceiling for just an instant as if the answer were written there before replying. "Eighty three jeva and four pence," he said exactly. "The exchange may also have changed, but that was the rate when I left Collinsworth."

Keltin blinked. He'd never heard of such a high bounty for a beast. The fifty he'd received for the forest devil near Brakerville had been his highest take within the last year, and that had only come after two months without a single pence gained. But here was a rich bounty for not just one beast but as many as he could kill.

"Has anyone made a guess at how many creatures there might be?" he asked in an effort to steady his excited nerves.

"Only that the sightings and attacks have taken place over the entire province, which suggests a very large number of the beasts."

Of course. There was only one way that the bounties could be set so high. With so many beasts to contend with, the nobles were taking the chance that most hunters would not return to collect. It was an expensive gamble, but one that these apparently desperate men had considered worth taking.

Keltin looked into the fireplace and watched the logs slowly die into ash as he considered. It would be good money. The best money he'd ever had from a job. It would be a comfort for his mother and sister, especially after the loss of Mary's employment. It would also mean paid rents for Mrs. Galloway, not just on time, but in advance, for once. But all that would only come if he survived the horde of beasts in Krendaria. He was no stranger to danger, but only a cautious hunter lived long enough to be called experienced, and Keltin was very experienced.

After a moment, Paulsen cleared his throat.

"So, Mr. Moore, I've told you the situation as exactly as I can, and I'm sure that you'll receive more specific instructions upon reaching Duke Gregson's estate in Carvalen if you decide to go. Have you come to a decision on the matter?"

Keltin sighed and looked up from the fire. "It sounds very exciting," he admitted. "Forgive me if I need to take some time to think it over, however. I've only just returned from a hunt after all, and I'm still feeling weary and drawn from the road."

"Well, I understand that, but I hope you can come to a decision soon. I've already waited here for two days, and I have other places I must be moving on to."

"I'll consider it. Excuse me."

Keltin rose and left the parlor. Climbing the stairs near the front door, he walked down to the end of the hallway and entered his bedroom for the first time in more than two weeks. It was just as he remembered it. His bed was against a window looking down onto Mrs. Galloway's rose garden and out towards the center of town. A single trunk sat at the end of his bed and a nearby dresser contained what clothing he had that wasn't suited for hunting. A washbasin stood beside a small mirror by the dresser, and he took a long while scrubbing the dust of the road from his face and hands. He was just drying himself with a soft towel from a ring on the wall when Mrs. Galloway's gentle voice drifted up from the downstairs entryway.

"Supper is on, sirs."

Keltin came out of his room just as a tall figure appeared in the doorway opposite him.

"Ah Keltin," it rumbled gently, "I thought I heard you stirring across the way."

A gentlemanly Loopi from the east, Mr. Renlowah was Mrs. Galloway's only other regular boarder. While his inhuman appearance had unsettled many of the Riltvinians not familiar with his people's long soft fur or ape-like faces, Renlowah had shown himself a gentle soul with no desire but to establish himself in the humble trade of a gardener. Despite the rough nature of his work, the Loopi was dressed for supper in a dining suit that Keltin always felt lent a spirit of formality to the evening meals when he was home.

"Good to see you, Mr. Renlowah," he said, shaking the incredibly large hand that was proffered to him.

"And you, my boy. You look well. I suppose you were successful in Brakerville then?"

Keltin nodded. "I got the bounty without getting hurt. That's always the goal."

"Indeed. What type of beast was it then?"

"A forest devil."

"I don't believe you've ever mentioned that type before. What was it like?"

Keltin described the beast and his hunt as they made their way to the dining room downstairs. They found an appetizing dinner of farmer's stew and freshly baked bread with marmalade and cream. Mr. Paulsen was already seated at the table but rose to greet them as they entered. Mrs. Galloway soon appeared with pitchers of cold cider and milk and they all sat to enjoy the meal together.

"Well, Mr. Paulsen," said the good woman as she poured herself a glass of cider, "were you able to speak with our

Keltin?"

"Yes, though he's yet to give me his decision."

"Indeed?" Mr. Renlowah gave Keltin a curious look. "It's unlike you to turn down a bounty, my boy."

"This time it's a little different from the usual bounty."

Keltin briefly told them the situation in northern Krendaria as Mr. Paulsen had described it to him.

"How horrible," murmured Mrs. Galloway.

Mr. Renlowah nodded. "It seems that Krendaria is on the edge of a most tragic season in its history."

"I have to admit that it all feels much too big for me," said Keltin. "A single beast I can handle easily. I've hunted pairs and even a few small packs. But a horde of the things?" He shook his head.

"Keep in mind, Mr. Moore, that you will not be alone in Dhalma Province," said Paulsen. "Hunters are coming from all over the continent to join in this hunt."

Mr. Renlowah paused in buttering a slice of bread. "If that's the case, then I see little reason for you to pass by this opportunity, Keltin. Consider the adventure of it, not to speak of the rewards and the good that you might do for the people of Krendaria."

Keltin nodded. "Maybe you're right. Heaven knows I could use the money, and if I'm not the only hunter working on the bounty, it may just be worth the risk. Besides, I've never been out of Riltvin. This could be my chance." He sighed. "But there are other problems."

"Like what, for instance?"

"Well, I don't have the money to go."

"What happened to the rest of the bounty money from Brakerville?" asked Mrs. Galloway.

"I sent most of it to Mary this afternoon."

Mrs. Galloway flushed slightly and placed an apologetic hand on his arm. "I'm sorry, I shouldn't have asked. It's really none of my business."

"It's all right," he said, gently patting her hand.

"Keltin," said Mr. Renlowah after a moment, "while you

were at the courier's office, did you happen to see Mr. Jastin?"

"Yes, he helped me with the transfer."

"Did he mention when the Jackson coach was leaving? I was hoping to send along a letter to Mr. Gubbins and ask for some more flower bulbs before the seasons change again."

"Yes, he mentioned it was leaving in the morning… that's it!"

"What's it?"

Keltin grinned and turned to Mr. Paulsen. "I think I'll be able to go to Krendaria after all. I'll be on the Jackson stagecoach in the morning, heading east."

"But how will you pay the fare?" asked Mrs. Galloway.

"I won't have to. Mr. Jastin offered to pay me to ride with the moneybox on the coach." Keltin made a quick calculation in his head. "I should make enough on the trip to take another coach to Collinsworth, and then the train to Carvalen. I may even have a little extra to buy more ammunition and supplies."

"Well I'm glad to hear it," said Mr. Paulsen. "My employers in Collinsworth will be happy to know that I've found at least one hunter for them."

"Will you be heading with me on the morning coach as well then?"

"I'm afraid not. I still have a few more individuals I should try to find before I return. After all, you're not the only hunter in this region that I found through my searches at the Collinsworth Gazette."

Keltin, Mrs. Galloway, and Mr. Renlowah exchanged curious looks.

"Really?" said Keltin. "Who else did you read about?"

"Well, there's a Mr. Thornton in Riksville I wanted to contact next."

"Oh, I'm afraid Mr. Thornton won't be able to help you," said Mrs. Galloway. "He retired last spring. I think he lost an eye to a beast, poor man."

"I see. Well, then there's really only one other fellow I want to try finding, though I'm not sure I'll have much luck. No one seems to know his real name. The papers call him the Shadow.

According to the Gazette, he saved an entire miner's camp from a subterranean monster at the Brighton copper mine."

Mr. Renlowah smiled. "You may be in luck, Mr. Paulsen. I think I can help you find him."

"Really? You know where he is?"

"Certainly. He's sitting across the table from me."

Mr. Paulsen looked at Keltin. "You're not serious."

Keltin grinned and shrugged. "I was hired by the mine's owner to handle the problem," he explained. "I never dealt with the miners directly. I was in and out in a hurry, and the workers gave me the nickname Shadow. I suppose the papers liked it better than my own name."

Mr. Paulsen blinked and nodded. "Well, it seems that I've exhausted all of my potential leads in the course of one meal. I'm only glad I waited the two days to meet with you. I suppose we'll be traveling companions on the stage after all, if it hasn't already been completely filled."

"I'll run by Mr. Jastin's after supper and let him know we're coming."

"You should probably go now, Keltin, before it gets any later," suggested Mrs. Galloway. "Don't worry. I'll save you a piece of pound cake. Run on now."

Keltin dutifully rose from the table and went to find the courier's home. He found Mr. Jastin just sitting down at his own supper, and quickly described his reason in coming. Jastin happily told him that he was welcome to serve as the rifleman on the Jackson stage, and that he'd keep a seat open for Mr. Paulsen.

As he bid the courier a good night and stepped back out into the cool air outside, Keltin wondered just what he was getting himself into. He struggled to remember what little he had ever heard about faraway Krendaria. He tried to imagine the ancient city of Carvalen nestled among the Sky Top Mountains. He'd never been further east than Collinsworth, and had only been in a big city a handful of times. He tried to comfort himself by remembering that most of his time would be spent in the northern provinces, away from the throngs of people he was sure he'd find at the capital.

Thinking of Carvalen, Keltin looked around at Gillentown as most of its humble people settled in for the night. He had seen little of his hometown in the last year. Beast hunts and traveling from town to town kept him away so much that he sometimes wondered if he'd be better served by storing his belongings at the courier's office rather than renting his room from Mrs. Galloway. He'd never seriously considered it however. If only for a few days at a time, it was good to have a home to return to.

Passing by the Azure on his way home, Keltin saw a woman standing outside and smoking. He didn't recognize her and tried not to look in her direction. She called out to him all the same.

"Where are you bound, handsome?"

Keltin allowed himself a slight scowl, knowing she couldn't see his face in the darkness.

"Home," he said.

"So early? Maybe you'd fancy a quick stop before facing the missus?"

He made no reply and quickly left the Azure behind him. There were some things he was more than ready to leave behind him whenever he left for the wilds.

Returning to Mrs. Galloway's, he found supper already cleared from the dining room table. Mr. Renlowah and Mr. Paulsen both seemed to have retired to their rooms early, but Mrs. Galloway was still up and about as she washed dishes in the kitchen. She glanced up from scrubbing a pot as Keltin walked in.

"Did you find Mr. Jastin then?"

He nodded. "Yes, it's all arranged."

"Good, good. Oh, I left your dessert for you there."

She pointed to a generous slice of cake and a glass of milk set on the small table near the stove. The cake had a large helping of cream set beside it and Keltin savored each bite.

"I wish I could enjoy this sort of meal more often," he said.

"You might, if you ever stayed in town long enough for one

of the young ladies here to get a good look at you."

Keltin shrugged. "Maybe someday."

"You should take care with 'somedays' Keltin. They can be deceptive if you're not careful."

"Yes ma'am, I will."

"Are you teasing me, Mr. Moore?"

"Not on my life."

"I didn't think so."

Mrs. Galloway finished rinsing the last of the dishes and placed them in a rack to dry. She turned and looked over the kitchen for a moment, then gave a satisfied nod and sat down beside him with a sigh.

"Will you be wanting a travel sack ready for you in the morning?"

"If it's not too much trouble."

"No, it's no trouble. I'll put it together in the morning. Anything you'd like in it?"

"Could I have some more of this cake?"

Mrs. Galloway smiled and patted his arm. "Of course, but I don't think it will last you to Krendaria."

"I doubt it will last to Jackson."

They chuckled together as Keltin finished his dessert and milk. He was about to excuse himself when Mrs. Galloway seemed to decide to say something to him.

"Keltin, I was wondering. I know you'll be heading through Collinsworth on your way to Krendaria. I hoped you might do something for me."

"Of course. Was there some errand you wanted me to run for you? Something you want sent back here?"

Mrs. Galloway took a breath. "I was wondering if you'd go and see Angela for me."

Keltin went silent. He suddenly remembered the strange woman outside of the Azure and felt himself go cold inside.

"She's… she's still there then?"

"I think so. Her last letter was from there. But it's been so long, and she hasn't answered any of my letters. It's been months Keltin. I would have gone to see her, but…"

"No. You don't need to go to see her. I'll find her for you."

Relief showed plainly on the good woman's features. "Thank you. I know it's hard for you."

"Will you have a letter for me to give her?"

"Yes, I'll write it tonight. I'll give you the address that she's sent from before, but I'm not sure it's still good."

"Don't worry, I'll find her for you."

"Thank you, Keltin."

He nodded and rose from the table. "I better get some rest. I'll have a long day ahead of me tomorrow."

"Oh, of course. Have a good night."

Keltin turned and quietly went upstairs, knowing full well he would not sleep for a long time. Lying awake in his bed, he tried to think about Krendaria and hordes of beasts, but all he could see was a face that he had desperately tried to forget for a long, long time.

* * *

It was still dark outside when Keltin rose from his bed to begin preparing his pack for the journey. He replaced the dingy clothes he had worn for the last few weeks with fresh garments from his dresser before kneeling in front of the chest at the foot of his bed. Opening the heavy lid and gently setting aside the box filled with letters from Mary, he withdrew his grandfather's old infantry pistol. An early Grantville revolver with five chambers, it was old and battered, having seen battle in the Three Forest War, but Keltin always kept it clean and serviceable. He rarely took it on hunts, but something told him that he might need the added protection of a smaller firearm which he could keep close at hand.

Slipping the revolver into his hunting jacket, he slung his pack over his shoulder and eased open his bedroom door. Moving soundlessly out of sheer habit, he was a little surprised when the door across from his own opened to reveal Mr. Renlowah, already dressed and ready for the day.

"On your way then, lad?" he asked softly.

Keltin nodded. "I'm surprised that you heard me."

The Loopi smiled gently. "I've long been an early riser. I wanted to wish you luck."

"You've never gotten up to see me off before."

"And you've never left the country to go hunting either." Mr. Renlowah's kind face turned serious. "Listen to me Keltin, remember that things to the east are very different from here in Riltvin. In many ways, the people in the hill country are much less complicated than their neighbors. You may see things you'll wish that you hadn't. I just thought that you should be warned." The Loopi sighed and shook his head. "But listen to me. I got up to wish you luck, so I will. Good luck my lad, and return safely to us."

They shook hands and Keltin turned to descend the stairs as he puzzled over Mr. Renlowah's odd advice. Reaching the bottom floor, he could hear the sound of papers rustling and drawers being opened and closed in the parlor. He peeked around the corner and found Mrs. Galloway feverishly searching through a small desk against the far wall.

"Good morning," he said softly.

"Oh! Keltin, you startled me. I was just pulling things together. Your provisions are all packed for you and sitting on the kitchen table."

She finally found an envelope for the letter that was clutched in her hands. Sealing it closed, she added it to a small bundle of letters and handed them to him. "The address is on the letters," she said, her voice catching slightly.

Keltin took the letters and carefully placed them in an inner pocket of his jacket.

"I promise, I'll get them to her."

"Thank you."

The good woman gave him a brief, tender hug before pulling away and turning towards the kitchen.

"Well, I better see to getting breakfast set out."

Mr. Paulsen and Mr. Renlowah soon joined them for a quick meal of warmed scones and marmalade. Keltin bid Mrs. Galloway a final farewell before leaving with the banker to make his way to the courier's office in the early morning light. They found the stagecoach waiting, and the driver, a stocky fellow named Bilson, helping an elderly woman up the coach's steep steps.

"Good to have you along, Moore," he said as he climbed up into the driver's seat. "Though I don't know why Jastin makes such a fuss. It's a quiet road to Jackson. Still, I'll appreciate a hand with this luggage."

Keltin obligingly handed up the cases and trunks belonging to the several passengers before helping Mr. Jastin's oldest son to carry the moneybox from the office and install it under his seat on the buckboard. He swung up into his position at Bilson's side as the driver snapped the reins and steered the four horses down the sleepy street. Keltin placed his rifle across his lap and settled in for the long ride.

"Just make sure you don't fall asleep," said Bilson as they left the town and passed onto the eastward road.

Keltin was about to respond, when one of the wagon wheels jumped a rut and nearly threw him from his seat. Struggling to keep himself from falling off the coach, Keltin decided that nodding off on this trip would be his last concern.

CHAPTER 2 – WHAT TO TAKE, WHAT TO LEAVE

"Welcome to Collinsworth! Everybody off."

Keltin descended the short steps from the stagecoach with relief. Riding inside the Collinsworth stage from Jackson had not been any more comfortable than the bone-jarring trip from Gillentown. Extracting his rifle and pack from the storage net in the back of the coach, Keltin was grateful to know that the rest of his long trip would take place on rails rather than country roads.

Steam trains were still new to most of rural Riltvin, but in Collinsworth the rails of the Longston Line had become the veins carrying the growing city's lifeblood. Trees, grown in the fertile soil of the misty hill country, were cut, stripped, and processed in newly minted factories before being shipped to Krendaria, Malpin, and other nations eager for the quality of Riltvinian lumber. Even at the edge of town, Keltin could hear the distant grinding of saws and smell the acrid smoke of brush piles and coal.

Mr. Paulsen set down his traveling case beside him, took a deep breath of the smoky air, and smiled.

"Well Mr. Moore, we've arrived at last. If you'll just come

with me to the bank, I can give you a letter of referral to Duke Gregson."

Keltin nodded and followed the banker to the local branch of the Bachman Turnstein Bank in the city's growing business district. Entering the austere brick building, Keltin couldn't help but feel somewhat out of place among the finely dressed businessmen and tellers all quietly exchanging currency from a variety of nations. Mr. Paulsen left him only briefly in the foyer before returning with a small envelope addressed to Duke Gregson.

"Will you be taking the noon train?" he asked.

"No, I have some errands to run in town."

Paulsen nodded and extended his hand.

"Well then, good luck to you, Mr. Moore."

"Thank you."

The banker started to turn, then seemed to think of something else.

"Incidentally, should you happen to come back this way, may I recommend our bank as a wise investment for any bounty money you might acquire in Krendaria?"

Keltin gave him a slight smile. "I'll consider it."

"Very good. Farewell."

Paulsen left and Keltin turned to make his way to the train station. The last train to Carvalen was leaving at four. He bought a ticket and counted what was left of his payment from the Jackson stagecoach job. Seven jeva and some change. Not much to live on, but enough to buy more ammunition with a little left over. After a quick consultation of a newly printed map of the city at the station, he made his way to a likely looking market district and began his search.

He wandered among the various carpentry shops, general stores, and other craftsmen stalls for more than an hour before finally asking a passing constable for a reputable gunsmith. Keltin followed the man's directions to a clean building that stood closer to the homes of Collinsworth's working class than the market district. The shop itself seemed to be an extension of the smith's home with a partially enclosed area nearby that housed a large, well-kept forge. Keltin spied the smith and his apprentice at work, shaping a tube of metal that he supposed would eventually become the barrel of a deadly rifle. Leaving the man and his apprentice to their work, he stepped into the shop to find a pretty young girl of no more than fourteen surrounded by a collection of expertly made firearms as well as more mundane household amenities and farming tools.

"Can I help you, sir?" she asked, pulling a stray lock of blonde hair behind one ear.

"I need ammunition as well as fresh oil and polish for both of these," he said, laying his hunting rifle and his grandfather's old army pistol on the counter. The girl picked up the pistol first, turning it in her hands for a moment.

"I haven't seen very many five chamber revolvers. Who makes it?"

"It's a Grantville revolver. It used to be my grandfather's."

"You've kept it up very well," the girl said as she opened the gun's chamber and examined the pistol's interior. "There's hardly any powder buildup and no corrosion to speak of."

Keltin smiled. "I do my best."

The girl nodded and turned her attention to the hunting rifle. Despite its considerable weight she lifted it, checked its chamber, and sighted along its length.

"This has been modified," she said after a moment. "I'd almost guess it was originally a Capshire bison rifle, but not quite. The stock is oak for one thing, and the sights are different."

Keltin shook his head in amazement at the young girl.

"You certainly know your wares. No, this isn't Capshire make. It's actually a rifle my uncle Byron Moore made."

"I've heard my father speak of Byron Moore's work, but I've never seen one of his pieces before." She set it down gently on the counter. "It's very nice. Is your uncle still working up in the hill country?"

"He retired last spring. I've been looking for a good gunsmith ever since."

The girl gave him a bright smile. "Then I'm glad to tell you that you've finally found one. My father is very good. Not as good as your uncle perhaps, but definitely the best you'll find in eastern Riltvin. It's a shame that you aren't looking to buy one of his pieces."

"Perhaps next time," Keltin said with a friendly smile.

The girl gave a little sigh and nodded. "Well, let me show you what we have. What caliber of shot do you need?"

Keltin told her and she quickly retrieved a variety of boxes from the shelves behind the counter. Keltin selected a couple of boxes of Reltac Spinners, some Haurizer Smashers, a small box of acid-filled Alpenions, and some Capshire Standard rounds for the pistol. After a moment he picked up a second box of acid-filled Alpenions and sighed.

"You favor the Alpenions?" the girl asked.

He nodded. "It's the belferin acid," he explained. "It's fast and works best on joints and organs. I'll admit I'm somewhat partial to the rounds, but they're so expensive."

"It's the cost of making the acid, not to mention that they're somewhat of a specialty item. Few hunters want to use them, as the acid can ruin the meat of their game."

"That doesn't matter to me. I don't want to eat the things that I kill."

The girl glanced up at him a moment, then her eyes went a little wide. "You're a beast hunter."

"That's right."

"I should have known. If Byron Moore is your uncle…"

"I'm Keltin Moore. My family has been hunting beasts in the hill country for three generations."

The girl nodded slowly, placing her hand on the stock of his hunting rifle.

"And this is what you use?"

Keltin nodded. The girl seemed to consider that for a moment, then turned and left the store through a backdoor. A moment later she returned, carrying a box of ammunition he didn't recognize.

"You might want to try these," she said. "Father just got them this week. We haven't had time to stock them yet."

"What are they?"

"Capshire Shatter Rounds. They're designed to penetrate before blowing apart. They may cause nearly as much damage as the Alpenions, and they're certainly cheaper."

Keltin removed one of the bullets from the box and considered it for a long moment.

"Has your father tested them yet?"

The girl grinned. "No, but I have."

"And?"

"We'll need to build a new testing target."

"I'll take them."

"Very good. I'll just fetch your oil and polish and total it all up."

"Thank you, Miss."

"Jessica."

"Thank you Jessica." Keltin couldn't help chuckling a little. "I take it your father had no sons?" he asked.

"Oh, I have two brothers," she answered over her shoulder. "One of them is apprenticed to a baker here in town."

"And the other?"

"He's four."

Keltin shook his head with a bemused smile and counted out the jeva notes into Jessica's open hand. She returned his change and wished him well.

"Good luck on your next hunt, Mr. Moore. Remember us when you need to restock."

"I certainly will. Thank you."

Keltin stepped back out into the street and checked his pocket watch. Ten minutes to two. He had time for one more errand. One he had been putting off.

He removed the small bundle of letters from an inside pocket of his jacket and checked Mrs. Galloway's neat handwriting on the envelope. The delicately scripted name brought a painful lump to his throat, but he fought it down to look at the street address. He didn't recognize it, but decided that he wouldn't go back into the gunsmith's shop to ask

Jessica where the street was. A girl like her would probably have no idea anyway.

He wandered for a few minutes until he spotted a sorry figure slouched in an alleyway and cradling a bottle of cheap spirits. Keltin approached the miserable looking man.

"Do you know where Gallant Street is?"

The grimy man looked up, a natural suspicion in his eyes.

"What for?" he asked with a slur.

"I… I have someone I need to meet there."

The man laughed in a hoarse bark revealing a gap-toothed, rotting smile. "I'll bet you do. Looking for the 'Rose are you? First time, maybe?"

Keltin scowled. "Do you know where it is or not?"

The man waved his hand in a southerly direction. "It's down that way… and if you see Gabrielle, tell her I'll be back as soon as I get some money."

Keltin turned his back on the man and tried not to notice how hot his face suddenly felt. Walking in the direction that the man had indicated, Keltin couldn't help noticing how Collinsworth slowly changed around him. It seemed that all of the city's lumber mills were upwind of this part of town, and every building bore a dingy coat of coal dust over its whitewashed walls. The air was stagnant, and Keltin imagined his lungs soon looking much like the buildings that he passed. The people on the street looked haggard and worn, each of them eyeing him suspiciously as he searched for street signs. He noticed several shady characters watching him from cluttered alleyways, but they seemed to give a wide berth to both him and the hunting rifle in his hands.

He found Gallant Street and followed it, watching the numbers climb on the grimy buildings until he stopped in front of a large two-story townhouse. A faded sign near the door read "The Gallant Rose". Keltin drew in a deep breath and walked inside. The entryway was dimly lit by a single oil lamp, illuminating an ample woman sitting at a small table playing cards with herself. Seeing him enter, she lifted her bulk from the protesting chair and smiled.

"Hello there, I don't believe I've seen you here before. What can I do for you?"

"I'm here to deliver a message."

The woman's welcoming smile died and left a slight scowl on her jowled face. "Oh? To whom?"

Keltin's voice caught slightly on the name. "Angela."

"You can leave it with me. I'll see that she gets it."

Keltin was tempted to just hand her the letters and leave. The air in the Gallant Rose was close and full of stale perfume that made it difficult for him to think. He was about to hand over the package when he remembered Mrs. Galloway's glistening eyes when she had given it to him. His grip on the letters tightened protectively.

"I was asked to give it to her in person."

"Well I'm afraid she's… occupied with another visitor right now."

The woman gave him a sly smile and a wink. Keltin felt as if he'd been kicked in the stomach, but he kept his face a hard mask.

"I'll wait."

"It could be a while. Would you like to enjoy some company while you wait?"

Keltin clenched his jaw until it hurt.

"No."

The woman shrugged and showed him to a sitting room lit by several dirty windows. He chose a faded, stained chair in a corner and sat, placing his pack on the floor beside him and his hunting rifle across his lap.

Time passed. Another man came into the room and sat down. Several women came to him one at a time, each speaking softly to him until he finally got up and left with one of them. Keltin focused his attention through the window on a grimy building across the street during each hushed conversation.

At last, he heard a soft step on the worn wooden floor and recognized a familiar voice.

"Keltin?"

He forced himself to look up. She was skinnier than he remembered. Her long brown hair had been twisted into a mound of matted curls, her face a mask of unfamiliar makeup. He refused to look closely at the dress she was wearing as she came into the room.

"What are you doing here?" she asked.

Her voice seemed tight, uncertain. What was she thinking? Did she think that he had come to… Keltin put the thought out of his mind as he stood and closed the distance between them without looking her in the eyes.

"Your mother wanted me to give you these."

He reached into his pocket and withdrew the letters. Angela took the bundle and looked at it in confusion.

"My mother wrote to me? I haven't heard from her in months."

"She's tried sending you letters before, but you never responded."

"But I never got any letters."

"Well, she asked me to see that you got these ones and read them."

"Alright, but I don't know how I didn't get her other letters."

Keltin couldn't help giving a suspicious look over Angela's shoulder at the woman in the entryway, but she seemed to be ignoring them. Angela opened the most recent letter and read it silently. After a moment, she heaved a heavy sigh, folded it closed, and slipped it into her pocket along with the rest.

"Thank you Keltin," she said softly.

"You're welcome."

Keltin hesitated for a moment, unsure if he should say anything. But there was nothing to say. Nothing that would not hurt them both. He turned, picked up his pack and rifle, and stepped around her towards the front door. Angela quickly placed a hesitant hand on his arm. He stopped as if her touch were an iron chain.

"Will you be in town long?" she asked.

Keltin fought a lump in his throat. "No, I'm leaving on the

four o'clock train. I should be heading there now."

"Could I walk with you to the station?"

"All right," he heard himself say.

Keltin waited in the doorway as Angela took a ratty shawl from a hook in the hallway and draped it around herself.

"I'll only be gone for a little while, Ms. Nall. I'll be back soon."

"See that you are," the woman called as Keltin held the door open for Angela. "Don't forget whose regular night it is. He'll be expecting-"

Keltin slammed the door on the rest of Ms. Nall's words.

They stepped out into the street and began silently walking side by side.

"You're looking well, Keltin," she said finally.

"Thank you."

He tried to return the compliment, but couldn't.

"I'm glad I was able to find you."

Another long silence passed between them.

"Where are you going?" she asked.

"Krendaria. There's a duke there who needs help with a large group of beasts attacking some farmlands."

"Will it be dangerous?"

"Perhaps."

"Well, be careful."

The gentle words sang and blended with memory in his mind. He recalled the same words spoken in that gentle voice tinged with fear and concern over and over again. Keltin found himself speaking before he could stop himself.

"I... missed you," he said.

Angela turned to look at him. "Really?"

Keltin nodded. "For a long time."

"But not anymore?"

Keltin finally looked into Angela's eyes. They were the same eyes he'd stared into for hours. The eyes that had ruled his dreams and thoughts for so long... But they were different now. There was no light behind them. She stared at him with cold, hungry eyes, filled with emptiness. He didn't know these eyes.

"No," he said, his voice barely more than a whisper. "Not anymore."

They walked the rest of the way in silence. People watched as they passed and may have thought them an odd pair, but no one sought to intrude upon them. Keltin walked mechanically, wishing that Angela would leave him. Wishing that she would stay.

They came to the train station too soon. Keltin stopped, keeping his eyes straight ahead.

"I need to go." He took a breath. "Take care of yourself."

He forced himself forward, his back to the young woman on the corner.

"Good luck in Krendaria, Keltin."

He swiftly made his way to the sighing train. Running a hand over his eyes, he entered the railcar, not trusting himself to look back.

CHAPTER 3 – A CHANGE OF PLANS

Keltin woke for what seemed to be the fifth time in the last hour. Usually, he was grateful to be a light sleeper and could remember several times when it had saved his life while on a hunt. But as he struggled to find a comfortable position slouched against the window of the cramped passenger car, he couldn't help feeling envious of the old man softly snoring in the seat across from him.

The two-day trip through Riltvin had been uneventful. They had passed without incident over the Krendarian border the day before and there was still a solid night's traveling before the train would reach Carvalen in the morning. Keltin finally gave up on sleep and watched the scenery speeding past his window as evening fell on the countryside. He had spent most of the trip looking out his window as the thick forests of the hill country had slowly changed to copses of evergreens separated by farmers' fields and pastureland.

Keltin watched the passing scenery until the last of the light had faded. With a sigh he rose and quietly left the tiny room, making his way along the rattling hallway towards the dining car. He'd stretched the food in his travel bag as far as he could, but at last he'd have to delve into his meager funds for some sort of dinner.

The dining car resembled a fine restaurant, with oil lamps at each table and uniformed servers expertly swaying with the motion of the train as they balanced their trays and plates. One man eased by him with a bottle of wine and several glasses perched on his tray.

"Just have a seat anywhere, sir," he said.

Keltin sat, feeling ill at ease and very uncertain. He'd exchanged the last of his jeva notes and pence for Krendarian drechs and marks. He felt the unfamiliar currency in his pocket and wondered whether he'd have enough for a decent meal. The server returned and handed him a single-page menu while setting a small basket of rolls on his table.

"Will you be having anything to drink, sir?" he asked.

Keltin glanced around at all the other patrons sipping wine, spirits, and strong Krendarian beer.

"Just water."

Glancing over the menu, Keltin was surprised to see that the price of each entrée was less than he might have expected, though his grasp of the currency exchange was shaky at best. He ordered the cheapest meal available, and then set upon the rolls, stashing every other one in his empty tuck sack.

Dinner turned out to be a large, spicy sausage favored by Krendarians as well as roasted potatoes, greens, and more rolls with jam. As he ate, Keltin looked around the dining car and noticed a discarded newspaper at a nearby table. The banner at the top identified it as an issue of the Carvalen Gazette, and he examined its various stories and features.

The front-page story detailed some sort of debate currently going on in the nation's Parliament. The issue at hand was who should hold the key to government while King Lewis was yet an infant monarch. There were plenty of eager parties, including the Queen Mother Alamiss. Apparently, the women of the royal family have never had much political influence and the queen felt that this would be a perfect time to change that. According to the article, she would see the authority of queen as an equal to that of a king, but many conservatives within Parliament were against it.

Moving on through the paper, he looked for any mention of the beast attacks in Dhalma Province. He found the article between a report on a factory riot and an arsonist's fire. Duke Gregson was mentioned, as well as an appeal for any interested parties to inquire at his estate in the Upper Quarter of the city.

He was just about to go back and read about the riot when he was suddenly thrown from his chair by a violent motion from the railcar. He was up on his feet with rifle in hands before he realized that the train had come to a sudden stop. Looking around the dining car, Keltin was surprised to see that very little had been upset by the violent movement. Even the oil lamps on the tables remained upright and burning on each table. Reaching out to the lamp on his own table, he tugged at it and found it firmly secured to the table's surface.

The indignant voices of the passengers mingled with the reassurances of the servers. The door to the front of the dining car opened and a uniformed employee of the railway entered, looking out of breath and seemingly in a rush towards the back of the train.

"What is it? Why have we stopped?" demanded one of the finely dressed passengers.

"The track's been blown in front of the train," said the man as he tried to rush past.

"What?" The passenger stood squarely in the unfortunate man's way. "What do you mean? How? When?"

"I don't know sir, but we just barely saw the signal from the rail workers in time to stop."

A great clamor of voices filled the dining car once more. Keltin paused only long enough to quickly wrap the remains of his dinner in his newspaper and left the car. Dropping to the ground, he followed the small crowd of onlookers up the line of cars to the engine and the much larger crowd already assembled there.

The damage to the tracks ahead was extensive. Railroad ties were scattered like children's toys in the glaring light of the engine's headlamp. Keltin knelt next to one of the rails. Its broken end was ragged and twisted, like a broken bone reaching for its other half a stone's throw farther down the line.

Nearby, a soot-stained man who may have been the train's driver was speaking with a tired looking railway worker.

"…just last night," the worker was saying. "We heard the blast a half mile away. Blew it out from here all the way to the junction."

"Trash-picking arsonists," muttered the driver. "Why couldn't they keep their plaguing bombs in the capital?"

Keltin turned away and squinted into the darkness, trying to distinguish the lay of the land. It seemed to be mostly farmland, level and easy enough for walking. He'd covered much harder ground in the hills of Riltvin. If he started out now, he should reach Carvalen by some time the next evening. Shouldering his pack, he began walking. Following the demolished tracks, he left the train behind him and continued on, alone, to Carvalen.

* * *

Keltin was up before the sun and traveling again the next morning. Trudging along the side of the railroad tracks, he studied Krendaria's Sky Top Mountains looming in the distance. Dawn light stained the mountains' snowy canvass shades of pink and orange, and Keltin sucked in a deep breath of awe at the sight.

With the endurance of a man familiar with long hunts all over the hill country of Riltvin, Keltin traveled for the better part of the day before finally spying signs of the capital city. Passing a smaller station along the line, he paused long enough to check his distance and estimated that he would arrive in Carvalen shortly before nightfall. Grateful for his sturdy new boots, Keltin pressed on. His first sight of the capital came as the sun sank to the horizon behind him, bathing the city's gleaming domes and spires in the vivid colors of a north country sunset. Even from a mile away, Keltin was impressed at the masterfully sculpted stonework of the magnificent buildings before him. Drawing closer, he realized that his imagination had fallen far short in anticipating the size of the city. Collinsworth could have scarcely called itself a quarter of the Krendarian capital's size. Keltin tried not to feel an overwhelming insignificance as he passed through the outer portions of the city and on towards the Carvalen station. The acrid smell of soot and grease greeted him as he threaded his way around the railcars, each one eagerly awaiting the repair of the rails miles away. Stepping up to one of the platforms, Keltin tried to make sense of a sprawling, grimy map attached to the wall. After studying the unfamiliar streets for a moment he gave up and entered the station house. A bored-looking ticket agent glanced up from a smear novel he was reading behind his barred window.

"No trains running today. Maybe the tracks will be clear in a few days."

"I don't need a train. I need to get to Duke Gregson's estate here in the city."

The ticket agent snorted. "Good luck on foot. Safer to wait until the cabbies start running again."

"When would that be?"

"Who knows? They've been on strike four days now."

Keltin glanced out the window at the fading light. Unless he could find the estate soon, he'd have to settle on somewhere to spend the night. He turned back to the ticket agent.

"Well, where is the estate?"

"I suppose the Upper Quarter," said the agent as he went back to his book.

"And where's that? What direction?"

The agent sighed and lowered his book again. "Northeast. But you'd have to cross the Industrial Quarter to get there. I wouldn't advise that at night."

"Is there a hotel where I can stay?"

"Several. Closest is just across the way. The Emerald."

"Thanks."

The agent went back to his book and Keltin left the station. The street was dark and sparsely peopled. Street lamps stood dormant at every visible street corner. Keltin wondered if the lamplighters were also on strike. Crossing the street, he entered the large building across the way. Unlike the street outside, the inside of the Emerald was brightly lit and elegant in its décor. A uniformed bellhop glanced in his direction, seemed to take him in at a glance, and quickly disappeared through a nearby door.

The desk clerk was a dapper man with slicked black hair and curls at each end of an impressive mustache. He took in Keltin's appearance with a single glance and gave him a smile that was civil if not friendly.

"How may I help you, sir?"

Keltin glanced around the fine furnishing of the entryway. "How much for a room?"

"Seven and four."

"Just for one night?"

The clerk took a deep breath that strained his courteous smile. "Perhaps sir, I can suggest the Turnover Hotel for your needs."

"Where's that?"

"Seven streets to the west."

Without wasting the breath to say goodbye, Keltin turned and left the Emerald to make his way westward through the darkened streets. The day's walking had finally eroded away his considerable stamina as he wearily dodged growing piles of garbage in the street and on the walkways. He saw few people on the street, and what few there were seemed content to remain just where they were for the night. Tired as he was, Keltin's hunter senses refused to relax in the strange city. Every shadow was searched, each dark figure assessed and evaluated. It felt strange, being wary of people instead of beasts.

He noticed the dilapidated buildings beginning to lean dangerously against each other and guessed that he had entered the city's Lower Quarter. With two streets left to go before reaching the Turnover Hotel, Keltin was struck by a sensation he had come to trust beyond hesitation. He knew -he could feel- that he was being watched. The street was sparsely lit and he saw no sign of anyone else, but something was there. Something close.

"Hands up, gob, or I'll-"

Keltin spun and swung his rifle towards the sound. The gun's solid barrel connected with a meaty crack against the shadowy figure's head and sent him to the ground. Keltin leveled his rifle at the still figure, but it wasn't needed. The figure was lying still in the filth of the street. Kneeling cautiously, Keltin felt for a pulse and found it steady and strong. The light was too faint to see any detail in the would-be thief, but he was able to find the rusty knife that the man had been holding. Tossing the blade into a waste bin, Keltin turned and walked on quickly, eager to leave the scene behind him.

The Turnover Hotel felt close and smelled of mold, but Keltin only wanted somewhere off the streets. He paid a beetle-browed man for a room but ignored the licey bed, unrolling his sleeping mat on the wooden floor instead. The man who'd given him the room had muttered something about dinner, but Keltin didn't risk it. He nibbled the rolls he'd stashed from the train ride, and wondered again what he had gotten himself into.

Of one thing he was certain. First thing in the morning, come devil or storm, he would find the home of Duke Gregson and then leave for the wilds of Dhalma Province. In a single night he'd had his fill of this city and its problems, and was eager to return to the simplicity of a beast hunt. With thoughts of how he'd spend the bounty money, he laid down and prepared for what would surely be yet another sleepless night.

* * *

Keltin paused to study a begrimed street sign, reciting to himself the round-about route given to him by the beetle-browed man with an assurance that it would avoid the mobs of protestors in the Industrial and Commercial Quarters. Instead,

Keltin would have to spend the better part of the day weaving his way along the twisting roads and alleys of the impoverished Lower Quarter, keeping a wary eye at all times should somebody try to repeat the brief, violent scene from the night before.

While he doubted anyone would risk attacking a man so well-armed as he, he'd taken no chances and loaded his hunting rifle with five Capshire practice rounds. Nicknamed candleshot for their soft wax interiors, the bullets were useful as cheap ammunition for target practice, and would hopefully prove effective as a nonlethal round. Keltin had no desire to shoot another human being, but if he had to, he would much rather knock them flat with a round of wax than kill them outright with a normal bullet. Still, he was relieved to see that few people even looked his way, and none tried to approach him.

He'd been traveling for some time when a wicked stench threatened to turn his empty stomach. Rounding a corner, he realized that the district's sewer system had suffered a blockage and fetid pools had formed at each of the drains in the cobblestone street. Keltin skirted the slowly growing pools, trying not to gag and longing for the fresh pines of Riltvin. Pausing upwind of the open sewage, Keltin stopped to blink tears from his stinging eyes and examine his surroundings.

He'd come to a sort of tenement slum with tightly packed buildings brooding down on the trash-strewn street. Laundry hung between buildings in a futile attempt to dry and freshen it. Looking up the street, Keltin realized he was being watched. A man stood, frozen in the act of tossing the contents of a chamber pot from a doorway about a stone's throw down the street from where he stood. The headless handle of an ax was held firmly in the hand not holding the chamber pot, and Keltin wondered if the man had had occasion to use the makeshift club. He waited for the man to retreat back into his home before continuing on his way. Passing the house, he noticed a slight movement at one of the upstairs windows. He glanced up and spied the small faces of two little girls staring back down at him through the dingy glass.

They looked no older than eight or nine, but their eyes showed age beyond their years. Keltin felt his heart clench to see the girls' mirthless faces. How long had it been since they had laughed and played? How long had it been since they'd eaten a decent meal? The girls watched him until he left the house behind him, and he struggled to shake their silent gaze from his mind.

Keltin tried to tell himself that he had come to Krendaria to help these girls. The beasts in Dhalma Province were keeping the farmers from their crops, and keeping food from getting to the capital. By saving the Dhalma farms, he could put food into the mouths of those two girls along with all the other suffering people he saw around him. The thought was meant to comfort him, but as he passed through more and more of the city's lower district, he began to wonder if it would really be that simple.

Eventually the tenement neighborhoods gave way to what may have been the townhouses of some of the city's merchants and tradesmen. These streets were clear of garbage, and the quality of the homes was certainly better, though Keltin noticed that most of the street-level windows were covered by boards or blankets. Passing one house with a door torn from its hinges, he glanced inside and saw only the gloom of a home long-abandoned. He met no one on the street.

A few more minutes walking brought Keltin to a makeshift barricade of wagons and barrels completely blocking the road before him. A half-dozen men in uniform watched over the top of the barricade, all of them eying Keltin and his rifle uneasily. One man stood up from behind a partially charred wagon and leveled what looked like a very old smoothbore musket at him.

"Stop right there. This area is closed to normal traffic. What's your business in the Upper Quarter?"

Keltin carefully rested his rifle against his shoulder before replying.

"I'm a beast hunter from Riltvin. I've come to answer Duke

Gregson's call for hunters in Dhalma Province."

The sentry lowered his musket and nodded. "We've seen many of you come in the last few days. Come on through, but keep your rifle on your shoulder."

Keltin approached the barricade carefully and took the opportunity to examine the sentries huddled behind the makeshift wall. Each man looked haggard and tired, and watched the lower district with a strange mixture of fear and disdain. Some were armed with antiquated military-issue muskets, the rest carried little more than clubs. Keltin wondered just how long it had been since these men had been relieved of their post or given fresh supplies. He knew that Krendaria was currently at war, but certainly they could arm and provision their soldiers in the capital better than this. It was little wonder that Duke Gregson had felt it necessary to look beyond the Krendarian army for help.

"Which way to the duke's estate?" he asked.

"Down Appleby Street, number five. You'll see it on the left."

"Thank you."

The sentry nodded. "Good luck."

Keltin noticed an immediate change in his surroundings once he had left the sentries' barricade behind him. Each home was separated from its neighbor by either a low stone wall or precisely pruned hedges. Cheery lanes of ornate sculptures led to opulent mansions surrounded by vibrant green lawns. None of the homes bore any sign of damage or arson, and all the windows were thrown open to allow the early autumn breeze inside. Keltin thought of the two girls he'd seen earlier that day as he turned the corner onto Appleby Street. Had they ever played on a lawn so vividly green as the ones he now passed? Would they ever?

The sun had begun to disappear behind the Sky Top Mountains by the time he reached Duke Gregson's estate. It was an impressive, three-storied structure of polished pillars and expansive windows. An ornate iron fence and an intricately wrought front gate separated the extensive lawn from the outside world. A uniformed soldier stood at the gate, holding a rifle that looked at least twenty years younger than the antiques held by the men at the barricade.

"You're a beast hunter?" he asked.

Keltin nodded. "Is the duke still offering the bounty for beasts?"

"As far as I know, though none of the men here have left for Dhalma yet."

"Why not?"

"Don't know, but the duke has asked all the hunters to gather in the gardens behind the house. He'll be addressing everyone there later on."

The guard opened the front gate and Keltin followed a gravel path around the house to find an impressive collection of what must have been native Krendarian flowers surrounding marble fountains and statues. A stone patio attached to the back of the estate looked down on an open space that might serve as a reception area for parties held during good weather, though its current occupants little resembled a gathering of party guests.

Keltin guessed there were close to forty hunters assembled together in the duke's gardens. Most of them were human men, all dressed in a variety of styles that Keltin was largely unfamiliar with. Among the humans, he spied a few of the bestial northerners known as Heteracks, their oversized shoulders and distinctive horse-like manes setting them apart from the men around them. There were also a few long-limbed Loopi sitting closely together on the outskirts of the group. Also on the outskirts were another group of humans, though Keltin could see little difference between them and the other hunters, aside from the fact that none of them seemed to be armed.

There was little conversation as most of those gathered seemed content to wait for the duke to make his appearance. Keltin was simply relieved to sit on the stairs leading up to the stone patio and rest, though he would have welcomed something to eat. Night fell and servants quietly lit lanterns and brought gas lamps out onto the patio. Keltin was about to ask one of the nearby servants what was keeping the duke when a gray-haired man in a fine suit began clearing his throat at the top of the patio.

"Excuse me, gentlemen," he said. "His Grace, Duke Gregson, will attend you shortly."

"You told us that nearly an hour ago," said a great, burly man wrapped in furs, his fingers tapping on the handles of two long-barreled pistols shoved into his belt.

The man on the stairs stiffened. "He will be here momentarily."

The silver-haired servant retreated into the house as the burly man swore loudly.

"I've had better treatment from dirt-poor village heads. You'd think they'd at least provide us with a hot meal. I haven't eaten since breakfast."

Keltin might have agreed with him, but didn't care to speak with the man. None of the other hunters seemed inclined to answer him either, though a few of the Heteracks grumbled in agreement.

At last, the doors to the estate were thrown open and a small group of guards came to stand at the top of the stairs surrounding a tall, stern looking man. Duke Gregson seemed to be in his middle years, with hard eyes and a rigid bearing that suggested a man of decision and authority. Keltin rose and turned to better see the duke as he began to speak.

"Good evening. I thank each of you for coming here and answering the call for hunters. I have no doubt that you represent some of the finest members of your profession. I'm sure that with your help, the beasts in Dhalma Province will be exterminated and the farmers' crops spared from rotting in the fields. Make no mistake, the work you will do here will mean either life or death for many of Krendaria's people this coming winter, and may even quell much of the turmoil that you have no doubt seen afflicting our fair capital."

The duke heaved a heavy sigh before continuing.

"However, I must inform you that the situation has

changed somewhat since I advertised the bounties that you are here for. When I sent out that call for hunters, we were still unsure of just how many beasts were plaguing Dhalma Province. While we still do not know an exact number, what information we can gather from the region suggests that the number of beasts in the province has grown into the hundreds."

The small crowd murmured uncertainly.

"Don't misunderstand me," said the duke. "I do not plan on sending any of you on a fool's errand to confront this infestation alone. However, the fact remains that the Dhalma Province is essentially under siege while the bulk of the Krendarian army is campaigning to the south. I have appeared before Parliament, and with uncommon unity they have approved the only proposal I can see for success. The plan is this. I will hire all of you, tonight, not as independent hunters, but as an expert militia force serving under a military hierarchy to liberate Dhalma Province."

The duke was met with stunned silence. Keltin struggled to reason through what he had just heard. He'd hunted for the same bounty as other hunters before, but never together. Even among his own family, each hunter had usually worked on his own as soon as he was old enough to. The idea of being in a military unit was especially uncomfortable. Keltin thought of the men at the barricade and wondered if it would be similar men put in charge of them.

"I understand that this is not what many of you were expecting," said Gregson. "If any of you wish to walk away now, then that is your right. I understand that the recently damaged rail system should be repaired in another day or so. You should be able to leave by train by then, barring further problems. But for those of you who will be going to Dhalma, you'll be under the command of Baron Rumsfeld. He is a good friend of mine and a veteran of the Krendaria Larigoss War. He'll be accompanied by a small detachment of hand-picked Krendarian Regulars, as well as a band of travelers that will help establish your base camp."

"You mean Weycliff vagrants," called someone from the crowd.

"The wayfarers are knowledgeable in camping and feeding a company of your size," answered the duke coolly, "and Evik has assured me of the good conduct of his people."

Duke Gregson nodded to a man standing among the group of humans that had kept themselves apart from the hunters. Keltin looked at them curiously as the man nodded back. He'd never heard of Weycliff wayfarers and wondered what manner of traveling companions they might turn out to be. His thoughts were interrupted by one of the Heteracks calling raucously to the duke.

"You keep bad company, your Grace. Weycliff rats handing the food and monkeys in the ranks," he shot a black look towards the Loopi standing off to the side before continuing. "I brought my band of sleevak wranglers all the way from Olsivo for a big chunk of Krendarian coin, but maybe we'll just turn back home. Unless, of course, the prize has changed, perhaps? Say, seventy drechs a head?"

"You can keep your clumsy haggling," said a human hunter flanked by several other men all wearing a similar cut of clothing. "We Krendarians don't need your kind here. Your stone-brained sleevaks are no match for our well-trained, tamarrin hounds."

"Maybe we should test that? Or are you too scared for your little puppies?"

"Our hounds would tear your pets to pieces."

"Care to try it?"

"Enough!" roared the duke. "I will not have my estate turned into a fighting pit. We will need both the strength of the hounds of tamarrin as well as the ferocity of the sleevaks if we are to have a chance of saving the province. As for Grel'zi'tael and his fellow Loopi, his powers as a Sky Talker will be invaluable." The duke looked pointedly at the Heteracks. "Unless, of course, your sleevaks can combat living smoke."

The sleevak wrangler shifted uncomfortably for a moment before withdrawing into a sullen silence as Gregson turned his attention back to the rest of the group.

"I know that most of you are, by nature, more comfortable working alone, but this is necessary. Those of you gathered here tonight are Carvalen's only hope."

"That's fine and well," said the burly hunter with the double pistols in his belt, "but I didn't come all this way for pretty speeches. Are the bounty amounts still the same or not?"

Duke Gregson shook his head. "I'm afraid that despite the generous aid of the Bachman Turnstein Bank, my associates and I cannot afford to offer the same bounties for such a high number of beasts. The government has promised to assist in your payment as much as possible, and I do have investments that will mature by the end of the season, but that is only if the Dhalma Province can be saved and the capital city remains functional. Therefore, I will reward each hunter who participates in this endeavor with a generous sum at the end of the season."

"How much is generous?"

"Three hundred drechs a man, payable once the campaign is complete."

"And provided the city isn't in flames by then," muttered the burly hunter.

The duke met the man's glare steadily. "Frankly sir, if that is the condition of the city by the end of the season, it will matter very little to me whether you are compensated or not."

The duke sighed and turned back to the group. "I will give you some time to think about all that I have said. You are free to use the front grounds of my estate to camp for the evening if you do not have lodging in the city. For those of you who intend to participate in the campaign to liberate Dhalma Province, I will give you tomorrow to make whatever preparations you will need to before departing. Meet here at dawn the next day to formally place yourselves in the service of Baron Rumsfeld. He'll then lead you to the province. I bid you all a goodnight and God's favor in whatever choice you think best."

With that, Duke Gregson turned away and went back into his house. The hunters stood in moody silence for a long while before dispersing to hold quiet conferences among themselves. Keltin sat back down on the steps to think.

He struggled for a moment to convert three hundred drechs into Riltvin jeva in his head, but eventually gave up. It was far more money than he'd ever seen at once, he knew that much. It would be enough money to pay his rent for an entire year. Enough money to keep Mary from needing to get another job and allow her the life that his mother had always wished for her. And yet, he wouldn't be hunting alone. He'd be surrounded by hunters, taking orders like a soldier, dancing to someone else's tune. The idea grated against him.

Still, he was hundreds of miles from home, with no money to return with. This journey had been a gamble, and if he returned now, he would lose. No, he could not return home now. He'd see this through. At least being among other hunters would mean he was more likely to make it home at all.

Keltin drew a deep breath and looked up at the stars. He recognized Sherdai, the wanderer, and smiled at the familiar constellation that had so often watched over him on the hunt. Whether in Riltvin or Krendaria, he was a Moore. He was a beast hunter. He would survive to bring home a bounty to be remembered and a story to share for years. Decided, he rose and followed the gravel path back around the house to the front lawns, looking forward to bedding down on the duke's soft, green grass for the night.

CHAPTER 4 – WELCOME TO DHALMA PROVINCE

Keltin spent much of the next day waiting for the coming dawn. While many of the other hunters seemed to have a great deal of business in the city, Keltin was reluctant to return to the chaos beyond the Upper District. He left Duke Gregson's estate only once to cross the street and post two letters he'd written to Mary and Mrs. Galloway, telling them where he was and what had happened to him thus far. As always, he omitted any details that might overly distress them.

He included the address of the Duke's estate with each letter, as a servant had informed the assembled hunters that they could use the address and have their mail forwarded to Dhalma as often as was possible. Keltin was grateful for the service, and after posting the letters he spent the rest of the day maintaining his equipment and waiting, content to ignore the hunters gathered around him as they ignored him and made their own preparations.

The next morning dawned cool and bright and found Keltin already awake, watching the last star in the sky slowly fade. Most of the other hunters seemed to share his habit of light sleeping and were beginning to stir themselves among the small village of tents. The Loopi were not only up but were just finishing the packing of their equipment. Keltin watched them curiously. There were four of them altogether. The silver-haired one called Grel'zi'tael was obviously the group's eldest member, and the other three Loopi respectfully assisted him in gathering up the dried rushes that he had slept upon.

Keltin had no knowledge of the Loopi people besides Mr. Renlowah. The thought occurred to him that he should send a letter to Renlowah and ask him about the title of Sky Talker, which was completely unfamiliar to him and had been used to describe Grel'zi'tael. With that thought in mind he quickly packed his gear and penned a hasty letter to the Loopi at Mrs. Galloway's boarding home.

The front lawn was nearly deserted of hunters by the time Keltin had written and posted the letter in the box across the street. Following the path to the gardens in back of the estate, he was pleasantly surprised to find several of the Weycliff people handing out bowls of steaming porridge. One wayfarer in a vest festooned with a variety of buttons seemed to notice him standing somewhat uncertainly and brought a bowl of the warm meal to him.

"It's not elegant, but it's hot and should fill you up all right," he said with a pleasant smile.

Keltin returned the smile as he studied the man, the first Weycliff he'd ever seen up close. He had a shock of golden hair and twinkling blue eyes that seemed to contain some mirth only he knew of. Keltin wondered what sort of people these wayfarers were, and tried to see any difference in them as he ate. The smiling Weycliff in the button vest moved among the hunters distributing bowls, and soon approached the hunter in furs with the double pistols.

"What is this?" demanded the surly man as he took the bowl. "There's not a scrap of meat in here. You expect me to hunt beasts with only gruel to eat?"

The wayfarer's smile remained in place even as his bright blue eyes hardened. "Actually, I understand that gruel is more soupy. But if you'd like, I can see about getting you some."

The hunter gave the wayfarer a black look and deliberately turned the bowl upside-down to dump its contents on the gravel path, soon followed by the bowl itself. The wayfarer's face remained a mask as he bent down and retrieved the bowl.

"Don't expect seconds," he said as he moved on in distributing the porridge.

"I'm not done with you yet, trashpicker," said the hunter, placing a hand on one of his pistols.

"Keep it in your belt," said Keltin.

The hunter turned on him, along with several other onlookers who had been watching the scene.

"You've something to say to me?"

Keltin took a breath. Setting his empty bowl down on the garden steps, he rose and looked the burly hunter in the eye.

"I said keep your pistol in your belt. You should be grateful. The people in this city are starving."

The hunter glowered at him. "Tell me what to do again, milk-sucker, and I'll punch a hole in your gut and watch you drain dry. Got that?"

Keltin could feel two score of eyes upon him as the burly hunter waited for an answer. The man stood with his feet apart, both of his hands now on the handles of his long-barreled pistols. Keltin began to slowly close the distance between them, keeping his hands relaxed and at his sides.

"You seem awfully eager to use those pistols," he said. "Maybe you should make sure they're loaded and cocked before you start running your mouth. After all, you're not the only dangerous person here."

The hunter raised his gnarled hands from his pistols and held them before him as if he'd throttle Keltin from a dozen feet away.

"I don't need my killers to sockmouth a git like you."

Keltin shook his head. "I came here to hunt beasts. I have nothing to prove to a boil like you."

The burly hunter swore a black oath and stalked towards him. Keltin watched the man's rolling gait and noticed a slight limp on his left side. The hunter came within an arm's length of Keltin and suddenly swung a meaty fist for his head. Keltin ducked to the man's left and delivered a sharp kick to the side of his left knee. The hunter cried out with a curse and fell to the ground. The man continued to swear sulfuriously as he scrambling to draw his pistols from his belt. Keltin was about to throw himself down on top of the man when suddenly the burly hunter was pinned to the ground by a honed ax blade pressed to his throat. One of the Loopi, a young male with golden-brown fur, peered down at the man from a height of over six and a half feet.

"Do not move," the Loopi rumbled deep in his chest.

The Sky Talker Grel'zi'tael stepped forward to stand beside his younger countryman. He looked down at the prone hunter with a somber expression.

"To make war so quickly among ourselves is to declare the beasts of Dhalma victorious this very morning."

The burly hunter swallowed against the ax blade but made no answer.

"Look!" cried out a harsh voice nearby. "We haven't even arrived in Dhalma Province and already the apes are drawing weapons on us!"

One of the Heterack sleevak wranglers pushed to the front of the crowd watching the scene and thrust an accusing finger at the two Loopi. "You see? You can't trust them. Turn your back on a Loopi, and you might as well shove a knife in your own back."

"That would be a trick, if you could do it."

"Who said that?!" demanded the Heterack.

Two men stood up from where they'd been sitting in the shadows of the garden patio. One was a giant, nearly as tall as a Loopi and as broad as a Heterack. A cabbage ear and a nose that had been broken at least once before suggested he was no stranger to brawls. His companion, on the other hand, was a handsome man with a noble bearing. Looking to be in his middle years, he had a fine-sculpted face and clever eyes that seemed to take in every detail around him. Turning his clever eyes to the Heterack, the composed man spoke in a measured, even tone.

"Baron Rumsfeld said it, and if you're to be under my command, you'll never speak to me in that way again." The Baron turned towards the group. "Well, I'm glad to see that you're all making friends already, but I must agree with the Sky Talker. This in-fighting will end now. You are all under my command, and will remain so until either our mission is over or you are dead. Is that understood?"

The hunters were silent. Baron Rumsfeld waited a moment, then indicated the giant standing beside him. "This is Oril Bracksten. He served as a company sergeant under me during the Krendaria Larigoss War and will be doing the same during our campaign in Dhalma. You'll follow his orders without question, just as you will follow mine. You may not be military men, but if we are to succeed, you will each have to swallow your stupid pride and act as a cohesive unit. You can expect to be dead within a week if you don't.

"Now then, I want you all finished with breakfast and assembled at the front gates in twenty minutes. I'll leave you in Sergeant Bracksten's tender care until then."

With that, the Baron went back into the estate and the hunters slowly resumed eating their breakfast. Bracksten approached Keltin, the burly hunter sitting on the ground massaging his knee, and the young Loopi standing somewhat apart from them.

"What're your names?" Bracksten demanded of the three.

Keltin identified himself to the sergeant and the burly hunter muttered that his name was Hull Kuley. The young Loopi was called Bor've'tai. Bracksten turned on Bor've'tai first.

"You may have stopped the fight, but if you ever draw weapons on another member of this company again, you won't live through the day. Understood?"

The Loopi's face was impassive as he gave a single nod. "Yes, I understand."

Bracksten then turned to Kuley. "You've got a bad attitude and a real mouth, Kuley. You stay in line or I'll straighten them both out. Got it?"

Kuley grumbled but nodded.

"Good, and one more thing."

Bracksten pointed at the porridge Kuley had poured on the ground. "You made a mess over there. Go clean it up, before I make you eat it."

Kuley began hobbling to the puddle of porridge as Bracksten turned on Keltin.

"You must think you're a plaguing hero straight from the smear novels, Moore. Well, you're not. You're under my command now, and if I say you mind your own business, then that's what you do. You got a problem minding your own business, Moore?"

Keltin could feel his heart still racing from the brief exchange with Kuley and almost made a sharp retort, but managed to catch himself before saying anything he'd probably regret.

"No sir."

"Good. Keep it that way."

Sergeant Bracksten stalked off and Keltin stared at the man's broad retreating back. Kuley may have been a bully, but Keltin could deal with bullies. Sergeants, on the other hand… Keltin wasn't sure how he felt about sergeants. Drawing a deep breath to settle his pulsing blood, he turned to see that Bor've'tai was still standing nearby.

"Thanks for your help," he said to the Loopi.

Bor've'tai looked at him silently for a moment, then nodded. "It was the right thing to do. I was glad to help you, Keltin Moore."

"Just Keltin is fine, Borva…"

"Bor've'tai," the young Loopi supplied. "I would speak with you later, but I must rejoin my companions. Farewell."

He turned and walked back to Grel'zi'tael without waiting for an answer. Keltin watched him a moment and wished that he could send another letter to Mr. Renlowah and receive an immediate reply with some sort of insight into the general temperament of his people.

Breakfast was soon over. The wayfarers collected the last of the empty bowls as the hunters shouldered their packs. Following the crowd, Keltin circled the house and found three wagons hitched and waiting at the duke's front gate. Each wagon had been fitted with rows of benches in their beds to accommodate the hunters on the long trip north. The Heteracks and tamarrin hound trainers split off from the group to make for their own caged wagons as Sergeant Bracksten barked out orders to the remaining hunters to get up onto the wagons. Keltin wondered where Baron Rumsfeld had gone, and turned to look farther up the road beyond the main gate. He spied the baron standing beside what looked like a private coach with a small group of well-armed men in Krendarian uniforms. The baron seemed to watch the proceedings for a moment before stepping into his coach and closing the door behind him.

Keltin turned to find his own place for the journey ahead. The seats were filling up quickly. The closest wagon held a sulking Hull Kuley, and Keltin stepped around it to avoid the surly hunter. The next wagon was full, as was the next. By the time he'd decided to put up with Kuley after all, the last seat on the final wagon had been filled. Turning around, he saw that he was the only hunter still standing on the ground. He was debating going to Sergeant Bracksten when he felt a gentle clap on the shoulder. He turned and saw the mirthful eyes of the button-vested wayfarer.

"Looks like you could use a seat, friend. Care to ride along with me?"

Keltin shrugged. "Well, it would be a long walk otherwise."

The Weycliff man grinned. "Come along then, my wagon is around at the servants' entrance."

Keltin followed the cheery man to a small circle of brightly painted wagons near a second, smaller gate in the estate's outer fence. He climbed up onto the buckboard next to the button-vested wayfarer as the man steered the two mules before them towards the main road and the rest of the convoy. Sergeant Bracksten approached them on an impressive gray horse that carried the gigantic man's weight easily.

"You Weycliff will follow behind the tamarrin hound wagons. The sleevak wranglers will act as rearguard after you."

"If you'll pardon me, sir, I don't know how well our mules will take to being followed by the sleevaks."

"The Heteracks will maintain a distance of half a mile from the rest of the column, so you shouldn't have to worry about it."

The wayfarer nodded. "Thank you sergeant. It seems that our good Baron has thought of everything."

"That's why he's in command."

Bracksten turned to look at Keltin as if he'd just noticed him. "What are you doing back here, Moore?"

"There wasn't room in the other wagons. These people offered me a ride."

The sergeant shrugged and turned his mount to ride back to the front of the line. Keltin heard his thundering baritone from somewhere up ahead.

"All right, let's move out!"

Whips cracked and wheels groaned as the convoy slowly left Duke Gregson's estate behind them and turned to the north. Keltin's traveling companion transferred the reins to one hand and turned in his seat to better see him.

"My name's Jaylocke," he said with a friendly smile. "I'm glad I could offer you a ride. I wanted to say thank you for what you did back at the estate. There aren't many folks who would have stood up for somebody like me."

"Why not?"

Jaylocke gave him a quizzical look. "Are you completely unfamiliar with the Weycliff then?"

"I'm from Riltvin. I'd never heard of your people before coming here."

"Is that so? Well, perhaps we should head west to your homeland as a holiday if we make it out of this. Krendaria isn't the best place for Weycliff wayfarers even in the best of times."

Keltin shook his head. "I don't understand. Why are your people disliked?"

"Oh, there's the typical stories of theft, cheating, lechery, and magic of the blackest sort. We're an easy scapegoat for anything from soured milk to a virgin daughter suddenly beginning to swell."

"But it isn't true… is it?"

Jaylocke shrugged. "I suppose there's your fair share of dishonesty and moral looseness among some Weycliff, just as you'll find anywhere. But Evik runs a fairly tight ship. Don't worry. We're completely trustworthy, as wayfarers go."

Jaylocke winked and Keltin nodded, deciding to let the subject rest for the time being. Instead, he took the opportunity to examine the tamarrin hounds in the wagon directly ahead of them. There were four of them lying calmly in their cages. Each hound was long and muscular. The smallest among them was at least four feet at the shoulder, and each one sported a distinctive, feathery tail. Keltin had never seen a tamarrin hound, but even in Riltvin he'd heard of their incredible tracking and hunting skills. Beyond their natural instincts, each hound was trained with military precision and machinelike blind obedience to its master. It was a stark contrast to the Heteracks and their feral sleevaks.

Keltin couldn't see the caged sleevaks or their handlers at the back of the column and that was fine with him. Unlike the trainers of the tamarrin hounds, the Heterack wranglers never attempted to train their sleevaks, preferring to release the savage creatures in the vicinity of their quarry and then recapture the sleevaks again after they had done their work. Keltin remembered when he had experienced the tenacious ferocity of a sleevak firsthand. One of the first beasts he'd ever hunted had been a sleevak that had killed its wrangler and escaped the traveling sideshow it had been displayed in. He'd hunted it for more than a week and ended up emptying a chamber of Reltac Spinners and bloodying the Ripper for the first time in order to bring the beast down. Musing to himself, he considered how he would take one down now if the Heteracks lost control of their monstrosities. He decided on one Alpenion Round in the creature's second eye from the left, or perhaps one of his new Capshire Shatter Rounds just behind the head frill.

"You're a quiet traveling companion, Mr. Moore."

Keltin snapped from his reverie. "I'm sorry. Call me Keltin. I suppose hunting alone tends to make me naturally quiet."

"I imagine it's a useful trait to have on a hunt, but a life on the road without conversation would get tiresome after the first two or three years."

"Have you really been on the road your entire life?"

"I was born in a wagon and raised in half a dozen nations."

"But what about your family? Don't you ever miss them?"

Jaylocke grinned. "Evik, our troupe patriarch, is also my father. Most of our band is either immediate or extended family, and whoever isn't might as well be. We're a very close bunch. And you? Do you have any family?"

"I have a sister and mother back in Riltvin."

The wayfarer shook his head. "I couldn't imagine having so few blood relations. Still, perhaps it has its advantages."

"I do have other family. The Moores have a reputation as hunters in the hill country of Riltvin."

"Really? A bit of a local beast hunting celebrity, eh?"

Keltin shrugged. "I've survived this long."

The convoy continued to travel at a rolling pace and soon the last outskirts of Carvalen were behind them. The landscape flowed by in small thickets of trees and grassy meadows. The Sky Top Mountains curved around the horizon and surrounded them on all sides like the walls of a god-made prison. Keltin looked up at the snowy caps of the mountains around him and gave an involuntary shiver.

The rough country slowly changed to fenced-in pastures and fields of crops nearly ready to harvest. Farmhouses passed by on either side of the road, but not a soul stirred from the lonely looking buildings. Seeing the abandoned farmlands, Keltin took the opportunity to remove the unfired candleshot rounds from his hunting rifle and reloaded the chamber, alternating Reltac Spinners with the new Capshire Shatter Rounds he'd purchased in Collinsworth. Snapping the chamber back into place, he set the rifle aside and unlashed the Ripper from his pack, setting the covered weapon between himself and Jaylocke before returning the rifle to his lap. Jaylocke gave the Ripper a curious look.

"Do you find you have to use that often?" he asked, nodding towards the three-foot long weapon.

"Not as often as I used to when I first started hunting. I've learned that taking an extra second to aim saves on ammunition and makes close encounters less necessary."

"Hmm…"

Jaylocke held the reins in one hand and tapped a finger against his chin thoughtfully. "I suppose that makes sense, but what about now? You'll most likely be facing more than one beast at a time on this campaign, and the bullets may run out before the beasts do."

"I can handle myself. I've also got this." He pulled open his coat to show Jaylocke his grandfather's Grantville revolver. "Besides, I still know how to use the Ripper just fine."

"I'm sure you do, but it never hurts to improve your chances. If we find time, perhaps I could show you some tricks you may not know with that thing."

"Thanks all the same, but I think I'll be fine."

Jaylocke shrugged. "Just thought I'd offer."

Empty farmers' fields continued to pass by them as the mules' steady march ate away the miles between the convoy and wherever Baron Rumsfeld was taking them. Keltin tried to look for any signs of destruction, but all the farms lay eerily still and silent. He saw no sign of beasts, though he knew to keep his guard up as they traveled. Unlike natural wild animals, some beasts weren't frightened by large groups of men. Some even seemed to seek them out.

Keltin was watching a field of potato plants slowly slide by when he noticed Sergeant Bracksten riding down the column towards them. The large man signaled for them to stop and Jaylocke obligingly reigned in the mules.

"What can we do for you, Sergeant?"

Bracksten pointed to the nearby field. "The Baron wants a

few of your people to dig up as many of these potatoes as you can to add to our company stores for the campaign."

Jaylocke nodded. "That's good thinking. They'll rot in the ground anyway if we don't succeed. Might as well make use of them."

"Good. Get to work then. We'll see you tonight."

Bracksten turned to Keltin. "Well, Moore, since you're here already, I'm assigning you guard duty over the wayfarers while they gather food. If you feel you need more support, you can ask the Heteracks as they pass."

"Thank you sir, but I think we'll be fine."

Bracksten nodded and turned back to Jaylocke. "We'll be making camp in a few more hours. I expect you will find us easily enough."

With that, the sergeant turned his horse and trotted back up the road. Jaylocke slid out of his seat and jogged back to Evik's wagon to explain the situation. When he came back, he was accompanied by a Weycliff youth in a billowing green shirt.

"Maynid here will take over driving our wagon in the convoy. We'll ride up in Evik's wagon when we're done here."

Keltin dropped to the ground and reached up to grab his pack.

"Don't worry about your gear," said Maynid as he climbed up into the driver's seat. "I'll see it gets to the camp for you."

Keltin shrugged and took down his Ripper and hunting rifle. He followed Jaylocke to Evik's wagon where the Weycliff patriarch was issuing instructions to the three other wayfarers who had been selected for the work. Each of the workers was issued a short-handled shovel and began the laborious process of unearthing and cleaning the potatoes, loading them into burlap sacks, and stacking them in Evik's wagon as the rest of the caravan moved on. Keltin found a raised stump by the side of the road and sat with his rifle across his knees to keep watch.

Soon the Heterack sleevak wranglers were rolling past them. They made no offer to help and Keltin didn't bother speaking with them, though he did coolly assess the strength of the sleevaks as they attacked the iron bars of their cages in an attempt to get to him. He noticed that each creature's bony shoulder plates showed the scars of their handlers, and that each sleevak bore the distinctively cropped frill that designated it as belonging to a wrangler. Keltin was glad when the slavering monsters had finally moved on.

Time passed slowly as the wayfarers worked, and Keltin's thoughts wandered. The conversation with Jaylocke about the Ripper gnawed at him. Would he have enough ammunition to see him through this campaign? Would he eventually be forced to fight the beasts of Dhalma Province with nothing but the Ripper? Keltin fervently hoped that the Baron had thought to supply the hunters with additional ammunition. He was unaccustomed to relying on someone else to do his planning, and it surprised him to realize that his lack of control here worried him more than any beast ever had.

A slight stirring in a nearby wheat field drew his attention. Watching closely, he soon saw again what looked like nothing more than the gentle rocking of the breeze. But there was no breeze. Keltin rose slowly, letting the feeling return to his sleepy limbs as he kept his eyes on the wheat field. Jaylocke looked at him curiously as he finished filling a sack of potatoes.

"What is it?"

Suddenly a tawny blur erupted from the wheat field. Keltin snapped his rifle into position against his shoulder, hesitating for only a moment to take aim and study the creature. The beast was moving incredibly fast. Its overlong, four-jointed legs coiled over the ground like cracking bullwhips at it galloped towards them. Jaylocke called out a warning to the other Weycliff. The wayfarers quickly scrambled up out of the potato field to take cover behind the wagon by the road.

Keltin watched the rapidly approaching beast and lined up his shot. His rifle cracked with a loud report as he sent a Reltac Spinner for the thing's head. The creature stumbled for half a heartbeat before continuing its mad sprint forward. Keltin adjusted his aim away from the head. Knowing it would be next to impossible to hit one of the blurring legs, he aimed instead for one of the creature's shoulders.

He fired, and the beast somersaulted forward as one of its front legs went suddenly limp. It flailed among the potato plants for a moment and raised itself up onto its remaining three legs. Keltin fired a final shot aimed at its chest just below the throat. The beast staggered. Its angry hissing turning to a gurgling rasp and Keltin knew that he had managed to pierce a lung. The creature wobbled for a moment before collapsing, lying less than a yard from where one of the Weycliff had dropped his shovel.

Picking up the Ripper, Keltin turned to the wayfarers gathered at the back of the wagon.

"Stay here, I'll make sure it's dead."

The beast lay still save for the occasional spasm of its overlong legs. Now able to examine it closely, Keltin realized why his first shot had seemed so ineffectual. The beast's ghoulish head was almost all bone, with only a thin covering of flesh around its eyes and nose. Looking closely, Keltin could even see where his bullet had lodged more than half an inch into the beast's bony scalp.

A crunch of soil signaled Jaylocke's cautious approach as he stood nearby to examine the dead beast. Keltin glanced up at him. Jaylocke sucked in a deep breath and gave Keltin a bemused smile.

"Well, Keltin Moore, welcome to Dhalma Province."

CHAPTER 5 – VISIT IN THE NIGHT

Keltin couldn't remember the last time he'd been so uncomfortable. The sack of potatoes he was using as a seat dug painfully into his lower back as Evik's mules seemed to purposefully pull the wagon over every bump and rock in Dhalma Province. Exhausted as he was from the lingering weariness of not sleeping well on the journey to Krendaria, Keltin knew he'd never manage to doze off as they slowly made their way to the camp. With no other choice, he continued to search for a comfortable spot as he tried not to resent Jaylocke sleeping peacefully across from him.

Night was falling outside the wagon and the trees between the farmers' fields were becoming more plentiful, reminding Keltin of the hill country and forests that he was accustomed to. While it was good to be out of Carvalen and back in more familiar surroundings, Keltin was also painfully aware of the dangers that the densely growing trees could hide. Despite his fatigue, he continued to search for any signs of movement in the fading light until Evik finally called back to the small group riding in the wagon.

"Start coming to life, everyone. I see campfires ahead."

Keltin sighed with relief as the wagon finally ground to a halt. He jumped out to feel the reassurance of solid ground under his feet once again and stretched, taking the chance to evaluate the campsite that Baron Rumsfeld had selected. They were in the open courtyard of a large farmstead that most likely belonged to a rich landholding family that had long since fled to the capital. The property had an impressive barn and a sturdy looking farmhouse that looked to have recently had a fresh coat of paint. Keltin wondered for a moment if he would be lucky enough to be spending his nights in the farmhouse, but it wasn't to be. A soldier standing guard at the front door suggested strongly that the Baron had already claimed the farmhouse as his own personal command center.

Wandering a little around the farmstead, Keltin found that the barn had been given to the tamarrin hounds and their trainers, while the Heteracks and their sleevaks were making use of the pigpen and nearby storage shed for their housing. The rest of the hunters had their tents set up in the relative safety of a small, fenced-in pasture nearby.

Seeing the other hunters' tents, Keltin decided he ought to pitch his own shelter for the night. Looking around, he found Jaylocke's wagon and went to the driver's seat to grab his gear from where he'd stowed it under the buckboard. It was gone. Keltin remembered what Jaylocke had said about some folks calling wayfarers thieves. He felt somewhat guilty for suspecting any of Jaylocke's companions, but what else could have happened to his missing property? He was debating whether he should speak to Jaylocke or Evik about it when Maynid, the youth who had taken over the driving of Jaylocke's wagon, strolled up to him.

"Looking for your gear?" the young man said. "I set it up for you already. The old Loopi, Grel-what's-it, asked that I pitch it near him and the other Loopi. I didn't see any harm, and I hope you don't mind."

Keltin quickly swallowed the guilty lump in his throat and nodded. "Thank you. I don't mind sleeping next to the Loopi. Of course, I'm not sure how much sleep any of us will get with only that cattle fence between us and whatever's out there."

Maynid grinned and winked. "Oh, don't you worry about

that. Old Rumsfeld's a clever sort. He's already made some improvements to our new home away from home."

Approaching the fenced-in pasture, Keltin had to admit that the Baron had certainly gone to extensive lengths to ensure the safety of the hunters while they slept. A deep trench had been dug around the pasture and the unearthed sod had been used to create an additional barricade behind the fence. Sharpened poles sprouted like quills throughout the barricade, and sentries had been posted along the entire perimeter. It was an impressive defensive structure that was probably an effective deterrent to both infantry and cavalry in the field. But how effective would it be against beasts?

Keltin was considering the best way to get across the trench and barricade when he noticed a lanky man with a long-barreled rifle sitting on a stool and watching him from across the divide.

"How do I get over?" asked Keltin.

"You must have missed out on the grunt work," the man drawled with an accent that identified him as a native of Drutchland. "There's a plank of wood around the other side that we're using as a bridge to get over all of this. Where were you when the rest of us were playing at ditch diggers?"

"I was standing guard over the wayfarers while they gathered some more food for us."

"Any beast attacks?"

"Just one. It was light and fast with a head like a rock, but it finally went down with a bullet in the throat."

The hunter nodded his approval. "I'll remember that if I see one like it."

"Any sightings here?"

"None yet, but they're out there."

Keltin left the man to his guard duty and crossed the makeshift bridge over the well-made fortification. Weaving through the cluster of tents, he finally found his own familiar shelter at the outskirts of the camp. Nearby, the Loopi knelt together in a quiet circle as Grel'zi'tael murmured softly in prayer. Watching the Loopi, Keltin felt a pang of guilt as he realized that he'd missed Congregation that day. It had always been a challenge to participate in group worship when he was on the hunt, but he usually managed some kind of religious observance, at least on the Day of Rest.

With no other option available, he sat on his bedroll inside his tent and said a quiet prayer. He made the usual request for good health for his family and protection from harm for himself. Unsure of what else to add, he offered thanks for surviving the beast attack earlier that day and finished the prayer. Opening his eyes, he was surprised to see Bor've'tai looking down on him from outside his open tent flap.

"It's good to see you finally made it."

Keltin crawled out of his tent and rose to his feet as the Loopi tilted his head in the direction of the farmhouse.

"A wayfarer came by a moment ago saying that dinner is ready. Shall we go together?"

"All right."

Keltin fell into step beside the Loopi feeling somewhat uncertain about his new acquaintance. While Bor've'tai had never been anything but polite to him, he found his companion's silent, looming presence unnerving. Keltin tried thinking of some minor topic to discuss as they walked together, but was unable to.

It seemed that Keltin wasn't alone in his uneasiness around the intimidating Loopi as they came to the tables that the wayfarers had set out in front of the farmhouse for their use. All the other hunters kept Bor've'tai and Keltin at a healthy distance as they moved through the line for the thick stew that would be their supper. Keltin was relieved to see Jaylocke's friendly face as he stood beside the large, bubbling pot, ladling out generous portions of the steaming stew.

"How's your backside, Keltin?" Jaylocke asked with a grin. "I think I'll be sitting on potato-shaped bruises for a week."

Keltin chuckled, taking his bowl of hot stew and turning to find a place to sit. The tables and chairs were all mismatched and Keltin guessed they had been appropriated from the surrounding farmhouses. He was certain that the Baron would have gotten enough chairs for all the hunters, but as he looked over the crowded tables he found empty seats at only one table, the one occupied by the Loopi. Keltin walked to the seat next to Bor've'tai's.

"May I sit with you?" he asked.

"Of course, please do."

Keltin sat and began to eat the savory stew, wondering how he had somehow been lumped together with what seemed to be the misfits and outcasts in this campaign. Could it be the result of the fight with Hull Kulley? Was it really so strange to have stood up in defense of a wayfarer, or to be seen speaking with a Loopi? Looking at the hunters gathered at the other tables, Keltin realized for the first time that nearly all of them shared the features of men from Krendaria, Malpin, Drutchland, and several other northern and eastern nations. Keltin seemed to be the only Westerner among them. Were things truly so different outside of his native Riltvin?

Turning his attention away from the other tables, Keltin noticed the Sky Talker Grel'zi'tael watching him. The gray-haired elder smiled as their eyes met and Keltin was suddenly reminded of his grandfather's gentle face despite the Sky Talker's inhuman features.

"Are you all right, Keltin?" asked Bor've'tai.

Keltin gave a start and realized he must have been staring. "Yes, I'm fine. I'm sorry if I was rude."

"That's all right," said Grel'zi'tael gently. "You seemed to be remembering something. If I may ask, what was it?"

"It was nothing. It's just that... you reminded me of my grandfather."

Keltin worried that the Loopi might laugh at him, but the elder only smiled warmly. "That is a humbling compliment, my friend. Are you close to your grandfather?"

"I was. He died three years ago."

"We mourn your loss," said a young female Loopi sitting across from Bor've'tai.

"Thank you, but he had lived a good life. I think he was content at the end."

Grel'zi'tael nodded. "May we all be so well blessed."

Keltin returned the nod and tried to think of something more to say. He almost asked if they knew Mr. Renlowah, but realized how foolish that would sound. Luckily, Bor've'tai spoke again and saved him from embarrassing himself.

"Have you met all of my companions yet, friend Keltin?"

"No, no I haven't."

Introductions were quickly made. The young female across from Bor've'tai was named Shar'le'vah, and the fourth Loopi identified himself as Val'ta'lir. Keltin introduced himself again, and began to feel himself relax a little. These Loopi were friendly and kind, and made every effort to make him feel comfortable among them. After a moment, Keltin hazarded a question.

"Grel'zi'tael?"

"Yes, Keltin?"

"I don't understand something. Why do the other hunters…"

Keltin hesitated, looking at the crowded condition of all the other tables and the empty chairs nearby. The Sky Talker followed his gaze and sadly shook his head.

"Why does any man act the way he does? Ideas, feelings, beliefs. These are things that are not easily changed, only through patience and dedication."

"I suppose so. It just seems strange. I don't remember anyone acting this way in Gillentown, at least not around Mr. Renlowah."

"Mr. Renlowah?"

"He's a Loopi, and has a room at the boarding home where I live."

"The name is certainly Loopi," said Val'ta'lir, "though it sounds somewhat odd."

"Perhaps it is our friend's accent," said Grel'zi'tael. "It may also be an affectation that was assumed when this Loopi left his native land. The original pronunciation may be something more familiar, as in Renn'low'ah."

"Are there many Loopi in Riltvin?" Shar'le'vah asked

Keltin.

"I don't think so. Mr. Renlowah was the only one I'd ever met until seeing all of you at Duke Gregson's estate."

Shar'le'vah seemed about to ask another question when Sergeant Bracksten rose from his seat next to Baron Rumsfeld. The sergeant stepped up onto a low table serving as a raised platform and addressed the assembled hunters.

"Listen up! Baron Rumsfeld has some things to tell you bunch, so pay attention."

The hunters went silent as Bracksten stood aside and Rumsfeld took the stand, pausing a moment to wipe his mouth with a napkin before speaking.

"Good evening, gentlemen," he said. "I hope you've all enjoyed your dinner and plan on getting a good night's sleep, because tomorrow will be when the real work begins. I'm going to lay out for you the first stage of our campaign, so make sure that you listen closely.

"Each of you will be assigned to a squad of six men with a Squad Leader chosen from members of the Krendarian Regulars," he indicated the uniformed men sitting at his table before continuing. "Squads will be deployed from our home base one at a time for six-hour patrols during daylight hours. Your mission will be to secure the surrounding area and engage any beasts you encounter.

"In addition to squad patrol, each of you will be expected to serve on sentry duty when assigned, and be prepared for any additional duties that you may be given. Until further notice you'll be receiving all of your orders from either Sergeant Bracksten or your Squad Leader. Are there any questions?"

The assembled hunters were silent and the Baron nodded. "Very well. I bid you all a fair evening gentlemen, and good hunting."

Rumsfeld stepped down from the platform and Sergeant Bracksten addressed them once again.

"I'll be reading off the squad assignments now. Captain Tallow and his tamarrin hound trainers will be their own squad, as will Captain Rok's sleevak wranglers. The rest of you make sure to listen closely for your name and squad, because I won't repeat myself."

The sergeant proceeded to read off the squad numbers along with their leaders and members. Keltin's name was listed among the members of Squad Three, as was Bor've'tai's. The Loopi silently placed a large hand on his shoulder and squeezed. Keltin felt the reassuring pressure in the strong grip and realized that he was grateful to have a friend within his group. The sergeant finished listing off the squad members and gave one final message to the assembly.

"Patrols start tomorrow after breakfast. Squad Three will take the first patrol, so if that's your group, make sure you're geared up and ready to go."

Bracksten stepped down from the platform as the assembled hunters resumed their dinner.

"I don't like the idea of being separated from the rest of you," said Shar'le'vah.

"Do not worry," said Grel'zi'tael. "I believe that our fellow campaigners will set aside their personal animosities once the true work of hunting begins. I also trust the good Baron to keep an orderly camp. We will be safe here."

"You mean aside from the ravenous beasts all around us?" asked Val'ta'lir.

"That is true, but remember that we are in good company. With hunters like friend Keltin among us, I do not think we need fear the beasts overmuch."

"Well, we shall know better after our first patrol tomorrow," said Bor've'tai.

"Be careful," said Shar'le'vah, looking from him to Keltin.

Keltin gave her a smile as he finished his stew. "Don't worry. As long as I can get a good night's sleep tonight, I should be ready for just about anything tomorrow."

* * *

Keltin was up and pulling on his boots before the first screaming wail had died in the night air. Grabbing his rifle, he dove from his tent and swiveled around to find where the beast was coming from. His still slumbering mind was confused by the tents surrounding him, and it took a moment for him to remember where he was and realize that he wasn't the one being attacked.

Listening, he determined that the shrieking chorus of bestial screams was coming from the sleevak pens. Keltin pulled on his hunting jacket and followed nearly a dozen other hunters all hurrying to the source of the hellacious noise. Something large was trying to break into the sleevak cages, its enormous body little more than a dim outline in the lights from the nearby farmhouse.

Drawing closer, Keltin lifted his rifle and tried to quickly search the beast for a vulnerable spot. Its muscular body was larger than a wagon with arms and legs like columns of sinew and a head dominated by three massive tusks. A short, split tail lashed from below its back and Keltin wondered if he was looking at some gargantuan variation of the forest devils of Riltvin.

The sleevaks were in a frothing frenzy inside their cages as the tusked giant attacked the thick metal bars. Captain Rok was screaming at his Heteracks, but none of the sleevak wranglers seemed willing to risk drawing close enough to the massive beast to release their charges.

"Shoot it, you boils!" roared the head wrangler.

Keltin was still seeking the best place for his first shot when the hunters around him opened fire. The beast shuddered under the barrage of bullets and turned to peer through slitted, opal eyes at its attackers. Keltin aimed for one of those eyes but the beast turned quickly and sped off into the black woods beyond the farmstead at a lumbering sprint. Keltin lowered his unfired rifle and examined the damage of the beast's attack as the thunder of gunshots gradually ceased around him.

The iron bars on several of the sleevaks' cages were bent and contorted as if they had been laid on the rails before a locomotive at full steam. The sleevaks themselves were in a state of berserker rage and the Heteracks had their hands full trying to subdue the thrashing monsters. Sergeant Bracksten arrived in a matter of seconds, looking none-the-merrier for being roused from his bed. He turned on the head wrangler with a fury that mirrored that of the sleevaks.

"What happened here, Rok?"

"A beast," muttered the Heterack as he thrust a foul smelling hunk of meat into one of the sleevak's cages with a long pole. "It came out of nowhere and went straight for the sleevaks."

"We'll have to repair these cages, Rok," called another wrangler. "They won't hold the sleevaks in this condition."

"Wait till the drugged meat has settled them! You get close to them now and you'll get torn to pieces."

"How did it get this close to camp?" demanded Bracksten. "Didn't you have a man on watch?"

Rok snorted as he attached another slab of meat to his pole. "We've never had to stand guard over the sleevaks. Nothing has ever tried to attack a group of them, cages or no."

"Well, now something has. Put a man on watch starting right now, and make sure those cages are secure. If so much as one of your little pets gets loose, I'll give orders to these men to shoot down your sleevaks like any other beast, and you and your wranglers will take their place on patrol. Understood?"

Rok grunted before barking orders to his comrades as Bracksten turned to Keltin and the rest of the hunters.

"All right you lot, get back to bed. Remember, the real excitement starts in the morning."

Keltin dutifully followed the other hunters back to their tents. Laying aside his rifle and shuffling off his boots, he tried to return to sleep, knowing that whatever rest he got would neither come soon nor last long enough.

CHAPTER 6 – FIRST BLOOD

Morning came too early as Keltin dressed with his eyes closed, cracking them open only when it came time to arm himself for the day's patrol. He strapped on his belt with his grandfather's pistol in its holster, slung his Ripper over his shoulder, and took up his rifle in both hands. Thus equipped, he dragged himself from his tent to find Bor've'tai already up and ready, his only weapon a large woodsman's ax.

"You didn't sleep well."

The Loopi's blunt observation wasn't a question and Keltin nodded numbly in agreement.

"I haven't slept a full night for a week."

"I'm sorry, but I hope it doesn't affect your ability to hunt."

"I hope so too. Let's go see what breakfast is."

Breakfast turned out to be porridge again. Keltin ate without comment or complaint as he listened to the muttered conversations of the hunters at the other tables. The topic on everyone's mind seemed to be the tusked giant's attack on the sleevaks the night before, and Keltin managed to separate the odd statement from the low murmuring around him.

"What kind of beast attacks a pack of caged sleevaks?"

"Them sleevaks were scared, did you see it in their eyes?"

"Naw, sleevaks are too stupid to be scared."

Finishing his eavesdropping and his meal, Keltin rose from his seat to toss his bowl in the tub of water set out for dirty dishes. Maynid looked up with a sleepy smile from the bowls he was busily scrubbing.

"Good morning, Mr. Moore."

"Morning, Maynid."

"We heard you were going out with the first patrol today."

"That's right."

Maynid stood up from his low stool, his young eyes suddenly serious. "We want you to know that you," he glanced at Bor've'tai as he joined them, "*both* of you, have the good wishes of Evik's troupe. We send the support of our ancestors with you today."

Keltin was uncertain how to take the youth's sudden solemnity. He murmured his thanks and Bor've'tai nodded to the lad. Maynid gave them one last smile and returned to his dirty dishes.

"We should go to the farmhouse," said Bor've'tai. "The rest of Squad Three should be there by now."

Bor've'tai proved to be correct as they joined their fellow squad members outside the farmhouse. Keltin recognized the lanky sentry he had spoken with the night before and gave him a small nod of greeting. He didn't know the other three hunters. They stood together in an uneasy silence until the front door of the farmhouse opened and a man in a soldier's field uniform stepped out. His young face was clean-shaven and he carried a Krendarian bolt-action rifle along with a large pack that seemed to weigh nothing on his broad shoulders. The man marched up to the squad and addressed them in a sharp, precise voice.

"Right, you men. I'm Corporal Lewis, your Squad Leader. I want each of you to say your names clearly and slowly for everyone else to hear."

Each of the hunters dutifully introduced himself and Keltin tried to match each name to the face of the man it belonged to. Henry was the lanky sentry he had met the night before, and Pollik was a squat old man with few remaining teeth. Ru and

Weedon were both young men who looked like Krendarian natives and seemed to already have a history of hunting together.

"Remember these names," said Lewis when they had finished. "Your survival may depend on knowing them when you need to. Now, here are our orders. For the next six hours we'll be making a sweep of the area immediately surrounding the camp. We'll move in a shoulder-to-shoulder line with myself in the middle and ten paces between each of us. If you see anything, signal the men closest to you, and I'll decide whether we engage or not. Do not fire until I give the order. Understood?"

There was an awkward silence as Keltin and the other hunters looked at each other in confusion. Lewis seemed to either not notice or ignore their reactions.

"All right, let's move out."

"Corporal?"

Lewis stopped and turned on Keltin.

"What is it, Moore?"

"I wonder, sir, if there's a better way to do this than marching through the forest in a straight line."

Lewis' eyes narrowed, his clean-shaven jaw visibly tightening. "Bracksten told me about you, Moore. You just follow your orders and we'll all get along fine."

"All I'm saying is that I don't think we'll be able to stay hidden from the beasts if we move shoulder-to-shoulder. We're not trying to flush out grouse, we're stalking things that could just as easily stalk us."

"For that matter, why do we need to crawl through the bushes?" asked Pollik. "I've been trapping beasts since before some of you were born, and I imagine a number of other fellows here could help me rig up some nasty surprises out in the forest."

"Or we could wait for the beasts to come to us," put in Ru. "Weedon and I managed to take out a spiked thresher once without it ever seeing us by using a tree stand and a butchered goat for bait."

"That's enough!"

Lewis' face flushed an angry red as he quivered with rage. "You will do as you are ordered! This patrol's objective is to determine the level of danger around the camp. We'll proceed as I've outlined. Now, let's move out. We'll pick up our day-rations from the Weycliff before we go."

The corporal turned and marched off, leaving the hunters to fall in step behind him. Keltin watched the corporal's back and wondered if the young man had ever participated in a beast hunt, or had even seen traditional combat. He was still trying to imagine why the young corporal wasn't on campaign in the south as he stood in line to receive his cloth-wrapped lunch and fill his canteen at a tapped barrel of rainwater. Mama Bellin, the matron of the Weycliff and seemingly the only woman among them, gave him a small smile as she handed him his rations. Keltin forgot the corporal long enough to wonder again about Maynid's odd words from earlier that morning.

"All right men," said Lewis. "Let's head out."

They passed the last sentries at the edge of camp and entered the thick wood beyond. Once they were outside of the camp, Lewis organized them into their ragged patrol line. Henry was placed on the end farthest from camp, followed by Keltin and then Bor've'tai, with Pollik, Ru, and Weedon on the corporal's other side. Keltin decided that for the time being it was pointless to argue any more about it, and resolved himself to try to follow the corporal's orders.

At first, the day passed slowly with no sign of life, bestial or otherwise. Lewis advanced the line of hunters forward at a slow pace, stopping at each telltale sound or rustle in the undergrowth. Keltin divided his attention between searching the forest for beasts and trying to keep his fellow squad members in sight. Henry and Bor've'tai were easiest to keep an eye on, and he spied Corporal Lewis beyond Bor've'tai at regular intervals. He eventually gave up trying to see the other three hunters through the densely packed trees.

A low whistle from his left drew Keltin's immediate

attention. Henry had crouched down and was trying to signal him to do the same. Keltin lowered himself to the ground, turning to give Bor've'tai the same signal. He tried to see what Henry had found, but the narrow trees were packed too closely for him to see beyond the rangy hunter and his long-barreled rifle. A stirring from his right side signaled Bor've'tai and Corporal Lewis crawling towards him.

"What is it, Moore?" the corporal whispered when he was close enough to speak directly into Keltin's ear.

"I don't know. I think Henry spotted something."

Lewis tried making a signal that Keltin didn't recognize in Henry's direction, but the rangy hunter wasn't looking their way. With a curse, Lewis crawled towards the man. A low rustling came from somewhere among the trees. Henry planted his rifle against his shoulder and fired a single, cracking shot. Corporal Lewis sprang to a kneeling position and began firing his bolt-action rifle with practiced speed. The faint rustling sound became a mad crashing through the underbrush. Keltin was moving closer to see what Henry and Lewis were shooting at when he finally saw movement ahead and dropped low to get a good view of the approaching beast.

It was roughly the size of a man, with no limbs and no discernible head. It was covered in bony plates and resembled nothing so much as a gigantic, armored leech as it undulated forward like a landed seal. Keltin tried to find some chink in the beast's protective plating, but its lack of any limbs or a distinguishable head left him few options. Corporal Lewis made no attempt to find a weak spot in the beast's defenses as he continued to pepper the thing with blast after blast from his rifle. The creature shuddered under the corporal's barrage, stopping its blind rush in Henry's direction and turning towards Lewis.

"Get out of the way!" Keltin yelled, but the corporal stood his ground, firing with mechanical efficiency.

The beast was on him in a matter of heartbeats. It reared up to briefly reveal a circular mouth ringed with fine teeth before collapsing on top of Lewis, pressing the screaming man to the ground underneath its quivering body. Keltin put his rifle to his shoulder to try for an exposed underside of the creature when Bor've'tai leapt forward.

"Do not shoot," he commanded over his shoulder as he crossed Keltin's line of fire.

The imposing Loopi sprinting forward to the beast on top of Corporal Lewis and drew his ax back. In a single, fluid motion he brought the honed edge of his weapon down on the creature as if it were a knot-filled stump. The beast's sturdy exoskeleton cracked open with a sickening crunch under the Loopi's tremendous blow. With less than a breath of a pause Bor've'tai struck again, cutting so deep into the creature that Keltin feared that he may have gone straight through to Lewis still feebly struggling underneath it.

The beast made no cry of pain as it died, and Keltin was just lowering his rifle when shots rang out to his right, followed by a tortured scream.

"Get over here!" shouted Weedon in a near-hysterical voice. "It's got Ru!"

Keltin raced towards the sounds of gunfire and screaming. Ru was on the ground, a stork-legged beast using its jagged beak to savagely rip the man apart. Pollik and Weedon stood nearby firing as fast as they could, and Keltin pulled his rifle against his shoulder to take aim. He quickly realized that neither of the other two hunters could do much more than pour bullets into the beast's meaty hindquarters from their poor position behind the creature.

Taking advantage of his position in front of the beast, Keltin aimed at its spindly neck. He advanced the chamber of his rifle, ensuring that the first shot would be a Capshire Shatter Round followed immediately by a Reltac Spinner. The beast had no chance to scream in pain as its head fell limply to the side, the spine severed by Keltin's pinpoint accuracy. The thing collapsed on top of Ru's prostrate body. Weedon ran forward, tears coursing down his cheeks. The young man swore violently as he struggled to pull the beast off of Ru's still form.

"Plaguing beast! Cursed thing came out of nowhere. Why didn't you pay attention Ru?! Pollik! You were supposed to watch his back. You blind old fool, this is your fault!"

Pollik's face was grim as he approached Keltin, ignoring Weedon's impotent raging.

"It came without a sound from behind us," the old man said softly, spitting in the dead beast's direction. "It must have circled around behind the corporal's precious patrol line."

Weedon finally managed to shove the beast's carcass aside to reveal Ru lying still on the ground. Pollik shook his head.

"That boy's had it," he said in a low voice.

Keltin looked at Ru's terrible wounds and knew the old man was right. Weedon tried for a moment to tend the dead body of his friend, but was soon overcome with a violent wave of sobbing. Keltin turned away from the scene.

"What happened over there?" Pollik asked, pointing in the direction Keltin had come from.

"Another attack. It got the Corporal."

"Bad?"

Keltin nodded as Bor've'tai and Henry approached them. Henry swore a black oath when he saw Weedon crying over Ru's body. Bor've'tai took in the ugly scene with grim stoicism.

"How is the corporal?" said Keltin.

Bor've'tai shook his head. "He is dead. His wounds were not severe, but I suspect the beast was venomous. The corporal was already stiff with paralysis when we got to him."

Keltin covered his eyes with a hand still trembling with adrenaline and sighed. Two men dead already. How many more before this was all over?

"What do we do now?" said Henry. "Do we go on with the patrol?"

"Why?" demanded Pollik. "We told Lewis it was foolish. Now he's paid for it, and I'm not going to follow him into an early grave."

"I do not think Weedon will be able to continue," said Bor've'tai, looking at the man now silently crying against his friend's chest. Pollik spat.

"He'll move unless he wants to be left out here alone. He can grieve when we're not in the middle of this plaguing forest."

"We are not going to leave him," Bor've'tai said, his deep voice leaving little room for argument. Pollik scowled at him.

"Stay here if you like, ape, but I'm not going to-"

"Shut up!" Keltin snapped. "We're in too much danger right now to have time for pointless fights among ourselves."

Keltin readied himself for an angry retort from the old man, but Pollik only stared at him for a moment before shrugging with a dismissive grunt.

"Then what do we do?"

Keltin ground his teeth together as he tried to think. "We go back to camp," he said after a moment. "We tell Baron Rumsfeld that his ideas of patrols and sentries may work fine in a war with men, but *we're* the experts on hunting beasts. We'll tell him our ideas from this morning. The traps, the tree blinds with bait, all of it."

"What about Lewis and Ru?" asked Henry.

"We'll bring them with us."

"They'll slow us down."

"I know, but it can't be helped. If we want to convince the Baron that his plans are fatally flawed then we have to give him undeniable proof. But we'll have to hurry. We need to get back to camp before the Baron sends another patrol to their deaths. Are we agreed?"

"Agreed," said Bor've'tai.

"I guess that's the best we can do," said Henry.

Keltin nodded and looked to Pollik, who shrugged and spat.

"I'm all for getting out of this forest as soon as we can, but I'm not waiting on that boy," he said, pointing at Weedon.

"I will get him," said Bor've'tai. The Loopi moved to the kneeling young man and placed a hand on his shoulder.

"We need to go," he said gently.

"Leave me alone," said Weedon bitterly, trying to shake off the Loopi's hand.

Bor've'tai's grip tightened as he yanked Weedon to his feet, turning the young hunter to look up into the Loopi's deep brown eyes.

"We are going," he said firmly. "We cannot mourn now, and we will not leave you."

Keltin expected an angry protest from Weedon, but the young man only stared into Bor've'tai's intense, liquid eyes. The two hunters stood silently, locked in place and motionless. At last, Weedon sniffed and nodded, and Bor've'tai released him to recover his dropped rifle.

"Which way do we go, Keltin?" Bor've'tai asked as he and Weedon rejoined the surviving members of Squad Three.

Keltin looked around a moment to get his bearings. "I think we should go this way. We can cross that fallow field that we circled earlier. From there we can continue on to the road and then follow it to camp. Agreed?"

The others nodded. Bor've'tai volunteered to carry the corporal, and Weedon refused any help in carrying Ru. Henry kept watch behind them, and Keltin led the way. He'd never had to lead anyone before, and was more than a little uncomfortable with the unfamiliar responsibility, though he was too preoccupied with getting them all safely back to camp to give it too much thought.

As they carefully moved forward, Keltin quickly realized that not all of his fellow hunters were familiar with stealthily stalking through a wooded area. While Henry moved as quietly as Keltin did and Weedon managed well enough despite the obvious burden of Ru's body, both Bor've'tai and Pollik showed the clear signs of individuals who were not used to making themselves unheard and nearly unseen. Keltin halted the group for a rest, keeping his voice low as he addressed them.

"We'll be reaching the field soon, but we need to be careful. Keep low, and watch where you step. Weedon, I know you want to carry your friend, but can I help you? We need to get back as soon as possible."

Weedon made no protest. The group seemed to have taken

Keltin's words of caution to heart as they continued on in silence. A movement up ahead caught Keltin's attention. He signaled to Weedon, and they crouched down together with Ru between them. The rest of the hunters followed their example, waiting until the beast had slowly emerged from between the narrow tree trunks ahead of them. It was another stork-legged beast, but this one seemed to have missed the hidden hunters. A soft hiss behind him drew Keltin's attention to Henry, who lifted his rifle with an inquisitive look on his face. Keltin shook his head, pointing to his ear to indicate the noise of the shot. Eventually the beast moved on and they were able to proceed.

As it turned out, Keltin's cautious, silent method of travel revealed more beasts in just a few minutes than the late Corporal Lewis' sweeping patrol had found throughout the entire morning. They spied another giant armored leech, as well as several new beasts of various sizes and descriptions, including one that seemed like a blending of stag and serpent and a two-mouthed, hairy quadruped with quills nearly a foot long. Perhaps strangest of all was a 'beast' that none of them could actually see, except for a strange warping of the forest immediately around it, bending and twisting the trees for a moment as it passed before restoring them to their solid form as it moved onward. Keltin was at a loss of how they would handle such a beast, but he kept such thoughts to himself.

At last, they found the fallow field and took another chance to rest, watching for any signs of beasts at the wooded edges of the large square of untended earth. Once Keltin was satisfied that there was no immediate danger, they moved as quickly as they could through the open space until reaching the cover of trees on the far side. Keltin breathed a sigh of relief to see the familiar dirt track of the road nearby.

"We should be able to make it back to camp within the hour," he announced to the others. "That should give us some time to talk with the Baron about what we propose before the next patrol moves out."

"And just what are we going to propose?" asked Pollik.

Keltin frowned as he shouldered his portion of Ru's weight

once more. "I'm not sure, but if you're all willing, maybe we can put a plan of action together before we get back to camp."

"I hope we can come up with something good," muttered Henry. "This whole campaign may just depend on it."

CHAPTER 7 – DISSENTION AND LOYALTY

Keltin stumbled, tripping over Ru's stiffened foot. The dead man's weight shifted on his aching shoulders and he found himself staggering drunkenly just to keep his footing. Weedon grunted on Ru's other side but made no comment as Keltin regained his grip. They continued on, two men silently bearing the burden of a fallen comrade.

"Can I help?" asked Bor've'tai.

Keltin wiped the sweat from his brow and looked back at the Loopi. He was still carrying Corporal Lewis' weight upon his shoulders without a word of complaint, but Keltin could see the Loopi's muscular body trembling with the strain of more than an hour's constant taxing. Keltin shook his head and gave a weak smile.

"We'll manage."

Bor've'tai nodded. He cocked his head to the side, a frown of concentration on his dark features.

"Henry is returning," he said after a moment.

Keltin looked up the road. Sure enough, the lanky hunter came into view at the road's next rising.

"The camp's just ahead," he announced. "We've made it."

"I'll go on ahead and get some help," offered Pollik, his weathered face red and sweaty from the unaccustomed exercise.

The old trapper jogged awkwardly ahead of them and Henry turned to Keltin and Weedon still struggling forward.

"Can I help either of you two?"

Keltin was about to gratefully accept the offer when Weedon suddenly fell to his knees with a gasping sob. Keltin struggled to keep Ru from falling on top of the young man and Henry quickly moved to help him. They resumed their slow pace forward, Keltin's joints screaming for relief as Weedon followed behind them.

At last, the barn and farmhouse of the camp was visible. Pollik returned with several other hunters and Keltin sighed with relief as Ru was gently lifted from his shoulders. The hunters from camp all seemed to be asking questions at the same time. Henry was busy trying to tell what had happened when Sergeant Bracksten stepped forward. The giant of a man looked from Corporal Lewis to Ru, then turned to Keltin.

"What happened, Moore?"

Keltin told the sergeant of the beast attacks between gasping gulps of air. Bracksten listened, saying not a word until Keltin had finished.

"All right," he said. "I'll report this to Baron Rumsfeld. In the meantime, take the bodies to the east side of the house. Corporal Alvor and his squad will bury them there."

Keltin watched the faces of the dead men as they were carried away. Pale and stained with their own blood, how long would they haunt his dreams? Then again, the thought of nightmares seemed almost welcome to him if it meant rest. Lack of sleep and the hard march back to camp had sapped his last reserves of strength. He struggled to resist the temptation to let his trembling legs give way and sink into an exhausted slumber on the welcoming ground. It took him several moments to realize that Sergeant Bracksten was speaking to him and his companions.

"...all relieved of duty until I tell you otherwise. That's all for now. Dismissed."

Keltin hesitated. He wanted so badly to sleep, but Bor've'tai and the others were looking at him expectantly. Leaning heavily on his rifle, he called to the sergeant's broad, retreating back.

"Sergeant Bracksten?"

The large man did not stop.

"Sergeant Bracksten!"

The sergeant stopped and turned, his face twisted with unhidden annoyance.

"What is it, Moore?"

"I need to speak with Baron Rumsfeld."

Bracksten's eyes narrowed. "You got something to say that you don't want me to hear?"

"No, you should probably hear it too. But I need to talk with the Baron."

Sergeant Bracksten folded his meaty arms. "The Baron is busy. You can talk to me. I'll decide whether he needs to hear what you have to say."

A wave of fatigue hit Keltin again and he almost gave up trying to speak with Rumsfeld. Perhaps it would be best to just tell the sergeant their ideas. But the pale faces of Ru and Corporal Lewis wouldn't leave him. They had died for the blind obedience of military discipline. It had to stop, before more men died needlessly.

"What I have to say may mean the difference between life and death for every man in this camp. That's why I need to tell him myself. If you don't let me talk with the Baron, then I'll go to the other hunters and let them decide how important what I have to say is. It's your choice."

Bracksten's face flared crimson. "I've had enough of your backtalk, Moore. Turn in your guns. You're coming with me. We'll let the Baron decide whether to flog you for insubordination or hang you for stirring up a mutiny."

Suddenly Bor've'tai stepped between them, his ax held firmly in his hands. Keltin stepped to the side to see Bor've'tai's eyes smoldering with the same cold stoicism that they had held earlier that morning just before he cleaved the armored leech in two. Keltin put a restraining hand on the Loopi's muscular arm.

He had almost expected Bor've'tai's protective gesture, but to Keltin's surprise both Henry and Weedon also drew closer to him in a defensive stance. Even Pollik stood closer to him. Keltin didn't know how to react to the sudden loyalty of men he'd only met that morning. Somehow, facing death together had drawn all of them closer in a way he had never experienced before.

He turned back to Sergeant Bracksten to see the large man slowly reaching for the revolver on his hip, his eyes darting between the faces of each of the remaining survivors of Squad Three. Keltin realized he had to say something quickly before more human blood was spilled.

"I'll turn in my guns," he said, stepping in front of his squad mates, "if it means I can speak with the Baron."

Bracksten kept his hand on his revolver, giving a quick nod in reply.

"Follow me."

Keltin and his squad mates followed the sergeant to the farmhouse. Pausing outside the low picket fence surrounding the house, Keltin dutifully handed his rifle, revolver, and the Ripper over to Bor've'tai.

"I'll tell Grel'zi'tael and Evik what the sergeant said," Bor've'tai said in a low voice. "If they try anything, we'll be ready."

Keltin nodded, unsure of what he should say. He appreciated his Loopi friend's loyalty, but he hoped Bor've'tai's concerns were unfounded. The last thing the camp needed was for the hunters to start killing each other while beasts stalked them from the shadows. Turning his back to his friends, Keltin allowed Sergeant Bracksten to lead him past the sentry at the front door and into the farmhouse's entry hall.

"Wait here," said Bracksten, the heavy tread of his boots echoing on the hard wood floors as he went further into the house.

Keltin found a low bench near the doorway and sank down gratefully. He leaned against the makeshift pillow of hanging coats on the wall behind him and felt consciousness slide from his exhausted body. He had no idea how long he remained slumbering in the corner before a rough nudge from Bracksten's boot dragged him back to the world of the living.

"The Baron wants to see you."

Baron Rumsfeld sat at the head of a long oak table in a spacious dining room, a worried frown taking the place of the sardonic smile Keltin had always seen him wearing before.

"Come in, Mr. Moore. Sergeant Bracksten has told me what happened this morning, but I'd like to hear your report myself. Take your time, and leave out nothing."

Keltin forced his mind to alertness and repeated his story to the Baron. Rumsfeld listened intently, interrupting him occasionally to ask a specific question or to clarify some small detail. The Baron shook his head sadly after he had finished.

"I am very sorry to hear about the loss of Corporal Lewis. His father is an acquaintance of mine. And Ru's death will no doubt hurt the men's morale considerably."

A long silence fell on the room as Rumsfeld stared into space. Keltin waited, fighting the temptation to sink into one of the chairs and lay his head on the polished wooden table. At last, Baron Rumsfeld looked back to Keltin.

"Mr. Moore, I want to ask you a question. Do you feel like this morning's tragic events could have been prevented?"

"Absolutely."

One of the Baron's eyebrows shot up. "Indeed? How?"

Keltin hesitated. He glanced at Sergeant Bracksten and found him glaring from where he stood in the doorway, his hand still on the gun at his belt. The Baron turned in his seat to follow Keltin's gaze. Some silent communication seemed to pass between the sergeant and the Baron before he turned back to Keltin.

"Sergeant Bracksten informed me about your... enthusiasm to speak with me. He also said that you'd go to the other hunters if I didn't listen to you. As a nonmilitary man, you may not realize that talk like that could be seen as a precursor to mutiny, which of course I cannot allow. However, I am loath to flog a man for telling his mind, and I believe this campaign has already seen enough death today. Now, tell me what you wanted to say to me."

Keltin took a deep breath and looked the Baron in the eye.

"I don't think the way that you have organized this campaign will work."

"I see. And why not?"

"Because you're treating hunters like infantry and beasts like humans. This morning's patrol proved that. A rough line of half a dozen men marching shoulder-to-shoulder through the forest can't possibly stalk a beast effectively, not even if each of those men was an expert stalker, which they weren't. I don't know how you decided on the members of each squad, but my squad seems to be a random mix of trappers, stalkers, and baiters."

"I see. Anything else?"

"Yes. Your military structure may be fine for trained soldiers, but except for the few men that you've brought with you, no-one here has a military background. We're not soldiers, we're hunters. Most of us chose this profession because we prefer to think for ourselves. We aren't used to taking orders, and we're certainly not going to sacrifice our lives for blind obedience. I'm not making threats sir, but you need to understand that if this campaign continues like this, you're going to get more than just rumors of a mutiny."

Keltin finished, a little nervous of how far his frustration had driven him. He didn't dare look to see what Sergeant Bracksten's reaction was, and instead watched Rumsfeld for his response. The Baron sighed and leaned on the table, covering his face with his hands for a long moment. At length, he looked up at Keltin again, his voice soft and quiet.

"Mr. Moore, I'm not a hunter. I've never participated in the hunts of the Krendarian nobility. I'm an officer. I'm a graduate of Carvalen's Military Academy and I served my country by leading the 142nd Infantry on the Tamkin fields of the

Krendaria Larigoss War. I took this assignment from my friend, Duke Gregson, expecting to have a company of trained soldiers at my command. When the army declined our request for more troops, we had to improvise. That's why you're here, and that's why I'm here.

"I know that you are correct, Mr. Moore. You and your peers are not soldiers, no matter how much I might wish that you were. I just don't see what I can accomplish here without the military discipline I need from my men. I'm at a loss."

Baron Rumsfeld hid his face behind his hands once more. Keltin felt the frustration that had burned inside him cooling into a sad pity for the Baron. The man was obviously out of his element and could see no way out of the terrible predicament he had fallen into.

"Well, perhaps I could help. I've spoken with some of the others, and we have some ideas."

The Baron looked up, a puzzled expression on his face. "Ideas? For what?"

"The campaign, sir. We hunters may not be the soldiers that you wish we were, and I can't help that. But we do have one thing your soldiers don't have. Experience. We know how to hunt and kill beasts, and we have ideas of how to do that here."

The Baron's mouth hung open a moment. He pulled out the chair nearest to him.

"Have a seat."

Keltin slid into the offered seat as the Baron leaned towards him.

"What were your ideas?"

"First, reorganize the squads into multiple teams of hunters with similar experience. You've already started with the tamarrin hound trainers and the sleevak wranglers. Then, once you have your teams of hunters, let them each work in the way that they're accustomed to. Have the stalkers, trackers, tamarrin hounds, and sleevaks each take turns hunting in different areas of the countryside. You should also take all of them off sentry duty so that they can spend more time hunting and get the rest they need between hunts."

"But what about camp security?"

"Have the trappers set up their snares and traps in the forest immediately surrounding the camp, and use the baiters and blinds-hunters as an additional layer of protection out in the forest, rather than relying on sentries inside the camp."

The Baron nodded, his eyes starting to show some of the sparkle that Keltin remembered from the first time he had seen him at Duke Gregson's estate.

"I'm liking the way that you're thinking," he said. "Specialized teams would be much easier to manage and far more effective in the field. It would also allow us to cover more ground and engage more beasts than the patrols alone would allow. Should we also make the Loopi their own team?"

"No. Bor've'tai has told me that Grel'zi'tael is training all the Loopi in rudimentary Sky Talker lore, and from what I observed on the way back to camp this morning, each team will need their skills against the more... exotic beasts in the area. I recommend dividing the Loopi between the teams. Just don't put any of them with the Heteracks."

"Of course, that's most prudent. So, we will issue a Loopi to each team, excluding the Heteracks, along with one of my men to act as each team's commanding officer."

Keltin shook his head. "I don't think that's a good idea. We've seen this morning what happens when a soldier inexperienced in hunting is in command of a group in the field."

The Baron stiffened slightly, and Keltin realized too late that Rumsfeld could have taken what he had said as a personal slight instead of a criticism of the late Corporal Lewis. But the Baron's tone was level and controlled when he spoke again.

"Then what do you propose?"

"I think it would be best to choose a leader from among the hunters of each team, based on their experience and ability to lead."

"With you in charge of it all, I'm sure," grumbled Sergeant Bracksten, breaking his moody silence.

"I've never led a group of men," said Keltin. "I wouldn't even know where to start. I'm only suggesting what the other hunters and I feel is the best option for this campaign's success."

"And what would Sergeant Bracksten and the rest of the soldiers in the camp do?" asked Rumsfeld.

Keltin shrugged. "Soldiers know how to stand guard and patrol better than hunters do. I'd suggest putting them in charge of keeping the camp safe and secure."

Sergeant Bracksten's eyes bulged and his face turned a violet hue. "You cocky little git! You think I'm going to let you take over this command while I stand around guarding latrine ditches?"

The sergeant was interrupted by a sudden explosion of laughter from Rumsfeld. Both Keltin and Bracksten stared at the Baron in surprise as he fought to contain his mirth, shaking his head and holding up a hand to reassure his uncertain sergeant.

"I must say, Mr. Moore. I knew you hunters were brave, but I never realized just *how* brave!"

The Baron broke into laughter again for a moment before finally wiping a tear from his eye and turning back to Bracksten.

"Sergeant, why don't you assemble the corporals? I'd like to speak with them."

Bracksten gave Keltin a black look as he left, and Rumsfeld waited until they had heard the slamming of the front door before continuing.

"Don't worry about the sergeant. He's stubborn, but he's a good soldier and will follow my orders. Now then, unless you have any more recommendations, I've made my decision. We'll follow the counsel of you and your friends. I agree that the idea of specialized teams led by experienced hunters is our best chance for success here. We'll begin making the changes immediately. There's only one thing that I don't agree with you about."

"What's that?"

The Baron's eyes twinkled. "I think that you're wrong about whether you'd be able to lead a group of men. I can't think of a better man to captain one of the stalker teams."

"I'd rather not take on the responsibility."

"And that's why I'm giving you the position. You brought the survivors of your squad home safely, and you were willing to risk Bracksten's temper to stand up for your companions and the success of this campaign. In the end, Mr. Moore, I want you leading those hunters, and I'll only assemble the teams if you take the position. Understood?"

Keltin forced himself to nod. "Yes sir, I'll accept."

Baron Rumsfeld smiled. "Good. And don't worry. I always see that my subordinates are well taken care of."

Keltin was about to reply when the front door opened and Sergeant Bracksten rushed into the dining room.

"Sir, we may have a situation. Nearly twenty of the men are gathering just outside with weapons in hand."

"What do they want?"

"They aren't saying. I've assembled the corporals and the other soldiers before the front door in case they attack."

Rumsfeld turned to Keltin. "Do you know what they may want?"

Keltin had his suspicions, but kept them to himself and shook his head.

"No, I don't."

"Well then, let's go find out."

Baron Rumsfeld rose from the table and gestured for Keltin to accompany him. They followed Sergeant Bracksten to the front door where the small number of professional soldiers in the camp stared uneasily at the armed group before them. Looking at the gathered hunters, Keltin recognized all the surviving members of Squad Three among them. Grel'zi'tael was also there along with the rest of the Loopi, and even Jaylocke waved and grinned from where he stood among several Weycliff wayfarers all armed and looking ready for a fight. Rumsfeld looked over the group for a moment before focusing on Evik standing among his fellow wayfarers.

"What's the matter, Evik?" the Baron asked with a friendly smile. "Why the sudden congregation?"

The wayfarer leader shifted uncomfortably a moment before answering. "We'd heard about one of the hunters being called into the farmhouse to meet with you, and we were worried about him."

"And why would you be worried about him?"

Evik seemed to falter, unable to answer the Baron's direct questioning. Grel'zi'tael stepped forward, his somber eyes unflinching as he addressed Rumsfeld.

"Baron," he said, "there has been much talk in this camp, and little of it open for all to hear. If we are to avoid a debacle, I advise that we speak plainly with each other."

Rumsfeld held the gray-haired Loopi's gaze a long moment.

"Very well, Sky Talker," he said with a nod. "You are correct, and these men deserve some direct speaking." The Baron turned his attention to the assembled hunters. "No doubt, all of you have heard about the unfortunate events of this morning's patrol. I have also heard the reports, and I commend the men of Squad Three for their courage in the face of such fierce opposition. I have also had the occasion to reconsider the way this campaign is organized.

"There will be some significant changes made, and I ask you to be patient as we restructure the camp. For the moment, I can tell you that the pattern of squads and patrols will be replaced by teams of hunters chosen by their area of expertise and led by their fellow hunters. We'll have more information for you by dinnertime tonight."

"And what of Keltin?" called out Jaylocke.

The Baron smiled. "Mr. Moore has graciously accepted the honor of serving as a team captain, and I must say that I can only hope that all my captains will have such loyalty from his fellows. Now, if you men will excuse us, Mr. Moore and I have a great deal of work to do before this evening."

The Baron turned to go back into the farmhouse and Keltin followed, pausing a moment to acknowledge the many relieved smiles among the gathered hunters. He did his best to smile gratefully back at them, but he was already dreading the additional hours the Baron would require of him before he could finally get some rest.

CHAPTER 8 – SKY TALKER

Keltin waited as Grel'zi'tael led the Loopi in their morning prayers. Standing at a respectful distance, he yawned and stretched, feeling more rested than he had since first arriving in Krendaria. A full night's sleep and a hopeful outlook for the campaign had improved his mood considerably.

The day before had been spent in the company of Baron Rumsfeld and the other newly appointed team captains to discuss and improve upon the ideas proposed by Keltin and the rest of the Squad Three survivors. Plans were made and implemented quickly, and by the afternoon the stand hunters were already positioned in a protective ring around the camp while trappers laid their deadly snares even further into the forest.

While Keltin's original idea had been for the stand hunters to take their positions beyond the trapper's territory, he'd quickly changed his mind at yesterday's meeting. Captain Morgan of the stand hunters had actually seemed offended when Keltin had suggested the traps be placed between his hunters and the camp.

"You think we'd let anything get by us?" he had demanded. "You'd never have to reset a trap!"

Keltin hadn't expected Morgan's reaction, but Baron

Rumsfeld had come to his rescue by skillfully dealing with the situation, cooling Morgan's temper while explaining to the rest of the captains the wisdom in placing the traps beyond the stand hunters. All present agreed on the change of strategy, and the dinnertime report of three beasts killed by traps and stand hunters confirmed their decision.

Now it was time to start sending out the mobile teams. Keltin's team of stalkers and the tamarrin hound trainers would be first, leaving the camp in different directions to cover as much area as possible and to avoid any accidental interference with each other.

At last, the Loopi finished their prayers and rose from their rush mats.

"Are you ready to go then?" asked Keltin as he approached them.

Bor've'tai looked up and nodded. Keltin was about to turn back towards the farmhouse when Grel'zi'tael placed a hand on Bor've'tai's shoulder.

"I should caution you, my friend," he said. "I feel that today you will be called upon for the first time to use those things that I have taught you."

Bor've'tai's mouth became a hard line. "Then perhaps it would be better if Val'ta'lir went with Keltin instead. He is farther along than I am."

Grel'zi'tael gave Bor've'tai a curious look, but the younger Loopi dropped his gaze to the ground. Shar'le'vah stepped forward to place a hand on Bor've'tai's arm.

"I can go with Keltin, I don't mind."

The Sky Talker nodded, but his eyes remained on Bor've'tai. The younger Loopi finally looked up to meet the gaze of his elder.

"I will go," he said softly, "if you tell me to."

Grel'zi'tael shook his head. "It is not my place to command you. If you must seek direction, speak with your Captain."

Bor've'tai turned to Keltin.

"It is your choice then, Captain. Will you take me or Shar'le'vah with you today?"

Looking at the expectant faces of the Loopi, Keltin suppressed a groan. Couldn't anyone in this camp make a decision for themselves? He nearly said as much as he debated with himself for a moment before speaking.

"Bor've'tai, you've come here to hunt beasts. If you have a good reason to not come today, well, all right. But if you don't, then I'd expect you to come along."

Bor've'tai heaved a heavy sigh and nodded.

"Very well, Keltin. I am ready. Let's go."

Taking up his ax, the Loopi walked away, leaving Keltin to catch up with him at the team's meeting place near the farmstead's barn. Waiting for the rest of the team, Bor've'tai's customary silence seemed even deeper than usual.

"Is it very difficult being a Sky Talker?" asked Keltin after a moment.

"I am not a Sky Talker. Grel'zi'tael has only instructed me for a few months."

"Oh, I didn't realize."

"Val'ta'lir and Shar'le'vah were already among his students before I joined them, so they are both further along than I am. Of the three of us, Shar'le'vah seems to have the most talent. Perhaps it's because she is also Grel'zi'tael's granddaughter. I'm not sure."

Keltin nodded, unsure how to react to the normally closed Loopi suddenly volunteering information about himself and his companions. Was this Bor've'tai's attempt to explain his hesitancy in coming with the rest of the team today? Was he trying to apologize? Keltin was still trying to think of something to say when a coarse voice called out to them.

"Look out Captain, you'll catch fleas or worse standing so close to the apes!"

The young Heterack leered at them until he disappeared behind the barn on his way to the sleevak pens. Keltin glanced at Bor've'tai to see his reaction, but the Loopi's expression had not changed.

"How do you put up with that?"

"I hear nothing when they speak."

Keltin shook his head. "I don't understand. What do they have against you? I've noticed it since we were all at Duke Gregson's estate. Both your people and the Weycliff seem to have somehow gotten on the bad side of nearly everyone in the camp. I know that Jaylocke said that the Weycliff are wanderers and easy scapegoats for any local problems. Is it the same with the Loopi?"

"You've never been to Malpin."

It didn't sound like a question, but Keltin answered it anyway.

"No, I haven't. I've never been outside of Riltvin before this. Why?"

"I do not recommend the trip."

Bor've'tai slipped back into silence as the rest of the team began to arrive. Keltin had to put his concerns about the Loopi and Weycliff wayfarers aside as he tried to remember names and match them with the faces of his teammates. Besides Bor've'tai, he'd only known the members of the team since the night before when they had all sat together for dinner. Still, he took comfort, knowing that each of them knew the delicate business of stealthily approaching a beast, finding the killing shot, and bringing the creature down without ever being seen. Keltin spoke a few words of greeting and encouragement to the group before leading them to the eastern edge of the camp and into the woods beyond. Weedon was waiting for them among the dense trees.

"Good morning, Keltin," he said softly. The young man seemed to have come to terms with the loss of Ru, though his grief still showed clearly in his reddened eyes.

"Good morning. Are you the one to lead us to the trappers' perimeter?"

"Yes, follow me."

Keltin and his team followed Weedon, proceeding quietly and carefully through the forest under the watchful eyes of hunters in the trees above them. Weedon led them to the edge of the stand hunters' area and silently left as a grizzled trapper approached them. Keltin inwardly tensed as he recognized

Hull Kuley, the man who had bullied Jaylocke at Duke Gregson's estate. Kully gave Keltin and Bor've'tai a dirty look, but kept his tone civil as he spoke softly to them.

"Follow me close, and step where I do."

As they walked, Keltin noticed that Kully seemed to have almost totally lost the limp that he had given him in Carvalen. He considered voicing some regret over the discomfort he had caused, but decided instead to let the matter rest and focus on watching for hidden traps and snares.

The trappers had been busy. Old-fashioned covered pits and baited cages were accompanied by the latest innovations in the specialized field of beast trapping. Spring-activated jaw traps accompanied bladewire snares and other, even more devious contraptions. As they continued through the killing ground, Keltin and his team passed a small band of trappers installing sharpened stakes in a pit nearly six feet deep.

"Still setting new traps?" asked Keltin.

"Resetting it," Kully replied over his shoulder. "We had a winged strangler skewer itself on it last night."

They reached the outer perimeter of the trap field where Kully left them without a word of farewell. Keltin and his team fanned out, each hunter finding his own trail between the trees. They made little effort to keep in sight of each other at all times, though each team member was careful to check where his neighbor hunters were at regular intervals, lest he become separated.

Keltin heard the low call of a crested blue robin and sank to the earth, checking in all directions for his quarry. At dinner the previous night, the team had agreed on the crested blue's song as their signal to each other. The bird's call seemed the perfect choice. It was easy to learn, and -more importantly- the bird was only found in the hill country of Riltvin. Keltin began stalking in the direction of the call when it sounded again from another direction.

A moment passed, and a gunshot broke the silence of the forest, quickly followed by a second and a third. Keltin studied the woods around him for any sign of additional beasts drawn by the shattering noise. All was still, and he continued to the source of the first call. He found Bryan, one of his hunters, kneeling over the still body of a serpent stag.

"I had a clear shot," he said softly.

Keltin nodded. "Good job. Let's check the other call."

They found another hunter, Oliete, watching the convulsions of a beast that was new to Keltin. It had a half-dozen ropy appendages extending from a squat body on stubby legs. Its vaguely pig-like head had a gaping wound in the side, and a second shot seemed to have found it solidly in the middle of its mossy green body. Oliete pointed to the wound in the creature's side.

"That was my first shot," he explained. "It started to run when the other shot sounded, and I had to take what I could to slow it down."

Keltin nodded as he slid the Ripper from his shoulder and approached the still thrashing beast. He waited for an opening, then hurried forward and brought the blade-end down on the thing's stocky neck, severing the nerve running along its spine. The creature went limp, and Keltin retrieved his rifle from Oliete.

"Well done," he said softly. "Let's keep going."

The morning continued in the same slow, methodical way. Keltin and his team brought down three more beasts with little to no trouble, and Keltin couldn't help feeling some pride at seeing his plans working out so well. When he next heard the call of the crested blue robin he sank down to the forest floor and waited for the sound of a gunshot. But none came.

The forest seemed full of stillness. Keltin began quietly moving in the direction of the bird call. He heard the stirring of undergrowth ahead of him. The signaler's beast must still be moving forward, or else the signaler was moving into a better position. There was a gunshot, then a second. A third echoed among the trees and Keltin quickened his pace. Something was wrong. The stirring in the brush became a reckless, crashing racket.

"Help! Help me!"

The voice was Oliete's. Keltin disregarded stealth and ran in the direction of the desperate cries. He burst through a thicket of barren berry bushes and came to a staggering stop. Oliete was scrambling backwards, his rifle discarded and forgotten on the forest floor. The hunter seemed torn between a desperation to flee and a hypnotic fascination with the apparition pursuing him.

The beast was unlike anything Keltin had ever seen. It seemed nothing more than a bluish mist, billowing and wafting among the trees like the dense smoke of a campfire. It drifted as if on a stiff breeze, moving relentlessly towards the near-hysterical Oliete. Keltin's rifle rose to his shoulder as if of its own volition, but he hesitated. Where would he shoot the thing? He searched in vain for some portion of solidity within the moving cloud, something that his bullet could lodge itself into.

The smoke beast was nearly upon Oliete now. Keltin advanced the chamber of his rifle to a Shatter Round for lack of a better idea and fired. The bullet passed harmlessly through the amorphous creature as it settled upon Oliete. The hunter's scream was cut off with abrupt silence as he fell to the earth, clutching desperately at his throat. Keltin fired again but it served no purpose. The rest of his team came crashing through the trees, and Keltin turned desperately to Bor've'tai.

"Do something!"

The Loopi stared at the smoke beast with an unreadable expression. He looked back at Keltin, his liquid eyes set and hard.

"I will try."

Bor've'tai sank to his knees, setting his ax on the ground beside him as he placed hands on knees and closed his eyes. Keltin looked anxiously between the unmoving Loopi and the smoke beast. Nothing seemed to be happening. Bryan, standing nearby, swore and ran forward with another hunter. They plunged into the smoke beast, grabbed Oliete, and dragged him out of the bluish mist. Keltin was about to order all the members of his team to fall back when he felt the slight stirring of a breeze against his cheek. He looked at Bor've'tai. The Loopi was grimacing, though Keltin couldn't tell if it was from pain or concentration. The light wind seemed to pick up. The edges of the smoke beast became ragged as it tried advancing towards them.

Suddenly the wind died and Bor've'tai gasped, his broad shoulders slumping. The beast drew itself together into a tight, imperfect sphere, its smoky interior so dense that Keltin could barely see through it. As he watched, the bluish mist began to spiral within itself, slowly at first, but gradually building in speed.

"What do we do, Keltin?" said Bryan, his voice hoarse from the few moments spent inside the smoke beast.

Keltin glanced at Bor've'tai, still kneeling and breathing hard, his chin pressed against his heaving chest. Keltin turned back to the rest of his team.

"Get out of here. Go towards camp. Grel'zi'tael should be with the stand hunters. If that thing follows you, the Sky Talker will be able to stop it."

"Camp's over a mile away," said Garthen, a burly Krendarian hunter. "It'll be hard to stay ahead of that thing while carrying Oliete."

Keltin kept an eye on the smoke beast as it continued to turn in upon itself, beginning to resemble a strange parody of a dust devil in a farmer's field.

"You better get started then. I'll stay here and try to hold it off."

Garthen placed a large hand on Keltin's shoulder.

"It wouldn't do any good," he said. "Don't throw away your life."

Keltin forced himself to make a grim smile. "Don't worry. I have an idea. Now get out of here. Make sure Oliete makes it back."

Garthen frowned, but nodded. "Good luck, Captain."

Keltin nodded, keeping his attention on the rotating beast as Garthen and Bryan each placed an arm under Oliete's shoulders and took off through the forest, followed closely by the rest of the stalker team. Keltin didn't dare look back at them. The smoke beast had taken on the rough shape of an hourglass, its two halves rotating in different directions like some impossible double-tornado. Whatever the beast was doing, Keltin guessed he had little time before it attacked him.

Quickly he withdrew a thick handkerchief from a pocket of his hunting jacket and tied it over his mouth and nose. Placing his rifle on the ground, he took the Ripper and chopped a branch off of a nearby sapling, its leafs vivid with the change of seasons. Perhaps if he could break the creature apart with the leafy branch it would disorient it enough to allow him to escape along with the rest of his team. If not... Keltin forced any doubts out of his mind. It would work. It would have to work.

He turned back to the beast with the makeshift weapon and realized that Bor've'tai had not moved from his spot on the forest floor. The Loopi still knelt with hands on knees and chin on chest, seemingly oblivious to the swirling mass only a dozen paces away from him.

"Get out of here, Bor've'tai," Keltin snapped as he approached the beast. "You can't do any more here."

There was no time to see if Bor've'tai had heard him as he stepped forward to confront the smoke beast. He tried to find some weakness within the thing's two swirling halves, but he wasn't even sure what to look for. The beast, which had remained stationary except for its self-contained spinning, finally began to move towards him.

Keltin leapt forward, swinging the branch for the bottom half of its hourglass shape. The branch passed through the beast as if it were water. Keltin swung again, dodging and moving just enough to keep the creature from catching him. He struck the smoke beast again and again, doing little damage that he could see. The creature continued its relentless advance as they moved in a bizarre dance between the narrow trees.

Suddenly the beast stopped. Its hourglass shape began to lose its definition and Keltin wondered if he had somehow damaged it. The swirling mist ceased to spiral as its two halves combined once again into the smoky mass it had resembled when Keltin had first seen it. With a sudden burst of speed it moved forward. Keltin tried to leap backward. Horror swept through him as he felt his boot catch in the underbrush and he fell on his back with a crash. The smoke beast was upon him.

Keltin held his breath as the forest around him took on an unearthly bluish tint. He struggled to rise, but a great weight seemed to press him firmly against the loamy earth. He could hear nothing but the thrumming pulse of his own blood in his ears. Desperately he tried to roll away from the beast, but the bush that had caught his boot now hampered his escape as well.

His lungs began to burn as some sort of liquid fell on his exposed face, taunting him to wipe it away with his weighed down hands. More liquid fell, great cold drops that quickly soaked his clothing. Confused and starved for air, Keltin thrashed with the unthinking ferocity of a landed fish. At last, his tortured lungs overthrew his reason and he gasped a ragged breath.

Pure air filled him. Keltin coughed and gagged, mindless of all else but his body's struggle to gain all his breath back at once. He managed to get his coughing under control and sucked in another breath through clenched teeth. It tasted sweet and fresh. He opened his eyes to have drops of liquid fall directly into them. It was water.

Trembling and uncertain, Keltin turned his face to the side and opened his eyes again. The forest had resumed its natural hue, blurred not by the smoke beast's blue mist but by the dimming deluge of rain falling all about him. He sat up slowly and looked around. The beast was nowhere in sight.

Keltin rose to his feet. The forest was still, save for the rain beating a gentle tattoo on the trees, driving many of the weakened orange and brown leafs to the forest floor. He walked among the fallen leafs, trying to understand what had happened. He found Bor've'tai still kneeling, heedless of the rain soaking his golden fur and clothing. Keltin dropped to his knees in front of his friend and placed a trembling hand on his arm.

"Bor've'tai?"

The Loopi looked up slowly, his deep eyes full of tears mixing with the rain as it fell.

"Keltin," he said, his voice barely more than a whisper. "You live."

Keltin nodded, wiping rain from his own eyes. "Bor've'tai, did you do this?"

Bor've'tai looked up as if noticing the rain for the first time. He let the cool water fall onto his dark face a moment before answering.

"Yes, I did."

Keltin could scarcely believe it. He felt a foolish grin rise to his face.

"Well done."

"Thank you."

Keltin laughed, releasing all the fear and exhaustion within him into the watery air. "Let's go find the team and head back to camp. I think Grel'zi'tael has some good news coming his way."

Bor've'tai nodded. "Yes, but there's one thing I must do first."

"What's that?"

The Loopi gave a tired smile and looked up again at the falling rain. "I need to figure out how to stop this."

CHAPTER 9 – FRIENDLY FIRE

"We're just not accomplishing enough here. I'm beginning to doubt whether we have a chance any more of saving this province."

The Baron sighed and rubbed his fingers against the dark circles under his eyes. Looking around the table, Keltin saw the same signs of weariness in the faces of each of the captains of the campaign.

"We're doing our best, my Lord," said Captain Tallow of the tamarrin hound trainers. "My men and their hounds have been out nearly every day since we arrived here, and I know most of the other hunters can say the same."

"Don't mistake what I've said for criticism, Captain Tallow. All you men and your teams have worked miracles in Dhalma. More than fifty beasts slain in a week with only four men dead and ten wounded. But we're running out of time. So far, Grel'zi'tael has managed to hold back the seasonal rains that would normally have started the crops rotting in the fields by now. But even if there is no rain, it will continue to get colder, and we don't seem to be any closer to ridding the area of this hellish infestation."

Rumsfeld turned to Keltin. "Captain Moore, do we have any idea just how many beasts are in these woods?"

"I'm afraid not. Each time a team leaves the camp, they seem to encounter just as many of the creatures as they did the day before. Our only clue is that the number of beasts seems greatest to the north. This has been confirmed by both the traveling teams as well as the trappers and stand hunters."

"That's something at least," said the Baron. "Captain Pollik, do you think your men can begin extending their trap field to the north? If it's true that the greatest concentration of the beasts is in that direction, we'd be wise to gradually extend that boundary."

The weathered trapper nodded. "We'll get on it."

"I can also change around the position of my men and place more of them to the north of the camp," offered Captain Morgan of the stand hunters.

"Very good," said Rumsfeld. "I want you both to begin as soon as possible. In the meantime, I will consider how else we may use this new information. However, we have another problem. Evik reports that we're running dangerously low on provisions. His people have already harvested all the available crops within the boundaries of the stand hunters' perimeter. We'll need a team to provide an escort for them to go further afield and find more food to fill our larders. Captain Moore, what is the condition of your team?"

"To tell the truth, we're a little undermanned since we sent three of my hunters to fill the gaps in Henry's team after those whip legs and armored leeches hit them so hard the day before yesterday. With Oliete still laid low and Bryan down with a bad leg, that leaves me, Bor've'tai, and only two others. I'm not sure we'd be able to manage a hunting foray all on our own."

"What about serving as an escort for the wayfarers?"

Keltin considered for a moment. "If some of the wayfarers were armed, just in case we ran into real trouble, I think we could manage."

Rumsfeld nodded. "Good. We'll send you to the fields southwest of camp. I believe Captain Rok and his sleevaks will be hunting just to the northwest of you, in case you need additional assistance."

Rok snorted. "Just don't get in my sleevaks' way. They haven't tasted blood in almost an entire day, and that always gets them riled."

The Heterack grinned. Keltin made a point of ignoring him. "When would you like us to go, Baron?"

"Immediately. Evik's people should be getting ready. I've already told him you're coming. Don't make him wait for you."

* * *

Keltin hadn't been among the Weycliff very much since arriving in Dhalma Province. The long hours of hunting each day were divided by brief periods of sleeping, eating, and caring for his equipment and left little time for socializing with anyone beyond his teammates. As he approached the wayfarers' section of the camp he noticed that their brightly painted wagons had been drawn together into a tight, defensive circle. It struck him as odd that they would assume such a protective formation within the relative safety of the camp. Maybe they simply wished to create a small haven from the cruel jokes and insinuating words that would circulate whenever they left their wagon circle. Scanning the wayfarers working outside the circle of wagons for a familiar face, he spied Jaylocke placing a shovel head onto a new handle.

"Good morning, Jaylocke."

The fair-haired man looked up and favored him with a sunny smile. "Keltin! How did you manage a free moment from slaying monsters?"

"Baron Rumsfeld asked if I and what's left of my team could provide your people with an escort for today's foray."

"Hah! So, Evik managed to get you, eh? Good. I'll feel much safer keeping my head down with you looking over my shoulder."

"You may still need to keep a look out. There's only four of us, and the sleevaks will be running just to the north of where we'll be. No telling what they might flush out in our direction. I was actually coming to suggest to Evik that some of your people may want to arm themselves, just in case."

Jaylocke nodded. "That's prudent. Well thought out." He gave a final thwack of his mallet on the stubborn shovel handle. "Come on then, I'll take you to Evik."

Keltin followed Jaylocke around the circle of wagons to the elder's mobile dwelling. As he walked, he noticed movement inside the protective ring and glanced in its direction. There was a flash of red before a wagon blocked his view. Coming to the next gap, he looked again and was surprised to see a stunning young woman with long red hair. She was sitting on a low stool, her hands in a soapy tub filled with clothing. She was surrounded by several other young women, all chatting quietly with each other as they worked. Despite sharing the same small camp for nearly a week, Keltin was certain he had never seen any of the lovely girls before. Again a wagon blocked his view and he looked away to see that Jaylocke had stopped and was watching him, his normally sunny expression surprisingly subdued.

"I hope you'll not mention what you've seen here. We don't allow any of the other hunters this close to our wagon circle, and nobody else knows our secret besides Baron Rumsfeld."

Keltin glanced at the tightly drawn-together wagons. "I don't understand. Why all the secrecy?"

Jaylocke stepped closer to him, his voice soft and serious. "Keltin, perhaps you haven't heard all the stories that folks tell about my people, and maybe that's why it's so easy for you to accept us. But most others don't take the time to find out the truth. They trust what they've heard, no matter how terrible, and we suffer for their intolerance. Our people are traditionally travelers for many good reasons, one of which is the sad truth that's it harder to catch a quarry that's always on the move. We've suffered a great deal at the hands of others, especially our... gentler people."

"But Baron Rumsfeld is in charge here, and he respects your people."

"Perhaps, but we prefer to keep our dear ones safe. Even if we weren't Weycliff, we know what can happen when certain men are given the liberating title of 'soldier'."

Keltin had a sudden thought occur to him. "Is that also why I haven't seen any of the troupe's children?" he asked.

Jaylocke shook his head. "Maynid's the youngest among us. Evik's troupe hasn't had a new marriage in a long time. Though that may change, provided we are successful here, of course." He seemed to look through the wagon between them and the center of the circle with an expression Keltin couldn't immediately recognize.

"I trust you, Keltin," he said after a moment. "That's why I've allowed you to know our secret. I may not be among your circle of captains or your noble teams of hunters, but I can see which way the wind blows in this campaign. I know the danger grows with each man that falls. It may be that I don't survive this adventure, and I fear for the safety of our women in this camp. I need to know that there are good men here who would protect them as their own people."

Keltin swallowed against a sudden tightness in his throat and nodded. "I'll keep your people safe however I can. I promise."

"Thank you." Jaylocke's grin returned. "Come on then, let's get ready for another adventure."

* * *

A half-hour later Keltin and his team left the camp along with half a dozen wayfarers and a team of mules hitched to a large wagon from the farmstead's stables. Keltin felt uneasy as they rumbled their way down the dirt road leading away from the camp. The meeting with the Baron earlier that morning played out in his mind once more. As hard as they tried, it seemed as if the hunters were making little progress in Dhalma Province. No matter how many beasts they killed, there were always more. Like the Baron, Keltin found himself beginning to doubt whether they could save the province in time for the farmers to bring in their crops.

Forcing his thoughts away from the campaign and to the

task at hand, he took stock of the weapons that the Weycliff workers carried. They had only three rifles among them, all Capshire single-shots. Those who didn't carry a gun had only a single, large knife tucked into their belts. Keltin tried not to worry, telling himself that he and his stalker team would be able to handle any beasts that would find them.

They passed through the stand hunters' perimeter and followed their trapper guide along the road and through the killing field. The change of seasons was showing clearly everywhere that Keltin looked in the dense woods. Most of the leafs had already changed their colors and would soon litter the forest floor, making the stand hunter's job much easier but causing Keltin and his fellow stalker hunters endless little problems.

Leaving their trapper guide behind them, they proceeded down the dirt road between the silent fields shrouded in cottony fog. The morning mist had been lingering further on into each day and Keltin might have doubted Grel'zi'tael's prediction that the rains would not come if he hadn't seen Bor've'tai's control of the elements with his own eyes. An odd thought occurred to him. Could the Sky Talker somehow hold back the dropping temperature along with the rains? Did he have that much power? Keltin resolved to speak with Bor've'tai on the matter when they returned to the safety of camp.

It was easy to find crops ready to be harvested, and soon the bed of the wagon had a healthy collection of potatoes, greens, and peas. The next field they came to was a pumpkin patch several acres square. The gourds were orange and swollen, and the wayfarers began the task of severing the thick stalks and carrying the massive vegetables to the wagon. Keltin and his team took their positions around the wayfarers to keep a careful watch of the surrounding forest.

As Keltin stood guard, watching the mist coiling over the farmer's fields and through the trees beyond, he felt a sudden pang of homesickness. Autumn would have only just begun in Riltvin and its seaside rainforests. The wooded highlands of

Krendaria seemed small and sparse in comparison with the dense greenery of his homeland. It all felt like a world away.

With nothing to do but watch the woods for signs of movement, Keltin's mind drifted back to worrying. He thought about his mother and sister. He'd had no word from them since reaching Krendaria, though news had come that the Carvalen railroad had been repaired and that the mail was running once more. He had sent two letters back to the capital with the camp courier, but each time the man returned his mailbag held nothing for Keltin. The courier was due to return to camp again soon, and Keltin had been unsuccessfully trying not to get his hopes up for word, any word, from home.

He stirred from his thoughts as Frederick, one of the few remaining hunters on his team, gave the crested blue robin signal. Keltin quickly moved to where the veteran Krendarian hunter stood looking off to the north.

"There's a winged strangler hanging about over that way," he said, not looking away from the wall of trees at the other end of the pumpkin patch.

Keltin watched the woods and soon saw the gray wings and spindly body of the beast moving slowly from tree to tree.

"Looks like it's content to watch us for the time being."

Frederick nodded. "Stranglers are cautious. He probably won't move out until he sees one of our group split off by himself."

Keltin turned to Jaylocke who was stacking pumpkins in the wagon bed nearby.

"Jaylocke, we have a beast hanging around to the north. Make sure your people keep close to each other."

Jaylocke nodded and swung himself down onto the ground, taking up a shovel in one hand and a rifle in the other as he quietly spread the word among his fellows. Keltin looked back to the north. The winged strangler remained half-hidden among the narrow tree trunks. Moments passed, and he began to wonder if the beast would eventually move on without harassing them. He was about to go back to his own post when the creature suddenly broke from the trees and began sprinting across the field in their direction.

"Here it comes!" called Jaylocke to his people as Keltin lifted his rifle to line up a killing shot on the approaching beast. Suddenly there was a raucous noise from the north and three sleevaks emerged, all in hot pursuit of the winged strangler.

"Sleevaks!" cried Frederick.

The Weycliff workers scrambled towards the wagon as the bloodthirsty sleevaks doggedly pursued the longer-limbed strangler. The fleeing beast curved sharply around to the west and for a moment Keltin hoped that the strangler would lead the sleevaks away from them. But the gangly creature swerved hard to the south again, causing the shuffling sleevaks to trip and stumble as they tried to match its darting movements. One of the sleevaks managed to right itself quickly and plunged on after its prey, but the other two rose from the ground and seemed to notice the gathering of hunters and wayfarers less than thirty yards from them. Both the slavering creatures leapt forward, racing towards their new prey.

"Get your people behind the wagon!" Keltin called to Jaylocke as he lined up his shot on the nearest sleevak. It was too far away and the ground too uneven for him to trust a shot at the beast's bony skull and tiny eyes. He advanced the chamber to an Alpenion round, aiming the acid-filled bullet for the sleevak's shoulder joint.

A nearby blast of rifle fire came less than a second before he pulled the trigger, causing his bullet to impact harmlessly on the ground at the sleevak's feet as it staggered from the impact of the first shot. Frederick had fired the first blast, but the Krendarian hunter's attempted headshot had been poorly aimed. The sleevak stumbled, but quickly righted itself and came at them with an added burst of speed. Keltin barely had time to drop his rifle and grab his Ripper before the sleevak was upon him.

The sleevak didn't hesitate once it was close enough to attack. It leapt forward like a coiled spring, launching itself into the air and swinging its claws at Keltin's face. Keltin managed to get the point of the Ripper up and angled for the beast's throat, but the creature's bony frill caught the tip of the weapon as the rest of the sleevak's weight painfully jarred the Ripper from his hands. Keltin fell back onto the ground, scrambling for the revolver at his belt. He might have died that moment if the hook on the Ripper hadn't caught in the joint of the sleevak's left forelimb, forcing it to pause a moment to untangle itself from the weapon. Keltin got his revolver free and aimed for the beast's second eye from the left. Suddenly Frederick was in front of him, firing his rifle at the beast at close range.

"Move, you plaguing idiot!" Keltin yelled over the thunder of gunfire as he scrambled to his feet.

He raced around Frederick just as the sleevak finally freed itself of the Ripper and leapt towards the other hunter. Keltin fired three shots with the revolver in the direction of the beast's eyes, unable to take the time to aim. He breathed a short sigh of relief when the creature's head suddenly tilted in an unnatural fashion. It fell to the ground, one side of its body still as a corpse while the other continued to thrash around in the dirt. Keltin left the killing shot to Frederick as he quickly looked around.

Bor've'tai and Garthen were managing their own sleevak far more easily. The stupid creature had clamped its great jaws down on the head of Bor've'tai's ax, allowing the Loopi to wrestle with the beast while Garthen peppered it with bullets. Already it looked close to its mortal end. Keltin turned to the wagon and the Weycliff.

Two of them were struggling to keep the mules from bolting while more gunshots and cries came from the other side of the wagon. Grabbing his rifle, Keltin took a chance and rolled under the wagon, its wheels rocking back and forth as the mules struggled against their masters. He came up on the other side of the wagon and rose into a kneeling position with his rifle at his shoulder to quickly see what was happening.

He realized at once that the winged strangler must have circled around to the south and then turned to the north again, leading the sleevak directly into the thick of the wayfarers. The strangler was lying still on the ground several yards away, but the sleevak was still up and fighting. Someone was engaged in close combat with the beast, but Keltin couldn't see around the bodies between them. Sprinting to the side of the crowd, he was stunned by the spectacle before him.

Jaylocke, armed with nothing but a shovel, was moving in an exquisite dance of death with the slavering beast. The sleevak lunged forward again and again, but each time Jaylocke stepped aside with almost inhuman grace while simultaneously striking the creature with the sharp edge of his shovel. The sleevak's face and neck were covered in thin cuts from the shovel's blade, its bloody visage full of unthinking rage. Keltin hesitated to fire as Jaylocke continued to leap and spin, fearful that his shot might hit his friend.

At last, Jaylocke spun away to the side, giving Keltin a clear shot at the creature. He had no more Alpenion bullets in his rifle's chamber, but a Capshire Shatter Round did the job as it burst in the beast's brain, killing it before it hit the ground. Jaylocke leapt forward and brought the point of the shovel down on the thing's neck with a mighty thrust as if striking the final pose of his elaborate dance. He stood rigidly still for a moment before shaking himself and looking up. He grinned at Keltin.

"Thank you, my friend. This shovel is a poor weapon for delivering a killing blow."

Keltin could only nod in reply as the other hunters came around the wagon to see the two dead beasts lying on the ground.

"Is anyone wounded?" asked Bor've'tai.

Jaylocke shook his head. "We managed to bring the winged strangler down with rifle fire before it drew close enough to strike anyone."

"And the sleevak?"

Jaylocke glanced at the twitching body. "Sadly, our single-shot rifles were all used up on the strangler. I thought to buy our people some time in reloading them, but luckily friend Keltin finished the monster with his usual skill."

Keltin shook his head, his eyes moving between the dead beast and the shovel in Jaylocke's hands.

"How?" he asked.

Jaylocke chuckled. "That's a short question with a long answer my friend. But we don't have time for telling it."

"You're right. We need to get back to camp. Get your people together."

"What about the dead sleevaks?" asked Bor've'tai.

Keltin drew in a deep breath. "Leave them. The Heteracks will come looking for them soon enough."

"Keltin, they're not going to understand that we were defending ourselves."

"I have to agree," said Jaylocke. "The Heteracks already hate the Loopi, and have no love for my people either. I don't like to think what they'll do to retaliate for this."

Keltin inwardly cursed. There were enough troubles in this campaign without this sort of stupidity. He wished that he could assure his friends that Rok and his fellow wranglers would realize that this was just a tragic accident without laying blame, but he knew it was too much to hope for. Any Heterack in the camp would gladly slit a Loopi throat if he thought he could get away with it. He didn't understand it, but he had to accept it. For a moment he was angry at Bor've'tai and his deep silences. Why wouldn't he explain the animosity between his people and the Heteracks? What could have caused such hate?

Keltin gave the dead sleevak a savage kick and allowed his rage to bleed into the misty air. It was too late to wish for different circumstances. The sleevaks were dead, and they would have to do something quickly if they didn't want to be present when their handlers found them.

"We need to go. We'll let Baron Rumsfeld deal with the Heteracks when we're all back at the farmstead."

"And what if the Heteracks come looking for us before the Baron's men find them?" asked Jaylocke.

"Tell Evik to keep all of your people inside your wagon circle until this is resolved." Keltin turned to Bor've'tai. "You may want to pass along the same warning to Grel'zi'tael, just in case."

"I will."

"Good. Let's go."

The Weycliff workers assembled themselves quickly and were soon in the wagon as it rumbled down the dirt road back to camp. Keltin and his team followed, carefully watching the woods for any signs of danger from either beast or Heterack.

CHAPTER 10 – TO PRESERVE THE PEACE

Keltin cursed the wagon's slow, trundling pace and half-expected to find the Heteracks waiting for them as they finally arrived back at the camp. He cast a cautious eye in the direction of the pig pens, but all was still. They had arrived before the sleevaks' owners.

Jaylocke spoke to him in a low voice. "Listen Keltin, I'll gather my people in the wagon circle, but lunch should be served soon. It'll look strange if Mama Bellin and the others aren't out and serving the men."

"Then let it look strange. We can't risk anything until the Baron can talk with Captain Rok."

"All right, but keep in mind that a camp of hungry men may be less sympathetic to us than otherwise."

"I'll go to Grel'zi'tael and my people now," said Bor've'tai.

Keltin nodded and turned to Frederick and Garthen. "I suppose you two can do what you think best while I make my report to the Baron."

Garthen cleared his throat. "If it's all the same, Captain, I'd like to stick with you. After all, we're in as much hot water as the Weycliff or the Loopi, more perhaps, since we were the ones who actually killed those three boils. I think we should stay tight together until this resolves, one way or the other."

119

"I feel the same," said Frederick, "if it's all right, Captain."

"All right then, let's all go make our report to the Baron."

The three of them passed the sentry outside the farmhouse and went inside. They found the Baron with Captain Tallow in the dining room looking over a roughly drawn map of the surrounding farmlands. Rumsfeld looked up and seemed to read the whole story in the faces of the three men standing before him.

"Captain Moore," he said evenly, "tell me what has happened."

Keltin gave his report, feeling an odd sense of déjà vu as he remembered the last time he had made a similar report on the death of Corporal Lewis. As he had before, Rumsfeld listened carefully until Keltin had finished. Captain Tallow gave the Baron a pointed look.

"I'm not the sort to say I told you so, my Lord, but from the day the Heteracks joined us, I've feared this was coming."

The Baron sighed. "As have I, but the Heteracks and their sleevaks were too valuable an ally to turn away." He turned back to Keltin. "I trust, Mr. Moore, that there was no way to prevent this unfortunate event?"

"Sleevaks can't be reasoned with, sir. We had no choice but to defend ourselves."

"Very well."

The Baron rose and went to the front door.

"Send for Sergeant Bracksten at once," he said to the sentry standing outside before returning to the dining room.

"Would you have me remain, my Lord?" asked Captain Tallow.

"No. Rejoin your men. Don't speak a word of this to anyone, but have your tamarrin hounds ready in case of any trouble."

"I can have my men run drills with their hounds out in the open. We'll be ready if the Heteracks try any foolishness."

"Just keep a level head on. We don't need any more complications today."

Captain Tallow left just as Sergeant Bracksten arrived.

"You called for me, sir?"

"Yes, sergeant. I'm afraid we've got a serious situation on our hands."

The Baron quickly outlined what had happened before continuing.

"It's too much to hope for to assume that the Heteracks will accept the actions of Captain Moore and his team as unavoidable self-defense. The presence of the Weycliff and a Loopi among the sleevaks' killers will only add to the situation's volatility. We must tread carefully, lest we spark a full-scale mutiny in our camp. The Heteracks alone could not challenge the rest of us, but they may have sympathizers among the other hunters, especially those from Malpin. What are your recommendations, sergeant?"

Bracksten answered quickly. "We shouldn't let word get out about this. No sense in adding fuel to the fire. Keep the members of the foraging party tucked away and make sure the Heteracks see plenty of my men with guns in their hands when they return to camp."

"Very good. I'd prefer to meet with Captain Rok alone to attempt resolving all of this. Do you think that's possible?"

The sergeant shrugged. "I could bring him to you, but he won't be happy to be separated from his fellows and their pets."

"Tell him that he may bring one other wrangler with him, and that the rest of his people have free reign of the camp, though the surviving sleevaks must be put back into their cages. You will serve as my guard while I speak with Captain Rok. Make sure you leave your weapons at the door, and that the Heteracks do the same."

"Yes sir."

"Dismissed."

The sergeant left. Rumsfeld turned back to Keltin.

"Now, Captain Moore, we need to look to the safety of your people."

"I know that the Weycliff are going to stay in their wagon circle until this is over, and Bor've'tai has gone to warn

Grel'zi'tael and the other Loopi."

"That's good. The Weycliff will be safe enough within their wagon circle, and I can have Bracksten's men bring the hunters' meals to and from the eating area. I'd like the three of you to remain here in the farmhouse. There are bedrooms upstairs that you can stay in while I meet with Captain Rok. I'd also like the Loopi to join you upstairs. I fear that they may be in the worst danger of any of us."

"I'll go tell Grel'zi'tael."

"Do so, and hurry. The Heteracks will be coming back any time now."

* * *

Keltin paced the worn rug lying over the wood floor, his eyes moving continually to the small window looking down onto the courtyard.

"For a hunter of some renown, you seem uncommonly nervous in waiting."

Keltin stopped and looked at Grel'zi'tael sitting in a rocking chair in the corner.

"It's different on a hunt. I feel like a prisoner here."

"Still, as prisons go, we're all fairly comfortable," said Garthen from where he lounged on the corner of a large bed.

"A prison's a prison," said Bor've'tai.

"This is not a prison," said Grel'zi'tael. "We are here for our protection."

"All the same," said Keltin, "I'd feel better if we weren't holed up in here."

The bedroom door opened and Shar'le'vah came in, her deep brown eyes moist with unshed tears.

"Grandfather?"

Without a word Grel'zi'tael reached out to her. She dropped to her knees and placed her head in his lap, trembling silently as he gently stroked her black and white fur. Bor've'tai rose and stood nearby, watching the two as his dark hands opened and closed awkwardly. Keltin and Garthen glanced at each other, both unsure of what they should do.

"Don't worry, Shar'le'vah," Keltin said after a moment. "The Baron will sort this out. Besides, we're all here, and Frederick and Val'ta'lir are in the room just next door. We'll keep you safe."

Shar'le'vah seemed to nod in response, though it was difficult to tell as she continued to hide her face against her grandfather's knee.

"Your words are kindly meant, friend Keltin," said Grel'zi'tael, "but we are troubled by things beyond Captain Rok and his fellows. Waiting here -in these upper rooms of the farmhouse- has cut too closely to painful memories of Malpin."

"What do you mean?"

Grel'zi'tael was silent. Bor've'tai let out a deep sigh and drew closer to Keltin.

"It is a difficult thing to discuss," he said softly. "What has happened in Malpin is common knowledge locally, and we have had little need to explain it to anyone."

"Well I'm not local, and I'm a little tired of everyone alluding to something I don't know anything about. Painful or not, I think I'm entitled to know something of the trouble I've gotten myself into here."

Keltin held Bor've'tai's unreadable gaze and waited for an answer. There was a part of him that realized it was just the feeling of being trapped that was causing his agitation, but his curiosity and the desperate nature of their situation maintained his stubborn attitude. Finally, Grel'zi'tael broke the silence.

"Bor've'tai, go with Keltin into the bedroom next door and explain to him as much as you are able. He has been a good friend to us, and he deserves to know why all of this is happening."

"Very well."

Bor've'tai turned and opened the bedroom door, casting one more look to Shar'le'vah before moving out into the hallway. Keltin followed and they entered the bedroom next door. It was much smaller than the one they had just left.

Scattered wooden toys and a small bed suggested it had been a child's room until recently. Frederick and Val'ta'lir looked up as they entered and shut the door behind them.

"Is Shar'le'vah all right?" asked Val'ta'lir. "She left us suddenly."

"Yes," said Bor've'tai. "She's with Grel'zi'tael."

"Good."

Bor've'tai nodded and turned to Keltin. "I'm sorry that I've never told you about Malpin. It's difficult to speak of, but I will do my best to make you understand."

"All right."

"Malpin has been a nation with many problems since the Three Forest War, and it grew much worse two years ago when the Vaughs finally acquired a majority of seats in the Assembly and put Polace Halev in the High Seat."

"Who are the Vaughs?"

"I'm not very familiar with them as I've lived most of my life far away from the capital of Kerrtow. I do know that they began as a close group of several Heterack families that used their wealth and influence to improve the position of their people in Malpinion society. They gained power as more Heteracks joined them, and many humans were adopted into their circle in mutually beneficial arrangements. They're now something between a political party and a vast noble family."

Keltin shook his head. "But the Vaughs were only trying to improve the lives of other Heteracks. That has nothing to do with Loopi."

"As I said, I don't know much about them, but I do know one thing. You can't ask for a second bowl of stew without leaving less for others to take. The Three Forest War depleted many resources. Businesses, land, workers. If the Vaughs were to receive more, they would need to take it from someone else."

"And that someone else turned out to be the Loopi."

Bor've'tai nodded. "The reasons for the Heteracks' hatred of us are old but strong and are deeply rooted in their mistaken belief that we were responsible for the death of their prophet

Ilep many centuries ago. The story goes that Ilep went into the wilds to fast and meditate on the secrets of salvation. When he returned, he was nearly dead from hunger. The Heterack Ilepenin teach that it was a community of Loopi that refused him both word and food, and he died under their impassionate eyes."

"How could they believe that?"

Bor've'tai shrugged. "I wouldn't pretend to know, but the Vaughs have used the people's old hatred as potent fuel for their political agendas."

"Do you think Rok and the other Heteracks in the campaign are all Vaughs?"

"I doubt it. More likely, they're here to try and make enough money to join the Vaughs when they return home. So, does that answer all of your questions?"

"I suppose, though I'm still not sure why you and the others had to leave Malpin."

"Polace Halev's first act in the High Seat was to introduce something called the Tolerance Laws, revoking many of the rights of certain types of Malpinion citizens, including Loopi. There was some violent opposition, and the Protection Act was created to make mob violence against Loopi all but legal. The League of Protection was formed to enforce the new laws, and soon most of the Loopi in Kerrtow were fleeing for the temporary safety of the countryside. Grel'zi'tael and the others were among them."

"But not you?"

"No. I was working in a lumber camp in the southern part of the country. When Grel'zi'tael and the others eventually made their way to our camp on their way south, I decided to help them, since they seemed unused to living outside of the city. We left Malpin and came to Krendaria, making our way to Carvalen in the hopes of beginning our lives again."

"But why did you take Duke Gregson's offer to come back to the north and be so close to the Malpinion border?"

Bor've'tai shrugged. "We needed money, and besides, we had seen the beginnings of the beast infestation as we traveled south. We knew what it would mean for this country if they were not stopped."

Keltin nodded and turned to look out the window, wishing once again that he was back home. He longed for simpler problems. Rents coming due, worrying about his sister and mother, tracking down a single beast somewhere in the countryside. He had always considered himself the sort of man who did a difficult job and left the greater powers of the world to their own business. He deeply resented how his difficult, though simple life, had become complicated by the problems of groups and nations that he had never visited or even seen before.

Watching the fading light of day, Keltin was startled to suddenly see Captain Rok and three of his burly Heterack companions coming towards the house accompanied by Bracksten and his guards. The Heteracks walked with swift, angry steps and Keltin pulled back sharply from the window to avoid being seen.

"What is it, Captain?" said Frederick.

"Heteracks. Stay here, we need to tell the others."

Bor've'tai and Keltin quickly returned to the larger bedroom.

"The Heteracks are coming," said Keltin.

Shar'le'vah stiffened.

"Bracksten and his men are with them," he added quickly, though it didn't seem to help her.

Angry voices drifted up to them from outside the window for a few moments, followed by the sound of a door opening downstairs. Keltin moved to the window and peeked around the corner. Two of the Heteracks stamped away from the front door to stand sullenly just outside the low fence surrounding the house.

"Close the curtains, Keltin," Grel'zi'tael said softly. "Soon it will be too dark to see out and too easy for others to see in."

Keltin drew the faded curtains closed as more voices came up to them from downstairs. Their tones were too low to make out what was said, and Keltin had to resist the urge to listen at the door. With nothing else to do, he sat down on the bed and waited.

Time crawled. Someone's stomach growled. Keltin realized that many of them had not eaten since that morning. He dug in his pockets and found a small package of jerked beef. He handed it to Grel'zi'tael with an apologetic shrug. The Loopi elder took the meager meal with a gracious smile and divided it between everyone in the room. Keltin noticed Bor've'tai kneel down next to Shar'le'vah and give her his portion. She favored him with a soft smile and a gentle, brief clasp of hands. They ate in silence.

The blue light filtering through the curtains outside faded to the blackness of night. It occurred to Keltin that their companions in the nearby room may not have closed their own curtains. He tried to brush the thought from his mind, but it continued to gnaw at him as the silent minutes ticked by. At last he stood up and moved to the bedroom door.

"I'm going to make sure that the others' closed their curtains," he whispered to Grel'zi'tael.

The Sky Talker nodded and Keltin eased the door open, stepping out into the hall and closing it behind him. The hallway was cold and dark, the warm light of gas lamps downstairs barely touching its shadowed corners. The voices downstairs were now much clearer, and Keltin could make out some of what was being said as he crept to the other bedroom.

"…I'm still willing to negotiate compensation for the loss of your property," -it was the Baron's voice- "but we must both be willing to compromise, if we're to make any progress here."

"You asked what I wanted in payment for the dead sleevaks and I told you. Either you pay or we leave. I'm not going to haggle with you."

Keltin paused with his hand on the doorknob, listening for the Baron's response.

"I understand that you are still upset, but…"

Keltin opened the bedroom door and stepped inside.

"Is it over then?" asked Frederick.

"No, they're still talking downstairs. I just came to see if you had closed the curtains. We don't want to be seen by anyone and make matters worse."

"Good thinking."

Frederick got up and drew the curtains together as Keltin moved back out into the hallway. Baron Rumsfeld's voice came to him again.

"…been very patient, but do not overestimate your position here. If you had controlled your beasts in the first place, none of this would have happened."

"If you're so unhappy with the work we've done, then we'll leave. It's that simple."

"Could we please stop running over the same ground and try to…"

Keltin closed the bedroom door and leaned against it. He knew little of negotiations, but it sounded like the talks were not going well. Minutes passed. The rap of a footstep on the wooden staircase shook him from his reverie. Someone knocked on the door. Keltin turned and opened it to see Sergeant Bracksten framed by the twilight at the top of the staircase.

"Baron Rumsfeld wants you downstairs, Moore."

"Are the negotiations over yet?"

"No. Come on."

The sergeant turned and Keltin followed, the echoing of their footsteps sounding uncommonly loud and empty. The soft light of lamps downstairs seemed almost blinding after the darkness of the bedroom upstairs, and it took a moment to clearly see the scene before them. Baron Rumsfeld sat at the dining room table looking drawn and tired. Rok sat across from him, his broad face dark and silent. Rumsfeld looked up and gave Keltin a slight nod of greeting.

"Come sit with us, Captain Moore," he said.

Keltin chose a seat next to the Baron, careful to avoid Rok's hard eyes.

"Captain Rok and I have discussed the unfortunate events of this morning in the pumpkin patch. We have had some difficulty in agreeing on an acceptable restitution for the loss of the Heteracks' property. I have offered more than fair financial compensation for the three sleevaks, and am even willing to offer more if Captain Rok will agree to my terms."

The Baron glanced at the Heterack but only received a stony silence in return.

"Unfortunately, Captain Rok maintains that he will accept only one of two possibilities. Either the Heteracks and their sleevaks leave the campaign immediately, or else we expel all the Loopi in the camp to fend for themselves."

Keltin's jaw clenched and the cold dread in his chest turned to a fiery pit. He turned to Rok and thought he could see the hint of a sneering smile. His hands ached for the handle of the Ripper. Rumsfeld seemed to see the silent exchange between them and covered his eyes with a weary hand.

"The reason I called you downstairs is to ask you a question. In your opinion, and for the good of the campaign, which group would be of more benefit to us in Dhalma?"

"That's a cutthroat's question," said Keltin, trying to keep his voice steady.

"Running a campaign is sometimes a cutthroat business, Mr. Moore. As the commanding officer here, I am forced to make difficult decisions. Understand, however, that they are mine to make alone. I am not asking you to choose who will go or who will stay. I am only asking your opinion of which group would be the better ally to keep for the good of the campaign. You're the only captain serving here that I feel will tell me truthfully, and without bias."

Keltin felt a painful tearing inside of him. His friendship with the Loopi challenged him to side with them at once, but the long lessons of honesty and integrity he had learned since he was a child threatened to overwhelm him. He spoke cautiously.

"It's difficult to compare the help that the Heteracks and Loopi provide in this campaign. The sleevaks are effective killers, and bring in at least as many kills as the tamarrin hounds or the stalker teams. But the Loopi, especially

Grel'zi'tael, are our only defense against the more bizarre beasts out there."

"And how many times have the Loopi helped us against one of these more exotic beasts? Think of every time you have either witnessed it or heard of such an encounter."

There was a strange note in the Baron's voice, and Keltin wondered if it might be desperation. He ransacked his memory for a moment before answering.

"I know of at least three separate times, but that doesn't mean that there haven't been more."

"Only three?"

Keltin looked in the Baron's eyes and suddenly realized that the Baron had already made his decision. He struggled to make his tightening jaw relax enough to speak.

"Don't forget the aid that Grel'zi'tael has given in holding back the full change of season and the rains."

Rok snorted, and the Baron sighed.

"Understand, Mr. Moore, that I'm not necessarily questioning the Sky Talker, but you have to admit that claims of controlling the weather are difficult to confirm at best. At any rate, you've answered my question to my satisfaction. You may return upstairs. The sergeant will come to get you when the negotiations are finished."

Bracksten came to stand behind Keltin's chair as he sat in stunned silence. He felt like it was all a nightmare, a terrible farce that he was watching from far away. He looked at the faces before him. Rumsfeld was staring at the table without expression, but Rok's shadow of a sneer had grown into a triumphant smile. Keltin saw that smile and a taunt cord inside his soul seemed to snap. He rose to his feet, but did not leave.

"Is there something else, Mr. Moore?" asked the Baron.

"Just this. Casting the Loopi out of the camp in the middle of this forsaken province is a sure death sentence, and you both know it. I'll not stand by to watch them punished for being who and what they are. If you do this, you'll lose me as well, because I won't fight alongside murderers."

Keltin turned on Rok. "I won't run away though. I'll still

hunt in Dhalma, but I'll hunt sleevak. I'll kill each one of your precious, plaguing beasts, and if any of the boils that you command try to stop me, they'll get the same."

Rok's eyes bulged. He leapt to his feet, knocking his chair to the floor. Keltin grabbed the chair in front of him, ready to lift it as a weapon, but Sergeant Bracksten was between them in an instant.

"Keep your seat!" Bracksten barked at Rok as he gave Keltin a hard shove backwards. "You two start a fight in here and I'll personally break both of your heads in before the guards outside get a chance to fill you both with bullets!"

Rok stared at Keltin, his eyes bright with hate. Keltin stared back, his body trembling with suppressed fury.

"You speak murderous words, Mr. Moore," Rumsfeld said softly.

"So do you."

Without waiting for an answer, Keltin stormed out of the dining room and climbed the stairs back to the bedroom. He threw the door open, stepped into the gloom, and slammed it shut behind him. Ignoring all else, he went to the bed and sat, burying his face in his trembling hands.

Keltin felt helpless, like a child caught between fighting parents. Hatred poured red hot onto everything he could think of. The Heteracks. The Baron. The sleevaks. Dhalma Province. Krendaria. Everything. Let the beasts take them all.

Long minutes passed as his blood slowly cooled. It surprised him when he felt tears on his cheeks and in his hands. He sat in silence, keeping his face hidden, unable to bring himself to face the curiosity of the others. Someone sat next to him on the bed. A large hand was placed on his shoulder. Keltin looked up and in the darkness could just see the outline of Bor've'tai sitting beside him. The Loopi said nothing as he gently gripped his shoulder. Keltin drew in a ragged breath and spoke softly to his friend.

"Whatever happens, I am with you."

He couldn't see the Loopi's expression, but he felt the grip on his shoulder tighten as the sound of footsteps came from the staircase outside. Keltin tensed, watching the play of light under the door that told him that whoever was coming was carrying a lantern. The door opened and Baron Rumsfeld himself entered the room. He turned to Grel'zi'tael.

"I apologize for the long wait, Sky Talker, but all has been resolved. The Heteracks and their sleevaks will be leaving the camp in the morning. I ask that all of you remain here until then, for your own safety."

There was a stunned silence from all those gathered in the bedroom. Even Grel'zi'tael seemed somewhat taken aback, though he spoke softly and evenly as he replied to the Baron.

"I commend you for the diplomatic way in which you have handled this situation. I assure you that my people and I will give you every support we can in these difficult times."

"I appreciate that."

"There is one thing, however. None of us have eaten in some time…"

"I'll see that you get something brought up to you."

"Thank you."

The Baron nodded and turned to Keltin, his eyes unreadable. "Captain Moore, I know that your team is undermanned, and I suggest that you find a solution quickly. Your team will be assuming the duties of the sleevak wranglers, in addition to your own. I expect you to be ready for the challenge."

Keltin returned the Baron's gaze steadily. "We'll be ready."

For a moment, it seemed as though the Baron's mouth turned up in a slight smile as he turned to go.

"Very good, Captain Moore."

CHAPTER 11 – FROM A DISTANCE

The chill of the morning air seeped through the window's thin glass. Keltin looked down at the activity going on below him in the pale light. Nearly all of the hunters had gathered together in the farmyard, their smoking breath mingling together in small, pale clouds as they spoke quietly with each other. Keltin wondered whether they had been assembled for the occasion or if they had come out of their own morbid curiosity. Sergeant Bracksten stood just outside the farmhouse with the campaign's remaining professional soldiers, each of them armed with Krendarian army rifles affixed with bayonets. Captain Tallow and his tamarrin hounds also seemed to be ready for trouble, the noble animals looking like wound springs as they sat beside their masters.

The crack of drivers' whips broke the silence, and the Heteracks emerged from around the pigpen in a rumbling caravan. The quiet procession was led by the two sleevak wagons, though the second wagon's cages all stood empty and silent. The remaining sleevaks thrashed and foamed at the sight of the tamarrin hounds, but the well-trained animals only stared back at them coolly.

The caravan moved out into the courtyard, pausing for a moment as the Heteracks in the second wagon were forced to jump to the ground and tie down an empty cage that had fallen to the earth. Keltin used the brief pause to study the caravan and was surprised to see some human hunters among the Heteracks. It seemed that the sleevak wranglers weren't the only ones dissatisfied with the campaign.

As the Heteracks in the second wagon finished their repairs, Captain Rok stood up in his seat. He turned slowly, looking out at the gathered hunters. Keltin wondered if he might make some sort of speech or declaration, but the sleevak wrangler only glared silently at the group before turning to look at the farmhouse. Rok raised his gaze to the bedroom window and for a moment Keltin looked into his dark, brooding eyes. Keltin felt his blood go hot just looking into those hateful eyes, but kept his face set and hard, watching the Heterack like he would any other dangerous animal.

Finally, Rok turned again and sat, whipping his mules to trundle on and out of the farmyard to the road beyond. Keltin watched until the last wagon had disappeared before turning to the others gathered in the upstairs bedroom.

"Is it over then?" asked Bor've'tai.

Keltin nodded. "They've gone. We should be able to leave soon."

It was a few minutes more before Sergeant Bracksten opened their door and told them that they could come out again.

"The Baron wants to see you at noon, Captain Moore," the sergeant added.

Keltin nodded and followed the others downstairs. Rumsfeld was nowhere in sight, but Keltin noticed a large leather bag resting in the corner of the entryway. The courier had indeed arrived the day before, though with all of the chaos in camp there'd been no opportunity to distribute the men's correspondence. Keltin suddenly felt a desperate need for any word from home.

He pulled open the drawstrings of the bag and carefully sorted through the envelopes and small packages inside. Several moments' searching yielded welcome treasure. Three letters addressed to him. One from his sister Mary, one from Mr. Renlowah, and a final one from Mrs. Galloway.

Clutching the precious envelopes, he stepped out into the chill morning air and searched for some secluded spot to devour them. A large firewood box to the side of the farmhouse provided him a seat away from the rest of the camp. He first opened the letter from Mary.

My Dear Brother,

I write to you with the same duplicity of expression that I always must confess to when you are on a hunt. I am glad that you have found work, but I am ever afraid for your safety. I find my fears are increased greatly knowing that you will be reading this in Krendaria, a nation in which you have never been before and I have never seen before either. You must tell me of its land and people, and as much of the campaign as you can manage. It may not put my mind at rest to know such details, but hearing your voice is comfort enough.

I have told Mother of your location and activities. I'm afraid that she did not receive it well, and has asked that I stop telling her of you. I am convinced that it is out of a deeper concern for your well-being that she does not want to know such details. Know that her love is still with you, as is mine at all times.

In your letters you have expressed concern about our circumstances since I lost my employment as a housemaid. Do not trouble yourself so. I am currently seeking employment as a governess, and I feel confident of finding a position soon. My upbringing as a schoolteacher's daughter and natural temperament speak well to my capabilities, and I am sure I will soon be placed with a good family.

I must regretfully end this letter prematurely. Know that I love you dearly and pray for your safety and happiness daily.

Most sincerely,
Mary

Keltin read the letter twice, savoring his sister's elegant handwriting and kind words. She would make a fine governess. He knew it, and would be sure to wish her well with her search in his next correspondence. Carefully placing the small pages back into their envelope, he proceeded to open the letter from Mr. Renlowah.

Keltin,

I am flattered to have received one of your precious letters. I know that Mrs. Galloway is always delighted to receive them from Mr. Jastin, and I think that her disappointment at receiving one for this address without her name on it was only reconciled by a sister-letter accompanying it that was meant for her.

It pleases me greatly to hear that you have met some of my countrymen, and I hope that you will take the time to make their acquaintance. The fact that you have met a Sky Talker is a rare and wonderful event. Sky Talkers preserve a very old and important part of our heritage, and I admit to some amount of envy in sharing such a close association with one.

I fear, however, that I have failed you in not telling you more of my people and our sad history in Malpin. Allow me to shed some light into the troubles we have seen, and perhaps explain a little of the behavior that you have no doubt witnessed by the time you read this.

Keltin read the following paragraphs, but it was already familiar to him from the explanations that Bor've'tai had made the night before. If only he had received this letter weeks ago. It may not have changed the events of the last two days, but it might have at least answered some of his questions and spared Bor've'tai the pain of revisiting unpleasant memories.

After finishing Mr. Renlowah's letter Keltin continued on to Mrs. Galloway's. Much of her correspondence was spent telling him gossip and other small events. Keltin read it all with a bemused smile until he saw a name that the good woman rarely mentioned to him.

…I also wanted to thank you for delivering my letter to Angela. I'm sorry to have asked such a painful favor from you. I only mention it because she has written to me, and I am so glad for it. She also

included a letter to you with mine, since she knew you would be in Krendaria and had no address to send it to. I've included it with mine without reading it of course, and hope that it gives you the same pleasant joy that her letter gave to me.

Keltin didn't finish his landlady's letter. He set the page aside and realized that the remaining pages were a slightly different size and were written in a different hand. For a long moment he stared at the first page of Angela's letter without reading it. He didn't want to read it. He had left her firmly in the past and had intended to keep her there. Opening old wounds was the last thing he needed this morning. But he couldn't help himself.

Dear Keltin,

Don't be angry that I'm writing to you. I just had to. Seeing you again, it made me remember all sorts of things. It hurt a little to remember, but I was glad to. They were good memories.

I can't imagine how hard it was for you to come here and deliver mother's letters to me. You were always such a straight arrow, doing what you thought was the right thing, no matter what you or anyone else might have wanted. I know you don't approve of what I'm doing. You think that I'm a completely different person. But I'm not. I'm living my life regardless of how anyone else may feel about it, just like you are.

Speaking of which, how is your mother? Is she still not talking to you? I wonder what she'd say if she knew what I'm doing with myself now. I don't think she ever liked me anyway. But Mary was always sweet. How is she? Do you remember the time that the two of us went walking in the rain and you came out to find us and bring us back? I remember how stern you seemed, especially when Mary caught a cold afterward. But later on, when it was just you and I, you told me how you liked the way that my hair looked when it was wet. It still looks that way when it rains.

Maybe when you come back from Krendaria we can go walking in the rain, just you and I. I'd like that. Please write to me, I'll be

waiting to hear from you. Be careful and be safe.
    Angela

Keltin folded the letter and began ripping it into smaller and smaller pieces, wishing he could make himself forget all the things it had said. Angela had managed with just a few words to casually stab his scabbed-over heart, and he hated himself for being too weak to ignore the letter without reading it. The same flood of anger and hatred from the night before returned in a rush. He hated Angela, Krendaria, the campaign, everything.

He longed for the simplicity of his life back home. To be back in the hills of Riltvin, saving a farmer's prize chickens from a wounded razorleg, or receiving the modest bounty for a terrorizing wood devil from a humble town mayor.

This was the reason why he was always alone. People meant pain and complications. As soon as this campaign was over, he swore to himself that he would return to the hills and never leave them again.

"Captain Moore?"

Keltin stirred himself from his dark thoughts. Quickly hiding the mangled scraps of Angela's letter, he looked up to see Maynid running towards him.

"There you are," said the young wayfarer, his cheeks rosy from cold and exercise. "Evik was hoping to meet with you."

Keltin sighed and felt the hot anger inside him turning into a weary lump of lead.

"What's gone wrong now?" he asked.

Maynid gave him a puzzled look. "Why... nothing, so far as I know. The Loopi came into the wagon circle and the Sky Talker has been speaking with the Elder. They wanted to see you."

"Inside the wagon circle?"

Maynid smiled, his young face warm and friendly. "That's what he said. Will you come?"

Keltin nodded, unable to return the smile. "Yes, I'll come."

He waited for the boy to dash back to his fellows, but the

young man turned and fell in step with him as they crossed the farmstead grounds. Perhaps Maynid wanted to talk. Maybe he wanted details of the day before, or just a chance to chatter as some young men did. But Keltin kept his silence all the way to the Weycliff's wagon circle.

Maynid led Keltin inside the protective ring. People milled about them, all laughing and talking happily together. Keltin recognized all of the men, but he knew none of the women aside from Mama Bellin. Among the female wayfarers were several very lovely young ladies, their faces bright and happy. One of them may have even smiled at him, but he refused to notice.

Moving among the chatting people, he found Bor've'tai and the Loopi standing with Evik, Mama Bellin, Jaylocke, and a young woman that he didn't know, though she seemed somewhat familiar. In a moment he realized that she had been the red-haired girl he had glimpsed between the wagons the day before. He quickly turned his attention away from her as the Weycliff Elder spied him.

"Friend Keltin," said Evik with a smile, "I am happy to see you. Grel'zi'tael has been telling us what happened in the farmhouse last night, and of course, Jaylocke has already told us about your heroic defense of our brothers in the pumpkin patch. On behalf of my family and clan, I thank you for what you have done for us."

Keltin looked at the kind, grateful faces before him and forced himself to smile.

"You're welcome, but I wasn't the only one."

"True, but everyone else has already been thanked."

Jaylocke stepped forward to take Keltin by the arm in a friendly clasp, then presented him to the red-haired woman standing nearby.

"Keltin, I want to introduce you to Ameldi, our troupe's finest singer."

Ameldi blushed a rosy hue as her emerald eyes darted to Jaylocke before she gave Keltin a modest curtsy.

"We are all grateful for your service on our behalf."

Keltin gave her a quick nod and turned back to Evik.

"Thank you for your kindness, but I need to prepare for my meeting with the Baron."

"Are you all right, Keltin?" asked Jaylocke.

"I'm just tired. I didn't sleep well in the farmhouse last night. Excuse me."

Keltin turned and left the wagon circle behind him. He had intended to spend some time trying to plan how he would handle the additional duties that the Baron had given him and his team, but he just didn't feel up to it. Returning to the pasture with the hunters' tents, he crawled onto his familiar bedroll and closed his eyes, trying to drive all thoughts of beasts and letters from his mind for a few precious hours.

CHAPTER 12 – WISDOM OF
THE FATHERS

"So what does the Baron propose we do now?" asked Bor've'tai as he and the rest of Keltin's stalker team sat together at the otherwise empty dining tables.

"We'll try to continue on as best we can," said Keltin. "We've still got the tamarrin hound trainers, and a fair number of stand hunters and stalker hunters are still with us. It seems that most of the human hunters that left with the Heteracks this morning were trappers, which is lucky for us, since mostly all that they were doing was maintaining the traps that have already been made. Sergeant Bracksten is going to assign what soldiers he can to fill the gaps in the ranks of the trappers, stand hunters, and Henry's team of stalkers."

"What about us?" asked Garthen.

"It turns out that we're actually the most complete group besides the tamarrin hounds after this morning. If we want to bring the numbers of our team back up, we'll have to figure it out on our own. Any ideas?"

"I suppose there's no chance of Oliete or Bryan miraculously recovering, is there?"

"I don't think so."

"And it goes without saying that the fellows we gave to Henry's team won't come back?"

"I think all three of them left with the Heteracks."

"Bunch of boils."

There was a moment's grumbling agreement before Frederick summed up the situation.

"There doesn't seem to be anyone left."

"I can think of someone," said Bor've'tai.

"Who?" asked Keltin.

"Jaylocke."

"The Weycliff?" said Garthen.

"Yes. We saw how he handled that sleevak yesterday with nothing but a shovel in his hands. Imagine if he had had a proper weapon."

"Do you know if he can shoot?"

"I have no idea, but even if he can't, I think he's our best chance for getting a real fighter to join our team. What do you think, Keltin?"

"I can't think of anyone better. I'll go to the wagon circle and see what he says."

"I'll see if there are any other hunters that want to join our team," said Garthen. "I may not find any, but it doesn't hurt to ask."

"Good. Let me know if you find anyone."

The various members of Keltin's team went their separate ways as he returned to the Weycliff section of the camp for the second time that day. He hesitated at the circle of wagons, uncertain if he should presume to enter the protective ring without an escort. A flash of red showed between the wagons and a sweet voice called out to him.

"Captain Moore, it's good to see you again. Won't you come into the circle?"

Keltin followed the voice to find Ameldi gracing him with a radiant smile. He returned the smile as best he could.

"I wasn't sure if I should enter without permission," he said.

"That's good of you, but you've done so much for us

already, for my part you are always welcome. What brings you to our camp?"

"I was hoping to speak with Jaylocke. Is he about?"

"He's just over there with Evik," she said, pointing behind him.

Keltin turned to see both men cutting up some of the pumpkins that had been gathered the day before. They looked up with pleasant smiles as Ameldi and Keltin approached.

"Hello Keltin," said Jaylocke. "Thought you'd come and conquer some bestial gourds with us?"

"No, I came to ask you something."

"What is it?"

"I need to find another man to add to my stalker team, and all the other hunters and soldiers are already committed elsewhere. I've talked it over with the others, and we agreed to ask you to join us."

Jaylocke considered silently for a moment, then turned to Evik. "Father, perhaps now would be the time to reconsider our earlier discussion."

Evik's smile had become a somber frown. "We have our purpose in this campaign, and a duty that we have agreed to fulfill for Duke Gregson and Baron Rumsfeld. Our lot is not the same as that of friend Keltin and his fellow hunters."

Ameldi's smile had also disappeared.

"Jaylocke…"

"It's all right Ameldi. Father, Keltin has saved my life twice, and each time he was acting beyond the duty that he accepted back in Carvalen. I could do no less for him. Besides, now that so many of the hunters have left us, there will be fewer mouths to feed and fewer hands will be needed for the camp labors. My patriarch, the gifts of the elders are mine to share, and I will do so. Will you give me your blessing?"

Evik sighed. "As a patriarch I can give you my blessing, but as your father I cannot say I will not worry about you."

Jaylocke smiled gently. "I'm sorry to worry you, but I must do what I feel is right." He turned to Keltin. "Friend Keltin, I offer you my service and life if need be. I'll take you as my captain, if you'll take me."

Keltin tried not to notice the way Ameldi stared at the ground biting her lower lip as he answered.

"Thank you, Jaylocke. As soon as you're able, I'll need to talk with you more. There are some things we should discuss before you come out on a hunt with us."

"What do you need to know?"

"Well, for one thing, what do you know about hunting?"

"In all honesty, I've never hunted beyond getting small game for the stewpot, but I have within me the blood of men and perhaps some women who will serve you as well as any hunter in this camp."

"I'm not sure I understand you."

Jaylocke grinned. "I think it's time that I share a little of the secrets of my people. With your permission, Father?"

"Go on, I'll finish this lot up. Good luck my son, and to you as well friend Keltin."

Jaylocke nodded and rose to his feet as Ameldi disappeared into a wagon without a word. He watched her go for a moment before turning back to Keltin. Together, they left the wagon circle and found a pair of barrels by an old tool shed where they could sit and talk.

"You asked me yesterday how I was able to fight off the sleevak," said Jaylocke. "It's a fair question. I've never trained as a fighter. My skills are in tumbling, juggling, and some singing, though I'll never hold a candle to Ameldi. However, I have a rich ancestry, and among them there has been an ample share of warriors and fighters. It was upon their strengths that I drew as I fought yesterday. The Weycliff hold our lineage in high esteem, and devote ourselves to maintaining our genealogies. We believe that we are the product of our forebears in a very literal sense."

"So your people practice a kind of ancestor worship?"

"In a way, though worship would be an improper word to use. We are a God-fearing people. It would be more appropriate to say that we reverence our ancestors, and call upon them for strength and guidance."

"How?"

"Take yesterday for example. When I saw that I would need to engage the sleevak in close combat, I called out in my heart to Kleadil, the uncle of my great-grandfather. Kleadil was a dervish in the service of Lord Hultir, and a master of the Deadly Dance. As I fought the sleevak, I felt my body move with the reflexes of my dervish uncle, though I'll admit I used some of my own skill as a tumbler when it was needed."

"So you actually thought of a particular ancestor to help you?"

"That's the only way it will work. Calls to the ancestors must be specific in both their purpose and who is called. Think of your genealogy like a great hall filled with people and you'll begin to understand how the Weycliff see their forebears."

"Does it only work for fighting?"

"Actually, yesterday was the first time I'd ever called on Kleadil. More often I call for Faldif my grandfather in times of difficulty, though I'll call Jelindil my great-aunt for aid in singing more often than I'd like to admit."

Keltin nodded, trying to digest all that Jaylocke was telling him. He had never heard of anything like it before, and doubted whether he would have thought it possible, had he not seen it for himself the day before. He wondered how much time Jaylocke and his people dedicated to studying, learning, and memorizing not only the names of their ancestors, but who they really were. He tried to think of what he knew of his own forebears, but beyond his grandparents he could remember very little, and his extended relations had always been few in number and far in distance.

"Finding this all difficult to believe?" asked Jaylocke after a moment.

"No, just... new. I'm curious. Could anyone call upon their forebears in the way the Weycliff do?"

Jaylocke shrugged. "I'm not sure. I've never heard of anyone else trying. To most, it would probably smell too much like witchcraft for their liking. Still, even if you couldn't call upon your own ancestors, you could still benefit from the blessings of mine… in a way."

"How do you mean?"

"Well, bringing me along with your team helps," Jaylocke said with a grin. "I can also draw upon some of the knowledge of my ancestors to instruct others. Do you remember when we first met, and I asked if you knew how to use that interesting weapon of yours? I can show you some tricks that Kleadil knew, as well as some drills that I know from a far-removed cousin who was a foot soldier in the Larigoss infantry. Would you like me to show you?"

"I suppose we can try, though I'm not sure I'll be much of a student."

Jaylocke rose and left for a moment, returning with a pair of shovels. He tossed Keltin one of them and then bowed his head silently for a moment. Keltin waited, wondering if his friend would look or act differently under the influence of his ancestors, but when the wayfarer looked up he wore the same friendly smile he always seemed to have on.

"All right, let's begin. First, show me how you stand when you're holding your weapon."

Keltin hesitated. He fingered the old, smoothed handle of the shovel awkwardly, reminded of the long hours of practicing his marksmanship under the loving but stern instruction of his Uncle Byron. For years he had endured Uncle Byron's tutelage, as well as the frequent advice of his father, grandfathers, and even his mother's brother, Uncle Ollin, a candle-maker who had never held a rifle in his life. The day that Keltin killed his first beast and collected his first bounty had marked the end of their instruction, and he had always remembered the date fondly for that reason especially.

Glancing up, he saw that Jaylocke was still patiently waiting for him. He forced the memories from his mind. He turned the shovel over in his hands for a moment before shaking his head.

"I suppose I don't really know how I stand when I hold the Ripper," he said. "To be honest, by the time the hunt gets to the point that I have to use it, I'm always deep in the thick of things. There's little time to think of form and stance when a spiked thresher is bearing down on you."

Jaylocke nodded. "Of course you're right, and that's why you must plan and practice what you will do before that moment comes, so that when it comes, you will be ready."

Keltin inwardly groaned, hearing echoes of similar lessons from Uncle Byron in his mind, but Jaylocke continued.

"However, we don't have the time to start from the beginning, and in truth, I doubt that would really help you anyway. You're a little backwards my friend, with experience coming before knowledge. You are alive, and so what you do must work, but perhaps I can improve upon it. Now, pretend I am a spiked thresher. Look out!"

Suddenly Jaylocke leapt forward, swinging the flat of the shovel at Keltin's head. Keltin jumped backwards to dodge the stunning blow, bringing his shovel up before him to strike back.

"Good!" cried Jaylocke. "Now don't move."

Keltin froze, his shovel still gripped tightly in his hands. Jaylocke moved around him, quickly examining his form.

"Where are you putting your weight right now?"

Keltin struggled for a moment to evaluate the way he was standing. "On both feet," he answered after a moment, "as evenly as possible."

"What part of your feet?"

To that Keltin was at a total loss. "I don't know. The entire surface, I suppose."

"Why are you standing that way?"

"It came naturally."

"Yes, but take a moment to consider. What are the advantages of standing the way that you are?"

"Well, I suppose... I suppose that it's a solid stance. I won't be thrown off my feet easily if I'm standing like this."

"Good! That's very true, and perhaps there are times when that's most important. But I want you to try something else. Lower yourself a little to center your body, then bring your weight up onto the balls of your feet."

"That's hard to do in heavy boots."

"I know, but I still want you to try it."

It was awkward trying to get into the new position, but once he had gotten the right balance Keltin found it felt surprisingly comfortable. Jaylocke examined his form again and nodded.

"Good. Now, here I come again."

Jaylocke sprang forward swinging the shovel. Keltin leapt back and was amazed to feel how much smoother the motion felt as he took up his stance once more. Jaylocke grinned.

"How does that feel?"

"It's different, but it felt comfortable."

"I'm glad to hear it. Now, let's take a look at your grip."

Keltin looked down at his hands, realizing he hadn't even thought about how he was holding the shovel.

"You've got a good grip," said Jaylocke, "and you're holding it far enough down the handle to move the blade freely while still keeping a strong hold of it. Now, is there any reason why you're holding it from opposite sides?"

Keltin considered why he held the shovel as if it were a rope that he was about to climb. "No, no reason in particular."

"Then try it this way," Jaylocke suggested, turning one of Keltin's hands over so that he gripped the shovel from the same side in both hands. "If you hold it this way you'll have greater control and flexibility with the blade. You can still thrust your weapon while being able to switch your hand positions more rapidly. For example, if you take this position" -he adjusted Keltin's hands- "you can swing it like you're splitting wood, or use this position" -again he made an adjustment- "to strike a blow with the blunt end of the handle. But always return to this position between strikes. Do you see?"

Keltin blew out his cheeks in a heavy sigh. "It's going to take some time to learn."

Jaylocke chuckled and hefted his shovel. "Shall we give it a try?"

Keltin took a breath and nodded. Jaylocke came at him

once more, forcing Keltin to jump away, but this time he pressed the attack back by thrusting forward with the point of his shovel. Jaylocke danced to the side and swung the flat of the blade at his chest. Keltin dodged to the side, swinging the butt of his handle at Jaylocke's stomach. There was a hardy knock of wood against wood as Jaylocke blocked the blow, and they continued the dance. Keltin felt sweat chilling on his neck in the cold air and a smile rose to his face even as he struggled to keep up with Jaylocke's swirling strikes and dodges. Jaylocke grinned in return, and they continued until both were heaving and sucking in throaty gasps of air as they fought.

At last, Keltin broke away and lowered his shovel. Jaylocke planted the blade of his weapon into the ground, leaned on it, and gave a hearty laugh. Keltin laughed too, releasing into the autumn air all the tension that had been threatening to overwhelm him. The fire that had guttered within his heart since he'd read Angela's letter seemed to crackle back to life as Jaylocke gave him a playful slap on the back.

"We'll make a dervish of you yet, Captain Moore."

"I suppose that's fine," said a deep voice nearby, "as long as he doesn't forget how to shoot."

Keltin turned to see Bor've'tai leaning against the shed and watching them.

"How long have you been there?"

"A while. You both did well. I assume that Jaylocke has accepted the invitation to join our company?"

"You assume right. Any luck finding another hunter for our team?"

"Yes actually. Weedon has agreed to come with us. He says that he's tired of waiting in the trees for beasts, though I worry that he may still bear the scars from the loss of his friend."

"At least we'll have another man along." Keltin turned back to Jaylocke. "I think I'm done for today. Thank you for the lesson."

"Of course, any time."

Keltin started to hand his shovel back and was surprised when Bor've'tai reached out and took it from him instead.

"Are you too tired to continue?" the Loopi asked Jaylocke.

Jaylocke shrugged and grinned. "I'm up for more, now that my blood's warmed."

Keltin thought he saw a twinkle in Bor've'tai's eyes as he returned the smile.

"Good, because now I want you to teach me."

"I'd be happy to, on one condition. Watch that feral strength of yours, friend Loopi. I'm sure Captain Moore wouldn't want you breaking any of my bones before I've given some beasts a chance to gnaw on them."

CHAPTER 13 – ON THE NORTH ROAD

The calls of the crested blue robin came to Keltin from several directions at nearly the same time, but he hesitated to return the call. The spiked thresher had lowered its head to the earth, its elongated snout snuffling at the forest floor. Keltin waited, trusting that the members of his team would not fire until he gave the signal. The thresher seemed to catch a scent and raised itself up, its long spikes glittering like obsidian in the morning sunlight.

Keltin gave the signal and two shots rang out from among the trees. The thresher's body contorted as the blasts hit it from two different directions. It bellowed a challenge even as it fell to the ground. Jaylocke and Bor've'tai swiftly emerged from the underbrush. The thresher turned and lurched in Bor've'tai's direction, forcing the Loopi to jump back or have his legs swept out from under him by the beast's heavy, clawed forelimbs. Jaylocke immediately took advantage of the beast's distraction. Using a scythe he had found at the farmyard and sharpened to a razor's edge, he leapt to the wounded creature's side. With a graceful arch he brought the point of the elongated blade down into the thresher's shoulder between three closely growing spikes. The beast convulsed, wrenching the scythe from Jaylocke's hands as the wayfarer dodged the thresher's wild swing. Bor've'tai used the opening to move forward and deliver a resounding strike to the creature's head with the honed blade of his ax.

With practiced haste, Keltin and the rest of the team surged into the small clearing. After only a brief glance at the thresher to make sure it was no longer an immediate threat, Keltin and the three other hunters spun and faced the forest again, their rifles poised and ready as Jaylocke and Bor've'tai finished the dying beast behind them. Sure enough, the rustling of foliage announced that something had been drawn to the sounds of battle.

A whip leg burst from the trees closest to Garthen. He barely had time to fire off a shot before the swift creature was upon him. Weedon, standing closest to the pair, fired two shots into the whip leg. The beast gurgled terribly from a bullet in its lung, and Garthen was able to push it off. He rolled away to safety as the whip leg became entangled in a thorny bush, thrashing wildly in its death throes. Weedon moved closer to make sure the beast didn't rise again as Frederick and Keltin continued to scan the surrounding trees for any more attacking creatures. The forest was still, and soon the sounds of the dying beasts faded to silence. Keltin turned to Garthen with concern.

"Are you all right?"

The hunter nodded with a grimace as he clutched his arms around his stomach. "One of the whips got me in the middle. Knocked the wind out of me, but I'm all right."

"I'd better check it anyway," said Jaylocke, leaving the still form of the spiked thresher. "We don't want any internal injuries."

Keltin nodded. "Good idea. The rest of you keep an eye open. We may have drawn more of them to us."

Bor've'tai and Frederick dutifully turned to face the surrounding trees, but Weedon's attention seemed bound to the dead whip leg. His young face was twisted into a fierce snarl as he delivered a savage kick to the still body.

"Weedon, leave it and look to the forest."

Weedon didn't reply as he slowly and deliberately stepped on the whip leg's throat before turning to the silent woods. Keltin watched the back of the young man for a moment and wondered what to do about him. He couldn't complain about the young Krendarian's skills in hunting. Despite his lack of experience in stalking, he had learned quickly, and was already a good shot. But his brooding silences were unnerving, and Keltin sometimes wondered if he had made a mistake in bringing him along.

Dismissing his doubts for the moment, Keltin turned to Jaylocke and Garthen. The wayfarer had already called for the assistance of his great-grandmother Landria, who had been a midwife for her village before marrying his great-grandfather and joining his troupe. Landria was Jaylocke's best source for medical knowledge, and already her humble, practical skills had cured a stomach problem of Frederick's and saved Bor've'tai from infection in a bite that he had received from a quilled terror. Jaylocke concluded his inspection of the injured hunter and looked up to Keltin.

"He'll have a lovely bruise for a day or two, but other than that he'll be fine." Jaylocke winked at Garthen. "Just be glad it didn't strike you any lower, or you and yours may have never needed the services of Landria's most important skills."

The members of the team all chuckled softly, even Weedon, and Keltin was once again grateful to have Jaylocke along. It was good to hear laughter again, even if it was only cautious chuckling in a dangerous wood.

"Which direction shall we continue in?" asked Bor've'tai after the good humor had died down.

"North," answered Keltin. "The Baron wants us to continue pressing further north each day. That's where the beasts are always thickest."

They set out with Keltin and Garthen taking the lead and the rest followed behind them. Already they had killed four beasts in one day, and Keltin allowed himself some hope that the campaign might be a success after all. While the area north of camp still seemed as infested with creatures as ever, fewer beasts were appearing everywhere else in the province. Perhaps they would be successful in saving the Dhalma crops after all, and Keltin might be home in time to see the first snowfalls of Riltvin.

The group paused as the trees ahead of them opened onto a wide dirt track winding through the forest. Keltin recognized it as the road that led from their camp into the northern territories of Dhalma Province, though he'd never followed it on any earlier forays. With that thought in mind he led the others to the woods just to the right of the track and continued north, always keeping the road in sight.

"Not much traffic on the road today," said Jaylocke softly.

"All the landholders and their workers have long since fled to the city," said Garthen. "I don't think anyone has used this road for nearly a month now."

"Except for Rok and those that went with him," said Bor've'tai.

"Do you think they went north then? It's a dangerous road to travel."

"That's the direction they took when they left camp."

"I'd say I hope they got through, if it were anyone else," muttered Frederick.

They continued their slow progress alongside the road. Several times Keltin noticed the telltale movements of beasts in the bushes ahead, but each time the creatures evaded them. Probably serpent stags or other, similarly skittish beasts. Keltin knew better than to try chasing the fleet creatures. Let Pollik and his traps handle them. He and his team would continue to focus on the more dangerous quarry.

Someone gave the crested blue signal. Keltin dropped to the ground and looked back. Weedon was silently gesturing to him. He crept closer to allow the young hunter to whisper in his ear.

"Look there."

Following the direction of Weedon's pointing finger, Keltin could see nothing at first. He strained his eyes, trying to make out some detail of the beast that would stand out from the surrounding foliage. He felt a pinch behind his forehead as a sharp pain stabbed him between the eyes. He quickly relaxed his aching eyes and realized that the forest itself was warped and distorted. As he watched, the center of the distortion moved slowly, bending the trunks of trees towards itself before continuing on and restoring them to their normal, solid state.

"One of these again," murmured Weedon. "I haven't seen one of those since... since our first day in the forest. Have you?"

Keltin shook his head. "There can't be many of them in the province. Nobody but us has reported seeing one."

Keeping a weather-eye on the warp beast, Keltin moved closer to Bor've'tai.

"I spoke with Grel'zi'tael about this thing," Keltin said softly. "He seemed to have some idea of how he would handle it. Did he speak with you about it?"

Bor've'tai nodded as the beast began to slowly move away from them. "Yes, but I do not think I could do it. The beast seems to affect the normalcy around it, and combating it would require imposing normality upon it. It would be difficult, even for Grel'zi'tael."

"It hasn't seen us," said Jaylocke. "We could let it pass on by, if we chose to."

"What do you say, Captain?" asked Frederick. "Do we try for it?"

Keltin sucked in a breath and shook his head. "No, let it be. We'll wait a moment after it leaves before continuing to follow the road."

He received no answer from any of the others and they watched the warp beast disappear into the forest. Keltin had to admit to himself that he was relieved to see it go, and wondered how many of the others felt the same way. Memories of the smoke beast -and how close he had come to being a victim of its deadly embrace- still haunted him. Bor've'tai had only barely conquered the creature, and Keltin was in no hurry to force his friend to confront something that even Grel'zi'tael might not be able to defeat.

They ate a silent lunch before pressing on, always alert and ready for an attack even as they rested. They continued north, finding and felling a quilled terror and a pair of armored leeches with no great difficulties. Keltin was glad to face more familiar quarry, and the mood of the team seemed to brighten as the afternoon wore on. He was about to call a halt and start them heading back to camp when he spied something moving on the road ahead of them. Signaling the team to stop and wait, Keltin moved stealthily forward to see what had wandered out onto the dirt road.

The scene that he found chilled his blood. Wagons lay torn and splintered on the road, their broken wheels reaching for the cold sky above. Bodies lay among the scattered contents from the wagons' beds, though it was impossible to make out any details of the slain from where Keltin crouched in the bushes. A razorleg skittered among the wreckage, its insect-like feet drumming a hollow tattoo on the upturned belly of a wagon as it scurried to one of the still bodies and began feeding. Keltin felt his throat go dry as he took in the grisly scene, and he had to make two attempts before he was able to signal his teammates. The others approached and huddled around him. Someone gasped softly. Another of them tried to stop from gagging.

Keltin lifted his rifle, pushing all other thoughts from his mind for a single moment. He aimed for the joining of the razorleg's feathered thorax and its small, hard abdomen. With a single shot he pierced the beast's second brain. The creature fell from its perch to the ground, twitching a moment before it became as still as the bodies that surrounded it. The team waited a moment to see if anything was drawn to the sound of Keltin's shot. Nothing came, and Keltin lead the others out into the road to take a closer look at the devastation.

"It's the Heteracks," said Bor've'tai.

One look at the bodies up close confirmed it. Keltin knew the faces of the dead as some of his former companions from just days before. There was little that remained of them, but Keltin and his fellows checked each for signs of life. There were none.

"I wonder what kind of beasts attacked them," said Jaylocke as he stood, dusting his hands off on his trousers.

"They were big, whatever they were," said Bor've'tai. "Look at the wagons."

"Fast too," said Garthen. "It looks like the Heteracks never got the sleevaks out of their cages."

Keltin examined the cages that had carried the sleevaks. Each one was torn open, the iron bars twisted and mangled like the crab pots of a Riltvinian fisherman after a shark had found them. The tattered remains of the sleevaks were still in the cages, hardly recognizable as the fierce predators they had been only days before.

"I've found Rok," called Frederick from the front of the lead wagon.

Keltin turned away from the sleevak cages to join him. The cold, black eyes of the fierce captain of the sleevak wranglers stared defiantly up at him. Keltin looked into the dead eyes of a person that he had hated so deeply and felt only a dull ache in his heart. Perhaps Rok had deserved to die like this. After all, hadn't he wished the same fate for the Loopi? It seemed fair and it may have been justice, but Keltin found no comfort in it. He turned away from the body to rejoin the others.

"What do you think did this, Captain?" asked Weedon.

"I'm not sure, but I've only seen one beast in the province that was big enough, strong enough, and mean enough to attack the Heteracks and their sleevaks."

"The tusked giant," said Bor've'tai.

Keltin nodded. "It could be."

"Which one is the tusked giant?" asked Jaylocke.

"The beast that attacked us on our first night in the province. It came into camp and attacked the sleevaks. A group of us fired on it, but it got away."

"Do you think that it was the same one that did this?"

"Maybe. I suppose it could have been another one, but I definitely think that it was the same type of creature. Look at the way it tore open the cages to get at the sleevaks. I wonder if this thing makes a habit of preying on other beasts. It could be the reason why we haven't seen it on any of our patrols. We're not it's normal prey. Beasts are."

Jaylocke whistled. "A beast that only eats other beasts. That's going to be one monster I'd as soon let you all fill full of bullets before I have to dance around its knees, if we ever meet it."

"Well, we need to get away from all these dead bodies before they draw more beasts down on us."

"Are we going to keep pressing north?" asked Bor've'tai.

"No. I need to report this to the Baron. Let's head back."

"Do you think we should spare a moment to see if there's anything useful we could scavenge here?" asked Jaylocke. "Some of these firearms still look serviceable, and there may be ammunition and other stores that we could use."

"No," said Frederick. "You may have no concerns about it, but I don't like the idea of stealing from the dead."

"Nor do I, and you can believe me when I say it's not a regular habit of mine. But whatever's here will only rust and rot on the road if we don't take it." Jaylocke turned to Keltin. "What do you say, Captain?"

"All right, but hurry. Everyone look for anything that we might need."

"I don't like the idea," said Frederick.

"Fine, then keep watch for any more beasts while we look around."

They made a quick search of the wagon train and were able to find several serviceable rifles, half a dozen boxes of bullets, and a goad stick used for handling the sleevaks that Jaylocke said would make a better weapon than his farmer's scythe. There was little else that was not spoiled or broken, and Keltin announced that it was time for them to be gone. Without a backwards glance, they turned and left the shattered remains of the proud sleevak wranglers behind them.

Keltin felt as if the stillness of the forest were pressing in on him as he walked along the road south. The sight of Rok's cold, glassy eyes haunted him and drove away the sense of hope for the campaign that he had felt that morning. Were they really any closer to liberating this nightmarish province?

"In a hurry to get home, my Captain?" asked Jaylocke beside him.

Keltin realized that he had indeed quickened his pace, but he didn't slow down. Moving nearly at a run, he led his team back to the south. The Baron had to learn of what had happened on the north road. Perhaps Rumsfeld would have a plan. Some brilliant scheme to make the death of all those hunters account for something. Keltin fervently hoped so.

CHAPTER 14 – A DESPERATE PLAN

Keltin was relieved to see the familiar outline of the farmhouse and surrounding buildings in the early evening twilight. Sergeant Bracksten approached them as he patrolled the barricade and trench that his men had extended to encircle the entire camp.

"You're in early, Moore," he said.

"We ran into some trouble."

Bracksten snorted. "This whole plaguing province is trouble."

The sergeant continued on his patrol as Keltin led his team into the camp.

"Looks like there's some new blood for the campaign," said Jaylocke.

He pointed to a small group of men in Krendarian uniforms standing outside the farmhouse. They looked fresh and alert and were obviously newly arrived from Carvalen.

"I hope they brought a whole company with them."

"Any reinforcements would be welcome about now," said Garthen.

"I'll agree with that," said Keltin. "I need to make my report to the Baron. I'll see you all at dinner."

He left his teammates and approached the farmhouse. The

new soldiers seemed uncertain how to address him until the campaign veteran standing guard called out a greeting.

"Evening, Captain Moore. The Baron asked to see you as soon as you returned to camp."

Keltin nodded in response and cut his way through the small crowd of soldiers now hurrying to get out of his way. A few even gave him an uncertain salute, which might have made him laugh out loud if his mood had been lighter. He found the Baron seated at the dining room table with a young man who Keltin guessed was the commanding officer of the group gathered outside.

"Captain Moore," said the Baron by way of greeting. "I'm glad that you've returned early. Sergeant Harris here has brought some reinforcements from Duke Gregson along with news from Carvalen, and I want to discuss it with you."

"I have news I need to discuss with you as well. We found Rok and his wagons on the north road. They'd been attacked. We found no survivors."

Rumsfeld heaved a heavy sigh and nodded. "Very well. Tell me the details quickly, and then we must discuss what we shall do about this campaign. Things have changed somewhat, and we will need a plan of action before dinner tonight."

* * *

Keltin left the farmhouse and went straight for the supper line. Most of the camp was already seated and eating. Mama Bellin gave him a generous portion of pumpkin stew and he did his best to return her friendly smile before finding his place among the members of his stalker team.

"We weren't sure if you were going to make it," said Jaylocke as Keltin sat and began devouring his dinner. "What took you so long?"

"The Baron needed to discuss the campaign. He'll be announcing it all soon," Keltin said between mouthfuls. "We'll have to talk about it afterward."

Any further conversation was cut off as Baron Rumsfeld

stood up on the raised platform in front of the seated hunters.

"Good evening."

Rumsfeld's voice was low and even, but all the noises among the tables fell suddenly silent. The crackling of Mama Bellin's cooking fire seemed to fill the dark farmstead grounds. The Baron continued.

"I'll not burden you with sweet words or stirring speeches. In the last few weeks, you men have seen horrors that would have turned an army to retreat, and you've faced them day after long day. While we've lost some good men, you've managed to kill more beasts than we can number."

Keltin wondered if the Baron would mention Rok and the other deserters, but the man pressed on without a word about them.

"But the beasts continue to come. While most of the creatures have been cleared from the south and sightings to the east and west are becoming more rare, the beast sightings from the northern patrols continue to be very high. For this reason, I have decided on a final strategy for this campaign before the season's crops are forever lost to us.

"First, we will draw a line across the province from east to west, centered on this farmstead. With the reinforcements that arrived today from Duke Gregson, we will establish a protected border across Dhalma to protect workers that will begin arriving in the south fields by the day following tomorrow. We shall consider the northern crops lost, and can only hope that the southern crops will be enough to fill the empty stomachs of Carvalen and hold back a bloody revolution.

"At the same time that the majority of us will be establishing this defended boundary, a small team of our best hunters will move some distance north and establish a secondary headquarters deep in the beasts' territory. It is our hope that this group will draw much of the beasts' attention away from the south, buying more time for the field workers and taking much of the strain off of the thinly dispersed defenders along the boundary.

"Your team captains will give you further instruction on how and where each of you will participate in the final defense of the southern farms. I wish good luck to all of you, and bid you a fair evening."

The Baron stepped down from the platform and returned to his table. It took some time for the low sounds of the hunters' evening meal to return. Keltin ate mechanically, his attention fixed on his bowl of stew as the members of his team watched him. It was Bor've'tai who finally broke the silence.

"It was us the Baron spoke of, wasn't it?"

Keltin shook his head.

"I wasn't going to speak for any of you," he said. "I agreed I would go, that's all. I suppose the Baron assumed there'd be at least one more man who'd go with me, or else he'd have just said I was going."

"What makes the Baron think anyone would volunteer for a crazed scheme like this?" said Frederick.

"He's offered to double our payment if we go north," said Keltin.

"Not much good if you're dead."

"Or if Carvalen is in flames by the time we get back," said Garthen. "Duke Gregson won't be paying anyone if his head ends up on the block."

"Don't say that," said Weedon. "The people of Carvalen only want to see their families fed. They'll settle down once the food of the southern crops starts coming into the city."

"Don't be simple," said Frederick. "There's more going on in the capital than a hungry lower class. We've got a child for a king, and all of Parliament has their heads in the mud. Nothing's going to satisfy an angry mob but noble blood, and lots of it."

"I tell you, that won't happen," insisted Weedon.

"How do you know what desperate men will do when they have to watch their children starve?" said Garthen.

Keltin heard the argument grow hotter and angrier but listened to little of it. He finished his stew and stared into the empty bowl, his thoughts a swirling turmoil within him. After a moment, he became aware of eyes upon him. Glancing up, he saw Jaylocke watching him curiously.

"I think that friend Keltin may have more reason than money for going north," he said.

The arguing hunters fell silent and looked at Keltin. He returned his attention to the table in front of him, trying to put the strange emotions within him into words.

"When… when I came to Krendaria, I came to make the money that I needed for a rent payment and to send to my mother and sister. Of course, I also knew that I'd be helping people. That's why I became a beast hunter, to help people and make a living at it. But it's never been like this for me. I've always worked alone, and even on my most dangerous hunts, I knew what I needed to do.

"But this time, I don't know. Time's running out, and something needs to happen to try and keep the beasts away from the southern fields. If I can draw the beasts' attention long enough to get that food to those who really need it, well, I think that this mad scheme is worth the risk. It's up to each of you to decide for yourself whether to come with me or not."

Bor've'tai immediately placed a hand firmly on his shoulder.

"I will go with you," he said. "I will fight and follow you as far as you travel."

Jaylocke chuckled and gave Keltin a wink. "I've already sworn my total allegiance to you. It'd be a sad, paltry pledge if I backed out of it again after only a few days. You'll have me along as well."

Garthen heaved a sigh and shook his head.

"Well, I'll not be outdone by a Weycliff and a woodcutter," he muttered. "I'll come along as well, Captain."

"As will I," put in Weedon.

Keltin was about to reply when someone clapped a hand on his other shoulder. He looked up to see Henry, the lanky captain of the other team of stalker hunters.

"Well Keltin," he said, "I hope that you've had more luck among your men, because I'm the only one from my team willing to go with you."

Frederick cleared his throat. "Well, since you've already got a sixth man, I suppose I'll go with the other team of stalker hunters to help protect the southern farms."

Keltin nodded. "I understand. Good luck, Frederick."

The other hunter shook his head ruefully. "I think you lot are the ones who'll be needing the luck."

* * *

Keltin set his pen aside. Flickering light from his campfire played over the page filled with his uneven handwriting. He started to fold the letter, hesitated, and opened it again to read it one more time.

Dear Mary,

Thank you for your letters, as always they have been a great comfort to me. I know that I have already sent you a reply to them and that you will likely receive this message before you have had a chance to respond, but circumstances have changed and I need to take this final opportunity to write to you.

The campaign is not going well. The northern farms are lost, and we are focusing all of our efforts on protecting the southern farms. For that purpose, I will be leading a small team of hunters north to establish a secondary camp to kill as many beasts as we can and try to buy enough time for the field workers. I won't lie to you. It will be very dangerous. I am not sure whether I will come back from this.

I have given instructions that the payment for my part in this campaign will be sent to you and Mother. I wish that I could say I know you will receive it and will be provided for regardless of what happens to me, but the situation in Carvalen is so tenuous that I will have to be content that I've done the best that I could to see to your needs.

Please give Mother my love, and tell her that I am sorry. I have done what I felt was right, and am prepared to face whatever consequences will follow. Know that my prayers are with you, and it is my greatest hope to see you again in happier times.

Until then,
Keltin

Keltin folded the small sheets of paper and slid them into the waiting envelope. Slipping it into his pocket, he left his tent and went to the small box that had been provided to the hunters for their outgoing mail. He dropped off his letter to Mary along with a second, shorter message to Mrs. Galloway before continuing on in the direction of the Weycliff wagon circle, hoping to find Mama Bellin or Evik awake to discuss the rations for the expedition north.

It was a dark night, but Keltin managed to find his way by the light of the many low-burning campfires and soon saw the silhouettes of the wagons looming before him. Turning to circle around the outside of the ring, he was startled to hear a familiar voice nearby.

"Won't you speak to me at all? I'll be gone by the morning."

The voice was Jaylocke's, and had come from the wagon he had just been walking past. Keltin paused as his curiosity temporarily overpowered his usual reluctance to eavesdrop. The painted canvass cover muffled some of the sound, but he still managed to make out the soft reply to his friend's question.

"What would you have me say?"

Keltin recognized Ameldi's musical voice as Jaylocke answered her.

"You can say whatever you want, just say something."

"I've told you that I pray for your success, and look forward to your return. What more do you want?"

"Ameldi, there is something more. You seem... withdrawn. What is it?"

"Withdrawn? Haven't you drawn away from your family and clan since you decided to play at being a hunter?"

"I'm not playing at being a hunter."

The sound of Ameldi's sigh was full of frustration. "I know. You and your companions have had great success. You must be very proud of yourself, offering your services to Keltin like a cavalier in one of Evik's sagas. But do you think it impresses me? Do you imagine me to be your dutiful maiden on some lonely castle wall waiting for your return?"

"I'll admit I had expected you to be more supportive," came Jaylocke's hot reply. "You act like you don't care at all about the suffering of the people of this country."

Keltin realized that the discussion was quickly turning into an argument, and decided to leave before hearing any more. A twig snapped underneath his foot, and he cursed himself for being distracted and clumsy. Ameldi and Jaylocke immediately went silent, and he knew that they had heard him. With practiced caution, he inched his way forward, wishing he could move faster but knowing it would reveal him to those he had been listening to.

"I do care about the people here," Ameldi continued as Keltin struggled to stealthily get out of hearing distance. "I cast my vote to come here and support the Duke's campaign the same as you did. But I didn't think you'd risk yourself... risk *us*, for your dreams of honor and nobility. I didn't cast my vote for that."

"It was my decision. I thought you would understand."

"It seems that I don't, and that you don't understand me."

"Perhaps I should leave your wagon then," said Jaylocke, his voice cold.

"Perhaps you should."

There was an angry shuffling and creaking and Keltin froze once again. He listened as Jaylocke climbed out the other end of the wagon to the driver's seat.

"I'll see you when I return," he said. "*If* I return."

Ameldi made no reply, and Keltin heard the dividing curtain yanked viciously into place as Jaylocke dropped heavily to the earth, his swift footfalls carrying him out of the wagon circle and toward the main body of the camp. The sound of soft crying began to drift from within Ameldi's wagon. Keltin waited a moment, then turned to silently make his way back to his tent. He could talk with Evik and Mama Bellin in the morning. He wasn't in the mood to speak with anyone right now, and he'd need as much rest as he could get before the morning came.

CHAPTER 15 – WITH FAITH AND COURAGE

Keltin was up before the sun. Cold seeped through his bedroll and hunting coat, and he rose quickly to finish dressing. As he began to warm, he dismantled his small tent and stowed it with the rest of his gear. Shouldering his pack, he moved silently between the tents in the predawn light, careful not to wake those hunters who still clung to the temporary comforts of sleep.

The Loopi were awake, sitting together on their rush mats in their now-familiar morning ritual of prayer and meditation. Keltin gave them a respectful distance as he began to make his way to the Weycliff wagon circle. He was just passing them when Grel'zi'tael's soft voice called out to him.

"Good morning, Keltin. You're up very early."

"I couldn't sleep anymore. I was hoping to speak with Evik or Mama Bellin about provisions for the trip north, if either of them are up yet."

The Sky Talker nodded. "That is prudent, but I would not worry. Mama Bellin has that title for a reason, and she has likely been up for more than an hour already preparing food for your expedition."

Keltin smiled and shrugged. "You're probably right. I suppose I'll just wander around the camp a bit to clear my head."

"You are welcome to join in our prayers this morning, if you would like."

Keltin hesitated. He'd rarely prayed with others and had always preferred solitude when speaking with his Maker. He formed a polite refusal in his mind and prepared to give it, but the gentle eyes of the Sky Talker stopped him.

"All right."

Bor've'tai and Shar'le'vah moved aside to give him room to kneel between them. They all held hands and Keltin was reminded of the Moore family prayers when he was a child as Bor've'tai and Shar'le'vah's long fingers wrapped around his much smaller hands.

"We'll begin again," said Grel'zi'tael. "Val'ta'lir, will you start?"

The dark-furred Loopi nodded and bowed his head. "Great God of the Heavens, I give thanks for the reinforcements from Carvalen. Give me strength to aid them as we begin securing the western boundary, and give Shar'le'vah strength as she labors on the eastern boundary. May we all return to this circle when all is done."

Val'ta'lir fell silent and Bor've'tai began. "God of the World, I give thanks for the teachings of Grel'zi'tael, his kindness and patience. Help me to remember his lessons and wisdom in the coming days, that I may protect my companions to the fullness of my power. Keep each of us safe until we return to this circle."

Keltin felt Bor've'tai gently squeeze his hand. He felt his mouth go dry as he tried to think of what he should say.

"Dear Father in Heaven," he began after a moment, "thank you for my friends allowing me to join them this morning. I'm… I'm a little nervous about today. It almost feels like it'd be easier to go by myself, without being responsible for the men going with me. Please help me. I can't do it by myself. Keep us all safe."

Keltin finished his prayer and felt a gentle calm come over him. He squeezed Shar'le'vah's hand and received a soft pressure in return as she spoke.

"God of all Peoples, I give thanks for the wisdom of Baron Rumsfeld as he leads our efforts in the province. I ask that he continue to guide us with intelligence and forethought, and that his plans may be successful to the easing of the people of Carvalen's burdens. I also give thanks for Keltin, for his faith and loyalty. Give him the guidance that he desires."

Keltin felt the warmth inside him grow as a smile came unbidden to his face. It took a moment for him to realize that Shar'le'vah had fallen silent. Had she finished? Grel'zi'tael had not yet begun. Was the Sky Talker just taking his time in gathering his thoughts? After a moment, Shar'le'vah continued.

"God of Infinite Love and Kindness, give Bor've'tai and his companions safety. Return him to our circle, so that we may feel the strength and courage of his heart once more."

There was a silence again. Keltin wondered what the two Loopi holding his hands were feeling until Grel'zi'tael's voice came like the gentle sound of waves on a rocky beach.

"God of Eternity, I give thanks for the faith of these children around me. Bless them. Give each comfort to his and her heart, for this morning and the coming days. When doubt and fear threaten, replace them with faith and courage. Return us again to this circle when our tasks are done, with Thy blessing. Amen."

Keltin opened his eyes to see that the sun had risen. The light of day was upon the gentle faces of the Loopi gathered around him. They were somber, but in their eyes a shining hope seemed to reflect the glow of a new day.

"Thank you for joining us, Keltin," said Grel'zi'tael.

"Thank you, Sky Talker."

"We should leave soon if we are to be breakfasted and gone before the morning is over," said Bor've'tai.

"You're right. Let's see if the rest of the team is up and about."

They found Jaylocke and the others eating the remains of

the pumpkin stew, their gear already packed and lying nearby. Keltin eyed the packs as he began to eat.

"Do we already have the provisions for the journey?" he asked.

Jaylocke shook his head. "Mama Bellin and the others have been trying to finish preparing them while making the men's breakfast. We'll have to stop by the wagon circle before we leave."

Keltin noticed that his friend's usual smile was missing and silently considered his suspicions for its absence. They finished eating just as the rest of the camp began taking their seats for the morning meal. Keltin and his team shouldered their packs and headed for the Weycliff side of camp, passing Mama Bellin and Maynid hurrying by with a large pot of porridge.

"Good luck!" called Maynid as he rushed by. "May the ancestors be with you!"

They pressed on and soon stopped just outside the ring of painted wagons. To Keltin's surprise it was Ameldi that emerged from the protected circle, struggling to hold a heavy-looking haversack. There were dark circles under her emerald green eyes and her hair hadn't been brushed, but there was still an audible intake of breath from all the men among Keltin's group who hadn't yet seen the Weycliff's finest singer. Jaylocke gently took the haversack from her.

"Is this all of it?" he asked softly.

She nodded. "It's mostly green meal with a few potatoes. It should last you until you can start foraging from the north farms, as long as you find water to cook with."

"I should be able to."

"Yes."

Ameldi's eyes went to the ground as Jaylocke fidgeted with the haversack. Keltin wished he could give them some time, but the rest of the group was waiting. He cleared his throat.

"We should be going."

Jaylocke nodded and reached a hand out to Ameldi.

"Ameldi, I…"

The girl shook her head and turned, running back to the

safety of the wagon circle. Jaylocke stood silently and watched her until she had disappeared from view. Moments passed. Keltin tried to think of something to say. Helplessly, he turned to Bor've'tai. The Loopi met his eyes, nodded, and moved to Jaylocke's side.

"I'll carry the food," he offered. "I have less to bring than the rest of you."

Jaylocke passed off the haversack without argument. With a final look back at the wagon circle, he turned to Keltin and the rest of the team.

"I'm ready to leave now."

Keltin nodded. "Good. Let's go."

The morning was cold and still as they began their journey northward. They had only just left the trapper's killing field behind them when they spied the mossy green body and ropey appendages of a coiling creeper. Henry gave Keltin a questioning look, but he shook his head. The coiling creeper soon moved on and Keltin spoke to the others in a hushed voice.

"I want to get a little distance from the camp before we start killing beasts. We don't want to bring them all down on us before we're ready."

Everyone seemed to agree with this, and they passed several more beasts without being seen as they pressed north. By noonday they had already reached the furthest limits of the territory that Keltin was familiar with and halted for a cold lunch. Jaylocke found a nearby field of carrots and they munched the twisted vegetables as they rested in the relative safety of a thick copse of trees. Keltin was rubbing some of the cold dirt off of his meal when Jaylocke shifted himself to sit closer to him.

"Is it safe to talk a little?" he asked in a low voice.

Keltin listened to the still forest for a moment and nodded. "I think so, if we keep our voices down."

Jaylocke nodded with a thoughtful frown. "I wonder... do you know much about women, Keltin?"

Keltin resisted the urge to give a bitter laugh before

answering.

"What do you mean?"

Jaylocke sighed. "I'm not sure. I don't understand something. I'm not even sure how to ask about it."

Keltin inwardly groaned. Leading this group into unfamiliar territory was bad enough. He didn't want to deal with their personal problems as well.

"Have you tried calling on one of your ancestors for guidance?" he asked, hoping to shift some of the responsibility away from himself.

"Several, but it hasn't helped. Perhaps it's because I don't know what to ask for. I'm not sure."

"Well, I'm not sure I can help you either. I'm really not that good with the subject myself."

Jaylocke sighed and nodded. "That's all right, I understand. I'm sorry I bothered you. I'll just think about it some more."

Jaylocke fell back into a thoughtful silence. Keltin was sorry to see his friend so troubled, but was grateful that the subject had been dropped. The rest of the day passed slowly as they left their familiar hunting grounds and pushed north into the unknown areas of Dhalma Province. Keltin began to consider where they should establish their basecamp. The obvious choice was to use one of the abandoned farmhouses that they occasionally passed, but Keltin wondered if a movable camp would be a better way to keep from being surrounded and overwhelmed. He was still debating with himself as he called a halt in the darkening evening.

"We haven't camped in the forest before," said Bor've'tai. "Do we light a fire, or shall we have a cold camp?"

Keltin considered for a moment. "In Riltvin, when I would camp on a hunt, I'd usually risk a small fire for cooking on cold nights."

"Most beasts don't need a fire to find you," agreed Henry. "And we've got enough men to rotate watches without anyone getting too little rest."

"Let's light a small fire then. It's worth the risk to have something hot in our stomachs."

Nobody seemed to disagree and each hunter quietly began making camp. Keltin put up his tent and foraged some fuel for their campfire. Soon he had a modest fire burning and Jaylocke was kneeling next to him to begin boiling a pot of water.

"What's for dinner tonight?" Keltin asked.

"Green meal, the traveling entertainer's staple."

"What's that?"

Jaylocke opened the haversack and used a cup to scoop out some of the fine, greenish-gray powder.

"Mostly it's dried beans and peas, ground to a powder and mixed together. It's the peas that give the stuff its color and name. Mix it in hot water and it makes a paste that'll fill you up and keep you warm."

"How's it taste?"

Jaylocke shrugged. "A little salt, a little pepper, and it'll be two, maybe three times before you're sick of it."

Keltin gave a half-hearted chuckle as he looked into the fire and tried to consider their situation. Jaylocke waited for his water to boil and poured in some of the green meal powder, taking care to slowly stir it as he added what spices he had available.

"How are you, Keltin?" he asked after a moment.

Keltin sighed. "I'm wondering what we should do next. We're here to draw the beasts' attention to us, but we won't do any good if we get ourselves killed the first day. I've never done this before, and I'm having a difficult time knowing what to do."

"Have you asked the others what they recommend?"

"Not yet. I was going to try to put together a plan and then ask their opinions, but I suppose that won't work if I can't come up with anything."

"No one's expecting you to always know what to do, Keltin. We're all in unfamiliar territory here. You don't have to figure everything out on your own anymore. You're not alone."

Keltin smiled. "I suppose not. You know, for a while, there was a part of me that wished I could have done this mission by myself."

"But then you would have never discovered all the many wonders of green meal."

"I could have lived with that."

Jaylocke soon finished preparing their simple dinner and served out shallow pans of the green mush. Keltin savored the heat radiating from the steaming paste for a moment before trying a spoonful. It was bland and hot. There was little else to recommend it. Keltin ate mechanically as he spoke with the others between spoonfuls.

"I want to ask you all something. I've been trying to decide whether we should keep camping out in the open or secure ourselves in one of the farmhouses. It'd be safer in a farmhouse, but we run the risk of getting boxed in with no way out. What do you think?"

"It seems caution is a wiser course," said Bor've'tai after a moment. "As long as we're killing beasts, it doesn't really matter if we're temporarily trapped."

"That's true," said Garthen. "The point of this expedition is to kill as many beasts as possible, and if we stay in one place, the bodies of the creatures we've already killed will likely act as bait to bring more of the boils to us."

"But being out in the open means we can actively search for the beasts," said Henry. "If we stay in a farmhouse, the beasts could be less than a quarter of a mile from us and we'd never know it if we just stay indoors."

"You're assuming that just because we're headquartered in a farmhouse that we have to remain there," said Jaylocke. "If we aren't getting many beasts at our door, we can always go looking for them. I think the main point here is how safe we are at night. In a farmhouse, we have the security of walls around us, out here…"

He fell silent and allowed the night to press in upon them. Keltin had to agree with Jaylocke. It was nights like this that had developed his curse of light sleeping. Even with men on guard all night long, he had to admit that he'd much rather sleep with a roof over his head than tent canvas.

"All right," he said. "We'll look for a good farmhouse once

it's light. In the meantime, we'll take turns keeping guard tonight."

"I suggest we try to keep our gunfire to a minimum," said Jaylocke. "If we can kill something quietly, better to let the rest of the camp sleep, not to mention any other beasts that are in earshot."

"Agreed. Weedon, you take first watch. Then Henry, Garthen, me, Bor've'tai, and Jaylocke. Each man takes an hour and a half watch. Does anyone need a timepiece? No? Then let's get some rest. We'll have another long day ahead of us tomorrow."

The hunters all nodded and crawled into their tents as Weedon sat with his back to the campfire to keep the glare from blinding him to the darkness beyond its light. Keltin stretched himself out on his bedroll and tried to relax, trusting the brave and capable men around him to keep him safe until it was his time to stand watch.

He was somewhere between exhaustion and dreaming when a gunshot shattered the night. Keltin was up with boots on and rifle in hand before he was truly awake, and searched blearily along with the rest of the men for any sign of danger. Weedon was nowhere in sight. Another shot sounded, then a third. Keltin rushed towards the sound, followed closely by the rest of the team. They found Weedon standing over the body of a still beast, his rifle still held tightly in his hands. Straining to see in the darkness, Keltin realized that the dead creature was the same type of stork-legged monster that had killed Ru on their first hunt in the province. Weedon seemed consumed with the silent creature lying before him as he slowly raised his rifle to his shoulder once again.

Keltin took a cautious step forward. "Weedon?"

The hunter fired a fourth shot into the dead creature.

"Weedon! Stop!"

The young man shot it again. Keltin began to move towards the young man, but suddenly Bor've'tai was at Weedon's side. The Loopi took hold of the hunter's rifle barrel and forced it up towards the starry sky. Weedon struggled to wrestle his weapon away from Bor've'tai's iron grip.

"Let go of my gun, you plaguing ape!" he screamed. "I'll shoot you too! Let go or I'll kill you!"

Suddenly Bor've'tai struck out with the flat of his broad hand, hitting Weedon squarely in the center of his chest. The young man flew back and landed solidly on the ground, coughing and wheezing for breath.

"Runny idiot!" Henry growled at the gasping young man. "You'll bring every beast within a mile down on us!"

"We need to get back to camp," said Keltin. "We'll see them coming more easily with the fire behind us."

They were just turning to go back when something crashed in the underbrush nearby. Garthen fired into the darkness in the sound's direction. Keltin stood poised, waiting for the beast to emerge. Nothing came, and after a moment Keltin crept forward to investigate. Behind a bush, he found a strange, horned creature with over-sized hoofs and a long tail covered in wicked barbs. Keltin examined it closer and realized that Garthen's wild shot had hit it squarely between the eyes, killing it almost instantly in a fantastically lucky shot. Quickly rejoining the others, Keltin led them back to camp and stood with his back to the fire, ready and waiting. Time passed and nothing else emerged from the forest.

"I think we're through the worst of it," said Keltin.

Bor've'tai nodded. "It seems we had few beasts near us tonight."

"We were lucky," said Jaylocke.

"No thanks to some," muttered Henry as he glared at Weedon.

Keltin turned to the distraught young man. Weedon had thrown himself down on his bedroll, still coughing and wheezing as he lay with his arms wrapped around his chest.

"Do you think I should check him for injuries?" asked Jaylocke.

"I suppose," said Keltin.

Jaylocke crouched next to Weedon and reached out to begin gently probing his ribs. The young hunter jerked away from his touch.

"Stay away from me!"

Jaylocke gave Keltin a helpless look. Keltin waved Jaylocke aside and took his place next to the young man.

"Weedon," he said. "We need to talk."

"Go jump down a beast's throat."

Keltin's hand shot forward, taking a handful of Weedon's hair and yanking his head around to look up at him. Weedon started to cry out but was silenced by Keltin's other hand pressed firmly against his mouth.

"Now listen," he said. "You may think that losing Ru gives you some special right to make this expedition a personal quest for revenge. Well it doesn't. Your stupidity could have cost us dearly tonight, and I won't allow it. I'll give you a choice, Weedon. Either keep your vengeful fantasies in your head, or tomorrow you're on your own. We'll leave you here. Understand? I'll take your decision in the morning."

Keltin released his grip on Weedon's hair and stood up, turning to the startled hunters watching him. He ignored their stunned expressions and turned to Henry.

"I'll take the rest of Weedon's watch. I'll wake you in an hour."

Henry nodded and quietly returned to his tent. Keltin went to the log beside the campfire and sat, facing the dark forest. Soon the rest of the team had followed Henry's example, and Keltin was left with nothing but the crackling fire and the sound of Weedon's soft sobbing to disturb the black silence of the night.

CHAPTER 16 – TRAPPED

Keltin crouched low in the narrow space between two rows of Krendarian maize that had already begun to rot in the field. He knew that there were at least four beasts circling around the field, trying to find his scent. This had been a mistake. While the maize field had provided him temporary cover, it made it impossible to see any of his companions except for Weedon, who was crouching nearby.

"They'll circle around behind us," Keltin murmured to him. "We'll need to be ready when they come between the rows."

Weedon nodded. He had not spoken a word since the night before, and Keltin was grateful for his silence. Better to have him silent and moody than loud and dangerous to everyone around him.

A sudden stirring came from among the maize plants nearby. There was a growl and a sudden thrashing as something crashed through the field. A nearby rifle fired with a deafening report. A piercing scream immediately followed. Keltin barely caught Weedon in time before he could dive through the tightly growing plants in the direction of the gunshots.

"They may think you're another beast," said Keltin as more gunshots filled the morning air.

They sat and waited, listening to the savage sounds of battle nearby. Suddenly a man's scream mixed with the cries of beasts.

"Help! Help me!"

The voice was Henry's. Keltin braced himself and plunged into the thickly growing maize with Weedon close behind him.

"We're coming!" he shouted.

Pushing through the stubborn plants, Keltin came out into another open track between rows. Henry was on the ground, a fierce razorleg viciously attacking his legs. Jaylocke was striking the beast with his gaff hook, trying to get under the creature's armored shell. There was a stir of movement and a serpent stag burst into the row just a dozen feet from the violent scene.

"Jaylocke!" Keltin yelled. "Get down!"

Without looking up Jaylocke immediately kicked both feet out from under himself, landing on his side and taking out a long knife to continue his attack on the razorleg. Keltin fired a shot over his head to strike the serpent stag just under the chin where its scales were softest. The beast lurched back and fell, its body quivering in the broken maize plants. Keltin raced towards Henry and Jaylocke just in time to see the wayfarer pry the razorleg's jaws open as Henry sawed its neck in half with a worn hunting knife. The creature thrashed its death throes as Jaylocke tossed it away and immediately began checking Henry's bloody legs.

Keltin didn't waste time asking how the man was as he took a guard position over the two of them. Looking around he saw a third dead beast lying nearby on the ground. It was a winged strangler, killed by a gunshot to its scrawny neck. A cautious voice spoke from somewhere nearby.

"Keltin, we're coming out."

"All right."

Bor've'tai and Garthen carefully emerged into the bloody clearing.

"Any more beasts out there?" asked Keltin.

"Just one more," said Bor've'tai. "Another serpent stag. It ran off after the first shots were fired."

"All right, keep an eye out for me."

Keltin turned back to Jaylocke and Henry. Kneeling beside them, Keltin looked at the bloody mess of Henry's legs.

"How is he?" he asked Jaylocke softly.

"I hurt like a soul in hell," Henry muttered through clenched teeth.

"He's torn up pretty badly," Jaylocke said as he ripped fresh bandages from a roll of fabric in his pack. "At least it didn't get down to the bone. Are razorlegs venomous?"

"No," said Keltin, "just mean. But you should still be worried about infection."

"I am."

Keltin looked at the blood seeping through Jaylocke's hasty dressings even as he tied them.

"He's not going to be able to continue."

"Not without some serious care, which I can't give him in the middle of this field."

Henry suddenly sat up, gripping Keltin's arm desperately.

"Don't leave me here!"

Keltin squeezed Henry's shoulder tightly. "We won't, I promise. But we need to get you somewhere safe."

Henry let his head fall back to the ground and made a sound somewhere between a laugh and a sob.

"There's no place safe around here."

"Maybe not, but we can still do better than this field. Bor've'tai, come with me to check out that farmhouse beyond this field. The rest of you follow as best you can."

"We should probably rig up some type of stretcher to carry Henry in," said Jaylocke.

"We passed a plow that was left in the field as we came in," said Garthen. "We could take it apart and use a tent canvass to rig something together."

"Good," said Keltin. "Get started. Let's go, Bor've'tai."

Cutting across the field towards the farmhouse, Keltin was able to get his first good look at the building they had been traveling towards when the beasts had attacked. It was a solid structure with two floors and a large barn standing nearby.

Drawing closer, the signs of age began to show in its faded paint and weathered boards, but Keltin was more interested in the defensive improvements to the house that looked like they had been both hastily and recently added. The entire bottom floor of the farmhouse was boarded up, and the low stone wall surrounding the kitchen garden on one side of the house had been extended with rough-hewn logs and piles of earth to nearly surround the entire property.

"It looks like these people tried weathering the storm of beasts rather than leaving," said Bor've'tai.

"Something happened. They didn't finish their wall."

"Perhaps they were taken by beasts before they could complete it."

"Maybe. The boards around the bottom level of the house still look secure though. Perhaps they decided to escape rather than remain here."

Drawing closer, Keltin could see signs of multiple beast attacks. The bodies of several creatures had been left to slowly rot where they had died, and broken glass under several boarded-up windows showed where beasts had tried to force their way into the house. Drawing level with the unfinished wall, Keltin noticed the body of a winged strangler that looked less than a day old. Kneeling down beside it, he found several bullet holes in its grotesque body. He was about to point it out to Bor've'tai when the Loopi suddenly dropped low beside him.

"I saw movement in the house," he said.

"Where?"

"An upstairs window."

Keltin looked up at the second floor that had for the most part remained untouched by the farmer's defensive additions. Searching the upstairs windows for signs of movement, he spied the silhouette of someone trying to look outside without revealing themselves.

"I see them. Someone's in there."

"I didn't think anyone was still alive this far north."

"Neither did I."

Keltin began to rise, but Bor've'tai placed a restraining hand on his shoulder.

"Carefully," he said. "These people have been through much and may be distrustful of strangers."

"We'll have to chance that. Henry won't last long out in the open."

"Agreed."

Keltin handed Bor've'tai his rifle. "Cover me."

Bor've'tai took the rifle, holding it awkwardly in his overlarge hands.

"I will try."

Keltin rose slowly, keeping his hands in plain sight as he approached the farmhouse.

"Hello in the house!" he called. "We're beast hunters and have a wounded man. May we take shelter with you?"

The silhouette disappeared. A minute or two passed, and a man came close enough to the upstairs window for Keltin to distinguish his features. He was of middle years, with several weeks growth of beard on his broad, haggard-looking face. He held a long-barreled rifle in his hands, though he kept it pointed away from Keltin.

"We haven't seen anything but beasts for weeks," the man called back. "How did you get through? Has the number of the cursed monsters finally begun to fall off?"

"Somewhat. Duke Gregson of Carvalen has called all able hunters to the province to try and save what crops we can."

The man turned and seemed to hold a brief discussion with someone Keltin couldn't see. He returned to the window after a moment.

"Come around to the kitchen garden entrance and I'll let you in. It's not safe to remain outside."

"The rest of my fellows are coming with our wounded man."

"That's fine. We have room inside for everyone when they arrive."

Keltin nodded and quickly went back to Bor've'tai to retrieve his rifle.

"They've agreed to allow us all into the farmhouse. Any sign of the others?"

"None yet. You go on in and inspect the place, I'll go back and see if I can help."

"Be careful."

Bor've'tai began to make his way back to the fields as Keltin circled around the farmhouse. Allowing himself through the low gate, he passed through a well-tended kitchen garden that had already been picked clean of anything remotely edible. He knocked on the boards that reinforced the back door and heard the clicks and shuffling of locks and braces against the entrance. The door opened, and Keltin stepped into the gloom of a modest kitchen lit only by the feeble light trickling through the boarded-up windows. The man from the upstairs window quickly shut the door behind him, drawing every latch and lock back into place before turning to Keltin.

"My name's Jonathan," he said, extending a work-hardened hand in the gloom.

"Keltin Moore, beast hunter from Riltvin."

"Have you seen anyone else in any of the neighboring farms?"

"You're the first, though I think many of the other farmers managed to escape down to Carvalen before the beasts grew too thick here. Why didn't you go with them?"

"My Master thought it best to weather the storm of beasts here, rather than trust our fortunes on the road."

"You're a servant here then?"

"I was the master's groomsman and gardener. My wife was his cook and housekeeper." He sighed. "I'm not sure what we are now."

"He's dead then?"

Jonathan nodded. "It happened less than a week ago. It's just the three of us left."

"Three?"

"The Master's niece is here with us. Poor thing's family thought they'd send her here to escape the turmoil in Malpin. No one thought the beasts would be this bad this year."

Jonathan sighed and shook his head. "Well, you might as well come upstairs with me. The light's better, and we can see your friends as they come."

They carefully made their way through the dim house and up the stairs to the second floor. A stout woman of middle years met them at the top step.

"Martha, this is Keltin Moore."

"It's a wonder you made it through the beasts, Mr. Moore."

"It hasn't been easy, Ma'am. I've got a wounded man that will need help once he arrives."

"I'll go set some water to boiling then. Excuse me."

She pressed past them to descend the stairs as Jonathan peeked his head into one of the nearby bedrooms.

"Miss Elaine? The beast hunter is here."

"All right."

Jonathan gestured for Keltin to enter. Pale light trickled into the bedroom through the large window looking out at the fields surrounding the farmhouse. A young woman sat in front of the window, a worn hunting rifle across her lap. She turned and rose as they entered, setting aside the rifle and smoothing out the wrinkles in her gray woolen dress.

"Miss Elaine, this is Keltin Moore, a beast hunter from Riltvin."

Keltin took her extended, slender hand and she gave him a welcome, tired smile, her azure eyes made all the brighter by the dark shadows beneath them.

"I'm so glad to meet you, Mr. Moore. You've no idea... we weren't sure we'd see another soul ever again." She glanced out the window as the light fell across her face, framing her delicate features. "I've been watching for your friends since you came in, but I haven't seen them yet. Which direction were they coming from?"

"West. We were attacked in a maize field."

"How badly was your friend hurt?"

"His legs were torn pretty badly by a razorleg. It didn't get to the bone, but we're worried about infection."

Elaine nodded. "We should heat water and fix a place for

him to lie down while we treat him."

"Martha's already boiling water," said Jonathan. "I'll prepare the dining room table for him."

"All right. We'll keep an eye out for them here."

Jonathan nodded and left. Elaine retrieved her rifle from the corner and sat on a low stool near the window to watch the cold farmlands beyond. Keltin studied the young woman. Despite the obvious strain she had been under for some time, her posture spoke of refinement and deeply trained poise. The rifle across her lap seemed an unfamiliar accessory, but her delicate hands gripped it firmly.

"Miss Elaine?"

"Oh, just Elaine is fine, Mr. Moore. I don't know why Jonathan and Martha even bother with formalities anymore. That world seems so far away now."

"But how did this happen? I mean, just the three of you, stranded in this farmhouse. How did you survive?"

"It was more than just us at first. Uncle Whellon had a dozen provisional workers in his fields that had been brought up from Carvalen, and a good foreman by the name of Transom. Between them, my Uncle and Transom were convinced that they could hold out better here than on the road south. As the last of our neighbors were fleeing for the city, Transom armed the field hands and set them to fortifying the farmhouse and building the walls around it.

"At first it seemed to be going well. Transom and the field hands were able to fend off the beasts, and even managed to continue tending some of the fields. But it didn't last. The attacks increased, and men began to get hurt. A few died. They wanted to go home, but Uncle Whellon and Transom convinced them that the roads were no longer safe for traveling and that we'd seen the worst of the monsters. But the beasts kept coming, and one day the field hands brought Transom's body back from where he'd been working on the embankment. The next day we awoke to find that all of the workers had gone, leaving just Jonathan, Martha, Uncle Whellon, and I."

"They abandoned you?"

Elaine nodded and sighed. "I suppose we should have seen it coming. Transom was the only reason that they stayed as long as they did. He was strong and handsome, and seemed completely invincible. When he died, they must have all lost what heart they had left. I don't know if any of them survived, but their leaving finally convinced Uncle Whellon that we couldn't stay any longer. We tried to leave, but we didn't get far before we were attacked. Something with coiling legs and glistening scales threw itself at Uncle Whellon. We managed to escape and return to the farmhouse, but Uncle Whellon was hurt terribly. He lingered and went into a fever. He said terrible things towards the end."

Elaine swallowed and turned her attention back to the window. She tensed.

"Something's out there."

Keltin immediately went to the window, rifle ready. Maize plants shifted for a moment before his companions emerged out in the open, carrying Henry in a makeshift stretcher between them.

"Those are my men. I'll go out and greet them."

"All right. Just knock at the door by the kitchen garden again and we'll let you in."

Keltin left Elaine at the window and tried to collect his thoughts as he made his way down the dim staircase. The farmhouse was well-suited for their purpose, with defenses already in place and a passably good view of the surrounding countryside. But Elaine and the two servants presented a real problem. Keltin had never considered finding survivors. What would he do with them?

He was still considering his few options as he met with the others and led them into the farmhouse. Martha directed them to a large table already covered with clean sheets. Rolls of bandages and a basin of steaming water also stood ready nearby. Jaylocke immediately set to work removing the bloodied bandages and tattered shreds of Henry's trousers. Martha wordlessly took the soiled fabric from him and handed him fresh bandages in return.

"Thank you for your help, Ma'am," he said as they worked together.

"I'm afraid we've had a lot of practice with this sort of thing of late."

"Will you need help from the rest of us?" asked Keltin.

"I think that I can handle it with this good woman's help."

"All right. Let's give them some room to work."

"The sitting room has been converted into a barracks of sorts," said Jonathan. "I'm sure you and the rest of your men are welcome to rest there if you'd like to make use of it."

"Thank you, we will."

The sitting room had been cleared of chairs and other furniture to make room for more than half a dozen sleeping pallets and two small beds. Keltin sat on one of the lumpy beds and heaved a heavy sigh. Bor've'tai, Garthen, and Weedon pulled the other bed closer to him so they could sit together in a tight circle. They brooded in silence for a long while before Garthen finally spoke.

"Well, what are we going to do now?"

Keltin shook his head. "I don't know."

"There weren't supposed to be people here. What do we do with them?"

"We should try to get them to safety," said Bor've'tai.

"How? Henry won't be able to travel and we can't leave him here."

"Maybe a few of us could go back with them?" suggested Weedon.

"No," said Keltin. "We had a hard enough time watching our back with six able hunters. It would be next to impossible to make it through that country again with three common folk and only a couple hunters to watch over them."

"They're hardly common folk," said Bor've'tai. "Keep in mind that they've survived all this time on their own."

"I'd like to know how they managed that," said Garthen.

Keltin quickly shared the story that Elaine had told him before returning to their current problem.

"I admit that they have held up remarkably well under the circumstances," he said, "but we can't expect them to be able to stay hidden with beasts behind every tree. It's just too risky."

"Then what do we do?"

"I think that it would be best to have a couple of us head back to the main camp and ask the Baron for reinforcements. Perhaps he can send some of the soldiers he got from Carvalen up here to escort these people back to safety. If they bring a wagon, they may even be able to take Henry with them."

"That seems best," said Bor've'tai. "Who will go?"

Keltin was about to answer when Jonathan appeared at the doorway in a rush.

"Mr. Moore, there's beasts outside."

Keltin jumped to his feet.

"Show me."

Jonathan led them upstairs to the north-facing bedroom window. Keltin peered out into the chill daylight and looked for signs of beasts. He saw them at the fringes of the farmstead grounds, among the shelter of the trees and in the thick of the fields. Each kept its distance from the other, but always they kept the farmhouse in sight. Keltin moved from room to room, checking each window. On all sides, he saw more of them.

"Why are they all coming around the house?" Jonathan asked in a whisper.

"Perhaps it's the smell of Henry's blood," said Keltin. "When we brought him here, we left a scented trail right to our own door."

"Those beasts out there are probably hungry," said Bor've'tai. "There's no more livestock or natural prey for them in the forest. There's nothing left for them to eat north of Baron Rumsfeld's line but each other and whatever is inside this house."

Jonathan swallowed. "So we're trapped."

Keltin nodded. "Looks like we're all in the same stewpot now."

CHAPTER 17 – THE GAMBLE

Henry's choked screams drifted up from downstairs as Jaylocke and Martha stitched his wounds closed. Keltin winced each time Henry cried out and wondered whether the beasts outside could hear him as well. Forcing himself to ignore Henry's pain, Keltin focused his attention on the open space between the barn and the maize field. The barb tail that he had shot for straying too close to the farmhouse lay still on the cold ground. A curious quilled terror had shuffled out to the dead body and started to feed on it. A nearby whip leg watched the spiny beast as it ate, unwilling to test its lightning speed against the terror's spiked defenses.

Henry's cries of pain died away after a few minutes, and silence returned to the farmhouse. Keltin welcomed the stillness as he studied the movements of the beasts outside. They seemed to alternate between either trying to sneak up to the house or contenting themselves with feeding on the remains of other beasts that had gotten too close. The situation was a stalemate. As long as there were dead bodies to feed upon, the beasts would continue to come, keeping Keltin and his friends trapped inside the farmhouse. In a way, it was exactly what Baron Rumsfeld had been hoping for. The more beasts that congregated around the farmhouse, the fewer of the monsters that would hinder the harvest to the south.

But Keltin hadn't expected to find any survivors in the north, nor had he considered what he would do with a man too wounded to travel. He cursed the Baron for making him a team leader. He had no mind for the sort of logistical planning that this mission had required, and now they were all paying the price for his lack of preparation.

The soft creaking of footsteps on the stairs pulled his attention from the window for a moment. Jonathan stood in the doorway, looking somewhat better for the rest that Elaine had suggested that he take as Keltin and his hunters took over the main chore of keeping watch.

"I can take a turn at watching if you need it," he said.

Keltin nodded as he rubbed his eyes. "All right. You can take over for me. I'll send Garthen up to replace Weedon."

Jonathan took his position at the window as Keltin went downstairs to the makeshift barracks. Garthen was already awake, and rose silently to go upstairs and relieve Weedon. Bor've'tai looked up at Keltin from where he'd been lying on the floor next to the low bed that wasn't long enough for him.

"I'll take the next watch," he offered.

"Are you able to? You haven't handled a rifle much, and you won't be able to use your ax from an upstairs window."

Bor've'tai shrugged. "I'll admit that I'm a poor marksman, but it shouldn't be too hard to hit something in the yard. Besides, I'm feeling a little useless right now."

"If another smoke beast comes around you'll be anything but useless. I was going to check on Henry before getting some rest."

"I'll come with you."

They moved into the kitchen and found Elaine feeding the stove with fuel from a badly depleted wood box in the corner.

"You seem to be running out," Keltin observed.

Elaine closed the door on the stove and stood, pulling a loose curl of her dark hair behind her ear as she spoke.

"We haven't been able to restock for a few days."

"Is there more wood outside?"

"Yes, but it hasn't been split small enough to fit in the stove."

"I'll take care of it," said Bor've'tai.

"But the beasts are still out there," Elaine protested.

"It's been too long since I've felt good, solid wood on the other side of my ax swings. Besides, I know how to handle a beast that gets too close."

Bor've'tai retrieved his ax and carefully went outside as Jaylocke and Martha wearily emerged from the dining room.

"How's Henry?" asked Keltin.

"He's sleeping now, or trying to. We got him all stitched up and wrapped in fresh dressings. It will be a day or more before we know whether we managed to head off any infection."

"I suppose I better see to getting some food prepared," said Martha.

"I can help you if you'd like," offered Jaylocke.

"All right. You can start by going to the cellars and seeing what we have left in the larders."

"Would you like to join me in the study, Mr. Moore?" Elaine asked. "We've been here some time, and I'd appreciate hearing what's going on in the world beyond this farmstead."

Keltin stifled a yawn and nodded. "Of course."

Keltin followed her to a small study that had become a storage place for much of the furniture that had been removed from other parts of the house. Keltin extracted two cherry wood chairs from underneath an upturned coffee table, allowing them to sit together in the dim light trickling between the boards covering the window. The moment he was off his feet, Keltin felt fatigue closing in on him and he had to fight to keep his eyes open as Elaine spoke.

"Have you had any word of conditions in Malpin? Are the beasts attacking there as well?"

"I haven't heard anything of beast attacks in Malpin. I suppose there could be, though I suspect that the approaching winter is already in the north, and that any beasts that were there are being driven south by the cold."

"That's some consolation, I suppose."

"Do you have family in Malpin?"

"My home is actually in Kerrtow, the capital city. My father is a solicitor there."

"How did you come to be here?"

"That's somewhat of a long story, but it started when the Vaughs came to power. Do you know much about them?"

"Only what Bor've'tai has told me."

Elaine nodded. "Your friend's people have been badly misused in Malpin, I'm afraid. My father is a good man, and took many cases fighting for Loopi rights. He lost them all. Later, when the Protection Act was created to protect mob violence against Loopi, he tried assembling a petition against it. But too many people were afraid of the newly formed League of Protection, and by that time most of the Loopi were either fleeing the city or had already left. Father eventually had to content himself with handling the estates of the departing Loopi families, selling the possessions they could not take with them to try and provide his clients with some money for traveling.

"Those Loopi that remained in Kerrtow were brutally attacked by League members and common citizens. As the violence in the capital increased, my parents worried about the safety of my younger brothers and I, especially considering my father's efforts on the behalf of the Loopi. They sent my brothers to a cousin who lives in the country, and sent me here to Uncle Whellon's farm."

"Didn't they realize that you'd likely be in even greater danger here?"

"There are always some beasts in Dhalma around this time of year. Uncle Whellon assured my parents that I would be safe with him, and I was. Until now."

The sound of a gunshot came from upstairs. It was followed by a second, and then there was silence. Keltin listened for the sounds of a rushing attack outside, but heard none and relaxed once again.

"I don't think I'll ever get used to that," said Elaine.

She pressed her hands to her temples and took a deep

breath. For a moment, her resolve seemed to fade, and Keltin was suddenly reminded of his sister Mary when she would wake to the sound of some creature howling late at night. He remembered rushing to her from his own bed across the room, holding her trembling shoulders as their father went outside to investigate. Sometimes there was silence, sometimes a gunshot, but always Mary seemed to find comfort in the strength of her father and brother and would soon return to sleep.

Jaylocke appeared, gently tapping on the open door.

"Keltin? Sorry to interrupt, but I was hoping to speak with you for a moment."

"All right." Keltin turned to Elaine. "Excuse me, please."

Elaine quickly composed herself and nodded. "Of course. Thank you for talking with me. I should go and see if Martha can use my help in the kitchen."

Keltin followed Jaylocke back into the front room and up the stairs where the rest of the team had gathered by the north-facing window to allow Garthen to participate in the discussion while remaining at his post. Jaylocke sat on the nearby bed and ground his fists into his sleepy eyes.

"When we get out of this, I swear I'll sleep for a week. So, Captain, have you decided what we should do?"

"We don't seem to have much choice. The beasts have stayed thick around this place since we arrived and we can't travel with a wounded man. We'll have to send a small party south for support from the Baron."

"Who do we send?"

"I'm open to suggestions."

"I should stay with Henry," said Jaylocke. "Even if his injuries don't get infected, he should have someone here who can look after him. Besides, I'm not as stealthy in the forest as the rest of you."

"I suppose you're right," said Garthen. "I'll go south, though I don't like the idea of leaving the rest of you like this."

"Then you'll just have to hurry back," said Jaylocke.

"I suppose I should go with you," said Keltin. "Between us, we've got the most experience at moving quietly."

Bor've'tai shook his head. "I think you should stay, Keltin."

"Why?"

"Because with Garthen gone, you'll be the only true marksman among us. We'll need someone with a cool head and a steady hand to keep the beasts from our door."

"But you'll still have Weedon with you."

Bor've'tai made no reply. Keltin turned to Weedon. The young hunter sat staring at the floor.

"Weedon? What do you think?"

Weedon shrugged, his eyes still on the floor. "I don't care. Go or stay. It doesn't matter."

Keltin turned to Bor've'tai, but the Loopi only shook his head.

"You need to stay, Keltin, as do I. We are both needed here."

"It's all right," said Garthen. "I'll take him with me. It'll help to have another pair of eyes as we travel."

Keltin nodded. "All right. It's decided then. Good luck you two. We'll all be praying you make it through."

* * *

It was dusk. Keltin watched the telltale signs of a spiked thresher making its way around the barn to the south of the farmhouse. He had a clear shot several times but held his fire, waiting for the signal from Elaine standing partway up the staircase behind him. Once Garthen and Weedon were ready, he'd begin shooting as much as he could as Jonathan did the same at the north window. Bor've'tai and Jaylocke would accompany Garthen and Weedon until they were safely off of the farmstead grounds. It was a gamble, and Keltin prayed that the fading light would mask Garthen and Weedon's escape while remaining bright enough for the rest of them to see their targets.

"They're ready," Elaine called softly from the top of the stairs.

Keltin took aim at an exposed area of the spiked thresher's

chest that wasn't blocked by its massive, obsidian spikes. He squeezed the trigger. The explosion of the gunshot filled his ears as the thresher lurched to one side. He fired again and dropped the beast before it even knew where the attacks were coming from.

Even as the creature fell, the downstairs door opened and the four hunters dashed outside. An armored leech that had remained hidden under an abandoned wagon surged in their direction. Bor've'tai saw it and broke off to meet its leg-less, galloping attack with a running swing from his ax as the others made for the stand of trees south of the farmstead grounds. Keltin watched around them, trying to spy any more beasts moving in the gloom. Jaylocke raced on into the trees, leading the way for the others behind him. Suddenly Weedon stopped, took aim, and began firing into the woods. Garthen kept running after Jaylocke, yelling something over his shoulder as he disappeared among the trees. Weedon emptied his rifle into the shadows and immediately began rummaging in his pockets for more bullets.

"Move Weedon!" Keltin cried from the open window.

He never knew if Weedon heard him. A stork-legged beast burst from the trees and closed on the young hunter trying desperately to reload his rifle. Keltin took aim, but the beast was already on Weedon, knocking him to the ground and slashing at him with its murderous beak. The light was too weak and the distance too far to manage a killing shot at the beast's scrawny neck as it violently pecked Weedon's thrashing body. Keltin advanced his rifle's chamber to a Capshire Shatter Round and fired it into the creature's body, hoping that some of the fragments would pierce an internal organ. The beast shuddered with the shot but continued its frenzied attack. Keltin fired Reltac Spinners into its body as close to the base of its long neck as he could, trying to score a hit in its lungs or heart. At last the beast croaked a gurgling groan and staggered away from Weedon a few steps before falling still on the cold ground.

Keltin desperately watched the hunter's still body, looking

for any sign of movement. A moment passed, and Weedon feebly reached out an arm to the farmhouse. Keltin turned and bolted down the stairs past a startled Elaine. Dropping his empty hunting rifle, he grabbed the Ripper from where it lay next to his bed and pulled his grandfather's revolver from his belt. Running to the kitchen, he sped past Martha who'd been minding the door and waiting for Bor've'tai and Jaylocke's return.

He rushed out into the kitchen garden and around the house, hurrying towards Weedon even as he watched for signs of more beasts. Bor've'tai had finished with the armored leech and was already kneeling beside Weedon. Keltin dropped down next to him and looked at the hunter's torn and bloody body. He knew the young man wouldn't live.

"You're going to be all right," he said, his voice thick in his throat.

Weedon gasped and choked, his hands feebly trying to put his destroyed body back together.

"Captain," he rasped, "I'm sorry. Please get word to-"

"Keltin!" yelled Bor've'tai.

Keltin looked up and only had time to raise the point of the Ripper before the whip leg was on top of him. He felt his weapon's point impact and slide off the creature's bony head. The butt end of the Ripper was jabbed painfully into his hip as the bend between the ax head and spike caught at the beast's shoulder, stopping the beast for an instant and saving Keltin's throat from its crushing bite.

They fell back together on the ground and Keltin felt the pull and tear of his hunting jacket as it absorbed the wild thrashes of the beast's cracking legs. With one hand on the Ripper, he fired his revolver into the beast's chest. Suddenly the beast was off of him as Bor've'tai swung his ax like a scythe in a wheat field, sending the beast flying through the air, its spine broken in two. Keltin rolled to his feet and went back to Weedon, but it was too late. Lifeless eyes returned his gaze.

"Run! Get back inside!"

The voice was Jaylocke's as he emerged from the woods at

a dead sprint. Bor've'tai and Keltin rose and ran with him back to the farmhouse, hammering on the door until Martha was able to get the door open for them.

"What was it?" said Keltin as she bolted the door shut again behind them.

"The tusked giant," Jaylocke said between gasps. "It was only a dozen yards behind me when I ran."

"Garthen?"

"I think he got away. I think it decided to chase me instead."

Keltin ran to the front room, retrieved his rifle and hurried back upstairs to look through the south-facing window. The tusked giant was already in the clearing. The light had faded quickly, and Keltin could only see the dim outline of the beast as it loomed in the darkness, its head and shoulders well above the low outbuildings around it. Cold dread ran through him, but the beast was not moving towards the farmhouse.

It bent down, and soon Keltin heard the crunch of bones and the ripping of flesh. The beast had found the bodies outside. Keltin felt his chest heave. Weedon's body was still out there. The last of the day's light finally vanished, the tusked giant moving from one place to another as it ate, finding more of the dead from the desperate struggle only moments ago.

"Is it still coming?"

Keltin looked away from the darkness outside to see Elaine's face framed by the faint light of a candle in her small hands.

"No," he said, his voice struggling through his clenching throat. "It's stopped. It's feeding on the dead creatures outside."

Elaine swallowed. "Did... did the others get away safely?"

Keltin forced himself to suck in a ragged breath and nod his head. "Yes, they both got away. They're free of this place now."

"That's good. Do you want me to keep watch?"

"No. I will. You should try to get some rest."

Keltin knew it was a useless, fool thing to say, but he didn't care. He turned and sat by the window, staring into the darkness until the light of her candle had silently left him. He listened to the tusked giant eating and knew that they wouldn't suffer any more beast attacks in the night. Nothing out there would dare disturb the monster outside as it ate. Keltin rested his head against the windowsill, gratefully allowing shock and exhaustion to drive him into a thoughtless stupor somewhere between sleep and wondering how they would survive the morning.

CHAPTER 18 – LYING LOW

Keltin watched as daylight slowly returned to the farmyard. Rubbing his bleary eyes, he focused on the tusked giant. The fading darkness revealed the monstrous beast lying with its back pressed up against one of the barn's exterior walls. Its massive, muscular arms were wrapped around its tusked head in a fashion that reminded Keltin of the wood devils he'd seen in Riltvin. In fact, looking at the tusked giant in the morning light, he noticed multiple similarities between the two beasts. Its tusks were serrated with barbed ridges, and its coiling hair gradually devolved into bony plates around its flanks and ape-like legs. Keltin took his time studying the beast, looking for any weaknesses in its massive body.

"Any movement from the giant?" asked Bor've'tai softly.

"No. It's asleep."

Bor've'tai nodded, sitting down next to him. "You should try to get some sleep too, Keltin. You're the only one that hasn't."

"I slept as much as I could. I've never been very good at sleeping. I listen too much, and my mind won't stop going. It comes from hunting alone in the hill country."

"I understand. You're used to watching your own back." Bor've'tai gently placed a large hand on Keltin's shoulder. "I'll watch the giant. You get some rest. Trust me to keep watch for you."

Keltin tried to protest, but stifled a yawn instead. With a nod, he quietly rose and went downstairs. Crawling into one of the empty beds in the front room he closed his eyes and tried to relax, letting his mind wander to peaceful snatches of memory. The sound of rain on a windowpane. The sweet fragrances as his mother baked. The softness of a downy quilt on a cold winter night.

He woke without knowing he had slept. Sunlight trickling in through the boards on the windows told him that it was fully day outside. He sat up and found himself alone in the downstairs room. Throwing off his rough blanket, he reached for his hunting jacket to ward off the chill permeating the house only to find that it wasn't with his pack. Confused, he searched for a fruitless moment, wondering if he had left it upstairs. Going up to the second floor, he found Bor've'tai still on watch with Jaylocke sitting with him at the window. His jacket was nowhere to be found.

The Loopi looked up at him.

"You've slept," he observed.

Keltin nodded. "Some. Is it my turn to watch yet?"

"No, it's mine," said Jaylocke. "Maybe you can convince this stubborn Loopi to leave me to it."

Bor've'tai shrugged. "I didn't want to wake you by going downstairs."

Keltin gave him a weary smile. "Well, why don't you take your own advice and get some rest. Who knows when you'll get another chance."

Bor've'tai went downstairs as Keltin sat at the window with Jaylocke. The tusked giant was still sleeping outside.

"It hasn't moved then?" asked Keltin.

"Not a twitch. No sign of any other beasts either."

Keltin nodded and noticed the single-shot rifle lying across Jaylocke's lap.

"How much shot do you have left for that thing?" he asked.

"It takes Matlik rounds, same as Jonathan's rifle. We've got a little more than a box between the two of us."

"Matliks won't do much good against that thing sleeping outside."

"I don't think any type of bullet will help if that thing comes at us."

"It might. I've still got a few Alpenion rounds that I've been saving. The acid in them is powerful and works especially well on a beast's joints. I could hobble it with a good shot into one of its knees. After that, I'd probably fire the rest of them into one of its eyes. I don't care how big its brain is. It'll shrivel in belferin acid like any other."

"I hope you're right, because I'm not sure how much good I'll be against that thing. I'm not a very good shot, and I still don't like my chances trying to stick it with a goad hook."

"I'm surprised that you don't have any ancestors that you could call on that were a good shot with a rifle."

Jaylocke shifted uncomfortably. "Oh, I'm certain I do. I think I even have a great uncle on my mother's side who performed as a trick-shot archer. But I don't know much about him, and there are... other problems with getting his help."

"What kind of other problems?"

"It's a little personal."

Keltin turned from studying the tusked giant.

"Jaylocke, if there's some problem with your ability to call on your ancestors' help, I need to know. I don't want to rely on you for help in some desperate moment and find out that you can't."

Jaylocke sighed and turned to meet his gaze.

"All right, Keltin. I've been having trouble calling on my ancestors."

"What? For how long?"

"It's been a problem for a long time, but it's been getting worse lately."

"Why?"

"You have to understand. My people's ability to call on our forebears for assistance isn't like a bottomless well we can continually draw from. Our ancestors are not some raw resource to be tapped. They still have their souls, their free will, and they can choose whether to help or not. Right now, most of them are angry with me and won't help."

"Why would they be angry with you?"

"It's difficult to explain. There's a covenant, a two-way promise that the Weycliff make with our ancestors when we call on them for help. In return for their assistance, we promise to gain a new skill on our own, something to add to the family's collective knowledge. Of course, it doesn't affect those that have already passed. It's intended to help those who come after us."

"So you have to learn something that none of your ancestors has ever known? That seems like it would be increasingly difficult with each generation."

"It is, though it isn't impossible. I'd only need to gain a skill that isn't in our clan's memory, so I don't have to worry about duplicating the knowledge of an ancestor that nobody remembers anymore. Still, there are a lot of ancestors, and my clan can still recall quite a few of them." He shook his head. "I've known I should be learning something new for a long time, but I just haven't gotten around to it. It's always been so easy to just call for help with anything I may need. If I felt like one ancestor was tired of me, I'd just move on to another. It hasn't been until recently that I realized just how many of them I've managed to offend."

Keltin was too tired to be angry, but frustration still burned inside him. Jaylocke had always been a reassuring presence, a source of good humor and optimism in the darkest of times. Now, when they were at their lowest, with a monstrous beast resting just outside, now was when Jaylocke decided to admit that he had his own problems. It was probably unfair to be upset with him, but Keltin didn't care.

"You picked a fine time to get around to telling me. You might have warned me that you've completely lost your connection to them before volunteering for this mission."

"I'm sorry, Keltin. I just wanted to help."

Keltin ignored him and turned to watch the beast outside.

"I can still call on some of them," Jaylocke said after an uncomfortable silence. "I'm fairly sure that Great-grandmother Landria will stay with me. She has a gentle heart, and she knows how much we may need her medicinal skills. Of course, it would be better if I could call on her Uncle Olvi. He was a field surgeon with the army, but he was one of the first to stop answering my calls. Too many questions about aches and pains when I was younger, I suppose."

"And what about your dervish uncle?"

"Kleadil?" Jaylocke smiled. "I think he'll stay with me to the end. Few others of my family seem to call on him, so he's more patient with me. He'll probably stay."

"Probably," Keltin repeated, not bothering to mask his frustration.

"I'm sorry. I didn't mean to have to tell you at a time like this. I thought I'd be able to... well..." he sighed and shook his head. "I'm sorry. But I want you to know that you'll still have me, whether my ancestors help me or not."

Keltin let out a long breath and looked into the sincere eyes of his friend.

"At least you finally told me."

They sat in silence for a while. Keltin didn't know what more he should say, and finally decided there was nothing to be said. He stood and walked away, leaving Jaylocke to his watch. Making his way to the stairs, Keltin noticed that Elaine's door stood slightly ajar. He intended to walk by without looking inside, but was distracted when he caught a glimpse of a familiar shade of brown out of the corner of his eye. Turning to look, he recognized the sleeve of his hunting jacket peeking around the partially open door. Curious, he gave the door a soft knock.

He tried knocking gently to keep the door mostly closed, but the well-built hinges swung open, revealing the rest of the bedroom. Elaine sat on her bed with Keltin's hunting jacket spread across her lap. Her delicate hands held a needle and thread as she stitched together the tears caused by the whip leg's attack the night before. She looked up as the door opened, her pale cheeks going a little pink when she saw Keltin.

"Oh, Mr. Moore, I didn't know you were up." She looked down at his jacket lying across her lap with a slightly guilty expression. "I hope you don't mind. I just feel so useless sometimes, and your jacket seemed in need of repair. I thought I'd try mending it for you. I'm sorry that I didn't ask you first. Here."

Keltin took the proffered jacket and carefully inspected her stitching. She had left the largest of the tears alone, focusing first on small rips in the inner lining that would be less visible, working her way out to other small holes wherever one of the whip leg's claws had caught it. Keltin studied her work critically, but had to admit that she had done a good job. He ran a finger over some of her stitching.

"What sort of thread did you use?" he asked.

"I used a spool that Martha gave me. It's the same type that she used to mend the field worker's clothes. She said it's very sturdy."

Keltin nodded and noticed a small pile of fabric scraps sitting beside her. She followed his eyes and laid her hand on the scraps.

"I went through some of Martha's patch scraps. I tried to find material that felt sturdy but was of a similar color. I haven't used any of them yet. I didn't want to put patches in your jacket unless you agreed to it."

"Thank you for your kindness. You've done a better job of fixing this than I ever have. Would you be willing to finish it?"

Elaine's eyes brightened and she smiled warmly.

"Of course. Which color do you want me to use to patch it?"

Keltin selected the shade that best fit the subdued brown of the jacket. Elaine took the scrap from him and compared it against the tears.

"This should cover most of it," she said. "You may need to choose another color for the rest, but I'll try to use as much of this as possible. I can find you when I'm finished."

Keltin nodded and turned to go, but realized he didn't want to. Watching Elaine mend his jacket brought back the waves of memory that had soothed him to sleep earlier. For just a moment, he wanted to forget that they were in real danger, that they may not see the day's end.

"May I watch as you work?" he asked.

Elaine looked up from cutting a section from the scrap fabric with a pair of small scissors. She seemed uncertain, and for a moment Keltin worried that she would ask him to leave.

"I... suppose so, if you would like. You can sit there."

She indicated an old-looking rocking chair in the corner. Keltin sat and watched as she finished cutting out the patch and began sewing it on.

"It's a very fine jacket," she said as she continued to work.

"It was my father's. He used to wear it on all of his hunts. He gave it to me after I bagged my first bounty."

"You learned to hunt from him then?"

"Yes, but not only him. My Uncle Byron is the one who really taught me how to shoot my rifle. Of course, Grandfather Milner was the one who showed me how to use his old military pistol, and Grandfather Moore taught me most of the little things about beast hunting that my father would forget."

"Was he the one who taught you to sew?" Elaine asked, holding up an old set of stiches along one of the jacket's sleeves.

"No, Grandmother Milner taught me that, though I wasn't much of a student."

"It sounds like your entire family has made a career of hunting beasts."

"On my father's side, yes. It's my mother and her family that have never really understood those of us that choose to hunt. For the most part, they seem to accept it as an oddity of the Moore family, but at times the Milners have taken special exception to the idea, especially since..."

"Since what?"

"...since my father passed."

"I'm sorry."

"It was a long time ago. He left on a hunt and never came back. My uncles and I searched for weeks. We finally found him a quarter-mile from a beast that had bled out from a gunshot wound to its stomach."

Keltin fell silent, his mind returning to that moment in the forest when he had realized his father was truly gone. He remembered the ache in his heart building to a torrent of tears as Uncle Byron had held him awkwardly, muttering comforting words and curses. Keltin shook himself and buried the memory deep inside him where it belonged.

"After that, my mother and sister moved to Maplewood where my mother could work as a school teacher, like she had been when she met my father. I think she wanted to be as far from the world of beast hunters as she could. I can understand it, but I miss seeing her and Mary. I send them a part of the money I make from each hunt, though I always wish I could send more."

"You sound like a very good son and brother," said Elaine.

Keltin shrugged. "I think about them often, especially Mary. Do you know you remind me of her? She's a lady now, with more elegance and refinement than her brother will ever have."

Elaine smiled. "She must be very special."

"She is. You know, I think the two of you could be friends, if you ever met."

Elaine was about to reply when Jaylocke appeared in the doorway.

"Keltin, you better come quick. The giant's stirring."

Keltin felt as if cold water had been thrown onto a warm fire inside of him. Elaine jumped to her feet like a startled bird, clutching Keltin's jacket in her white-knuckled hands.

"What do we do?" she said.

Keltin stood and took his rifle from the corner, slipping back into the comfortable skin of a confident beast hunter as he tried to calm her.

"I'll go with Jaylocke and have a look. In the meantime,

would you mind finishing with my jacket? It's getting chilly without it."

Elaine took a deep breath, and gave him a brave smile. "All right. Thank you, Mr. Moore."

"Thank you. We'll have to continue our talk another time."

...if there ever is another time, he thought to himself before rushing after Jaylocke.

CHAPTER 19 – BAD TO WORSE

Keltin watched as the tusked giant stirred and rose. It shook and stretched, rising to its full height before casting its gaze around the farmstead. Keltin pulled farther back from the window, willing himself to not be noticed by the monstrous beast.

"We should have killed that monster before it woke up," muttered Jonathan behind him.

Keltin didn't answer. He had no time to explain that he had already considered and disregarded the idea hours ago. While he wouldn't hesitate to shoot a beast in its sleep if it meant a quick, clean kill, he knew that it would have been nearly impossible with the tusked giant. It was simply too large for a single bullet of any type that he had to bring it down with one shot, and trying to coordinate a simultaneous attack from several hunters at once would be extremely dangerous at best. Better to wait and study. Better to prepare for what would come. With that thought in mind Keltin stepped away from the window, putting a hand on Jaylocke's arm as he moved past him.

"Keep an eye on it," he whispered as he quietly made his way back to Elaine's room. He found her sitting on her bed, her steady hands working swiftly on the final patch to his jacket. She quickly set it aside as he came into the room.

"Is it still out there?" she asked in a hushed voice.

"Yes. I need something from my jacket pocket."

"I put everything there," she said, pointing to a sizable pile on top of a dresser behind the door.

Keltin quickly found the box of Alpenion rounds and shook the remaining bullets into his hand. He had four left. Snapping open the revolver chamber of his rifle, he replaced the Reltac Spinners with the Alpenion rounds, adding a Haurizer heavy impact round or "Smasher" to fill the chamber. The Haurizers weren't bullets that he used often as they were designed for breaking bones rather than quick kills, but his supplies were running low and he had little choice. Perhaps he could use one to break a hole in the beast's skull and follow it with an Alpenion round to its brain. It might work.

"Stay here," he told Elaine as he finished reloading the rifle and left her room.

Keltin turned the corner and froze. The tusked giant stood less than a dozen yards from the farmhouse, its great eyes staring directly back at him through the upstairs window. Jonathan stood nearby in the hallway, trembling and praying under his breath as Jaylocke tried to hide from the beast by pressing himself against the wall next to him. Keltin willed his voice into a steady whisper.

"Come to the stairs," he said quietly.

The two men's movements seemed painfully slow as they drew behind the corner and out of the beast's line of sight.

"Could it see us?" Jaylocke asked in an unsteady voice.

"I don't know. The house is dark, but its eyes could be better than ours."

"What's it doing now?"

Keltin peeked around the corner. The tusked giant was still focusing on the house. It had come closer, and Keltin could hear the pumping bellows of its massive lungs. Its cavernous maw opened and a baying howl echoed from deep within it. Keltin nearly dropped his rifle to press his hands against his ears. From somewhere downstairs there was the sound of glass breaking.

The tusked giant launched itself at the house. Like a roaring wave it smashed against the outside wall. Timbers groaned and snapped as the once-solid building shuddered under the concussive impact. Keltin fell and immediately struggled back to his feet to look around the corner and through the upstairs window. The window was gone, leaving an empty hole in the wall surrounded by broken glass. Looking through the hole, Keltin could only see the bottom half of the tusked giant as it backed slowly away from the house.

Crouching low, Keltin hurried towards the demolished window. As soon as he could see the beast's head he stopped and took aim. The giant crouched for another run just as Keltin's Haurizer Smasher pounded it between the eyes. A smaller beast would have died at the moment of impact from the well-placed shot, the front of its skull reduced to broken fragments.

The tusked giant's head recoiled from the blast and for a moment it stood disoriented and confused. Keltin fired again. The beast shook its head, causing the precious Alpenion round to miss its mark and instead penetrate the soft flesh of the beast's bull-like nose.

"Rot!" swore Keltin as he saw the splatter of blood from the beast's snout.

The beast howled as the belferin acid burned its face. Keltin kept his focus on the creature's violently shaking head, waiting for another opening. At last the beast stopped, but its face was turned away. Keltin waited. The creature had gone strangely still. Keltin watched it down the sights of his rifle, trying to will it to turn its face towards him.

A span of heartbeats passed, and the beast suddenly turned and galloped to the sheltering woods to the east. Keltin let out a heavy breath as it disappeared among the trees. He'd only managed to give the beast a skull shaking and a bloody nose, but at least it was gone.

"Where's it going?" asked Jaylocke from behind him.

"I don't know. It almost looked like it was running away

from something."

"Could it have been us?"

"I doubt it."

"Then what?"

"Mr. Moore!" came Elaine's voice from her bedroom. "Come quick! There's something in the north fields!"

Keltin and Jaylocke hurried to join Elaine at her still-intact window facing to the north. Elaine pointed at a section of the field that seemed distorted and warped. It was moving towards the farmhouse.

"What is it?" she said.

"The last thing we need," muttered Keltin. "Jaylocke, where's Bor've'tai?"

"Here," answered a low voice.

Keltin turned to see the Loopi staring off into the north field, his eyes stony and hard.

"Are you ready to face that thing?" asked Keltin.

Bor've'tai sighed. "No, but I will try."

"Why don't we just run from it?" said Jaylocke.

"We can't leave Henry," said the Loopi.

There was a sound of hurried footfalls on the stairs and Keltin turned to see Jonathan desperately rush into the room.

"Come help me, quickly! A kitchen cabinet fell over in the shake that great boil gave us and it's fallen on my wife. I can't get it off of her!"

"Go," said Bor've'tai. "I'll deal with the beast."

Jaylocke tried to protest. "But, Bor've'tai…"

"It's crushing her!" pleaded Jonathan.

"Go," said Bor've'tai again as he knelt facing the north fields.

Keltin grabbed Jaylocke's arm and pulled him towards the door.

"Come on, we can't help him."

They turned and raced after Jonathan to find Martha pinned under a heavy cabinet and surrounded by the broken shards of dishes. Quickly gathering on one side of the bulky cabinet, the three men and Elaine lifted it up to rest on its side.

Martha moaned softly as the weight was lifted off of her, feebly trying to pull her bloodied hair out of her face with one hand as the other lay limp across her chest.

"Jaylocke," said Keltin.

"I am."

He kicked aside some broken glass and knelt next to the woman. With only the barest pause to collect himself, he carefully examined her as Jonathan hovered nervously nearby.

"Her arm's broken," said Jaylocke. "She may have some cracked ribs as well, but I don't think there are any internal injuries. We should get her away from all this broken glass before I do any more."

"Let's get her into the front room," said Keltin. "Do you think you can stand, Martha?"

"I think so, but my head is spinning."

"Don't worry, we'll help you."

They gingerly eased her up from the floor and helped her from the destroyed kitchen into the bed-lined front room. They were just lowering her to one of the low beds when Martha let out a startled yell and pointed to the far wall. Keltin turned to see the boarded-up section of wall across from them twist and distort.

There was no time to run or cry out. In an instant the distortion had grown out to fill half the wall, then it was upon them. Keltin's head exploded with pain. All sensation disappeared as his equilibrium spun like a child's top. Pain he couldn't identify seared through him. Freezing, burning, suffocating, crushing, drowning, dying. Then it was gone.

Keltin tasted bile and realized he was vomiting. Somewhere amid the ringing in his ears he heard the sounds of others retching nearby. Sensation returned slowly, and Keltin found himself on his hands and knees. Trembling and weak he sat up, his eyes struggling to focus the crazily shifting room.

At last his vision cleared, and he looked at a room twisted beyond recognition. Floor, wall and ceiling were swirled together like the mixed paints of a painter's pallet. Cold sunlight streamed through the large openings the warp beast had created in the once solid farmhouse.

"Is… is everyone all right?" he said, wiping his mouth with the back of his hand.

"No," came Jaylocke's rasping reply, "but I'm alive. Looks like everyone else is too."

"Thank heaven it's gone," said Jonathan.

"What made it leave?" asked Elaine.

Keltin looked up at the madly contorted ceiling.

"Bor've'tai."

Forcing his shaking legs to move, he struggled to his feet and up the stairs. He fell, but ignored the pain as he crawled into the north-facing bedroom. Bor've'tai was lying face-down, his body motionless on the twisted floorboards. There was no sign of the warp beast. Keltin reached his friend's side but hesitated to turn him over. Would the Loopi be twisted and disfigured like the farmhouse? Gritting his teeth, Keltin pulled Bor've'tai over onto his back. He was whole. Better yet, he was breathing. But his eyes were like a dead man's. Open and staring at the ceiling.

"Jaylocke!" Keltin called, his yell echoing painfully inside his own skull.

The wayfarer came up the stairs as fast as his disoriented body would take him. He took one look at Bor've'tai and dropped to his knees by his side to examine him.

"What's happened to him, Jaylocke?"

"I don't know. He's not injured in any way that I or Landria are familiar with. I can't even begin to guess what's wrong with him. I'd ask Grel'zi'tael if he were here, but…"

Jaylocke trailed off as footsteps echoed on the staircase. He gently shut the Loopi's eyes as Elaine appeared and drew near them. She looked at Bor've'tai anxiously.

"Is he…"

"He's alive," said Jaylocke. "For now, anyway. But I don't know when, or if, he'll wake up again."

Elaine bit her lip and nodded. She turned to Keltin.

"I just saw another beast moving around outside."

"They aren't waiting very long, are they?" said Jaylocke,

rising to his feet.

"No," muttered Keltin, looking down at Bor've'tai, "and our numbers are dropping fast."

"What can we do?" said Elaine.

Jaylocke closed his eyes and took a quick breath before answering.

"We should fall back to a more defensible position. That's what Kleadil would do in this situation."

"Fall back to where?"

"Does this house have a basement? It'd be easy to defend with one entrance and no other way in, and we'd be close to the food stores."

"A basement won't be as defensible as you may think," said Keltin. "Many beasts can burrow and dig, and holing up down there could mean sealing ourselves inside our own tomb with no way to escape."

"What else would you suggest?"

"I… I don't know."

"We could try hiding in the attic," said Elaine.

Keltin turned to her. "An attic? How big is it?"

"It's a little cramped, and we may have to clear it of some old storage, but we should all be able to fit up there."

Keltin nodded to himself. "An attic would be easy to defend once we take up the ladder, especially if it has some windows we can watch through and keep guard."

"I'm not sure how sturdy the attic will be after all the damage the farmhouse just took," said Jaylocke.

"I agree. We'll have to make sure it will hold us. But if it does, we won't have to kill every beast that approaches or even enters the farmhouse, since most of them won't be able to reach us."

"Except for the tusked giant."

Keltin heaved a heavy sigh. "Nowhere in the house will be safe if the giant comes again. It could dig us out of the basement and it could pluck us out of the attic. But at least we'll see it coming from up above. It's the best idea we have. Any more arguments against it?"

No one spoke.

"All right then. Let's hurry. I want to see if the attic is sturdy enough to hold us and start preparing our move up there before the next beast gets too close to the farmhouse."

CHAPTER 20 – AGAINST THE WALL

"Mr. Moore, I'm sure that I heard something moving downstairs."

Keltin bit back an angry retort as he struggled not to drop Bor've'tai on his head. Up in the attic, Jaylocke and Jonathan heaved on the Loopi's shoulders and slowly eased the large, unconscious body up the steep ladder. Keltin climbed the steps with Bor've'tai perched precariously above him until he could finally ease his burden onto the attic floor. Freed, he descended the ladder and caught his breath for a moment as Elaine anxiously hovered nearby.

"It's in the house," she whispered urgently.

"Then you should get up in the attic. I'll be back with Henry."

"He won't come," she said. "I begged him, but he only told me to bring him his rifle."

"He'll come, if I have to knock him out and drag him up."

"Be careful."

Keltin nodded as Elaine hurried up the ladder and disappeared into the darkness of the attic.

"Jaylocke," he called up softly, "come down when you've settled Bor've'tai. If I have to knock out Henry, I'll need help carrying him."

"Aye."

Keltin took his rifle and moved cautiously downstairs. The clicking of claws on the hardwood floor in the front room echoed up to him as he checked his revolving chamber filled with alternating Haurizer Smashers and Reltac Spinners. He was advancing the chamber to a Smasher round when there was a sudden crash and bellow from downstairs. Keltin moved quickly below the landing to see that not one, but two beasts had entered the house.

A coiling creeper, its ropy appendages flailing frantically, was being attacked by a winged strangler. The taller creature was trying to get a grip on the creeper's thick neck while the struggling beast savaged one of its opponent's long legs in its tusked jaws. Keltin knelt on the stairs and took aim at the creeper. The Smasher round hit the creeper just below the right eye, collapsing its skull and causing each of its flailing appendages to stand rigid for an instant.

The winged strangler tumbled on top of the creeper as the smaller beast's legs gave out underneath it. Temporarily tangled in the fleshy ropes of the creeper, the strangler looked up at Keltin and gave a bloody bellow. The sound was cut short as a Reltac Spinner passed through its brain and out the far wall into the fading daylight. Before the strangler had even finished dying, Keltin was searching through the large gaps in the outside wall for more beasts. The surrounding fields looked clear for the moment, and he rushed to the kitchen and the dining room beyond.

Henry sat upright on a worker's bed that had been moved into the room to make him more comfortable. His legs were wrapped in bandages and looked to be causing him a great deal of pain, but his eyes were fierce as he held his weathered hunting knife close to him.

"Glad you're here. That girl wouldn't give me my rifle, and I can't reach it from here." He pointed to his long-barreled rifle propped up in the far corner of the room.

"We're moving up to the attic," said Keltin. "Can you walk at all?"

Henry snorted. "These plaguing legs of mine are as good as two dead sticks for how stiff they are. I was about to crawl over to my gun."

"Jaylocke will be along soon, between us we should be able to get you upstairs."

"Don't bother. Go back upstairs with the others. I'm not going with you."

"Don't be an idiot, Henry."

Henry's eyes went dark. "Captain or no, you'd best watch what you say to me."

Keltin stared back, fatigue and stress driving away any sympathy he might have had for the wounded hunter.

"If a man who can't walk insists on staying in a house that'll soon be swarming with beasts, I'll call him an idiot as much as I like. You're coming up to the attic."

"I told you Keltin, I'm not going."

Keltin felt his hands balling into fists as the stubborn hunter stared defiantly back at him.

"We've already gotten Bor've'tai up there, and he was unconscious."

"Just give me my rifle, I'll hold them down here as long as I can."

Keltin spat on the wood floor near the bed. "Curse it, Henry, I've already killed two beasts that got into the house! You won't do us any good down here!"

"I won't go up there."

"Why not?"

"Just give me my rifle."

Keltin glared. Henry turned away. Something moved in the front room.

"Rot," muttered Keltin as he turned to the door.

He filled his rifle's empty chambers with more Smashers and peeked around the corner. A razorleg clicked along the wooden floor, apparently drawn by the smells of blood coming from the two dead beasts in the front room. Unaware of Keltin, the armored beast set about ripping mouth-sized bites out of the winged strangler. Keltin silently moved away from the door and bent down over Henry, his whispered words coming in a tight hiss.

"Listen Henry, I don't have time for your heroics. We need you upstairs. There's a razorleg in the front room. I'll kill it, and we'll make our way to the bottom of the stairs and meet up with Jaylocke."

"I'm not going anywhere."

Keltin's hand shot out and grabbed the man's shirt collar, yanking his upper body up from the bed to bring the startled hunter's face inches from his own.

"Don't make me threaten you, Henry. I'm too tired, hungry, and generally hexed to talk nicely to you anymore. Either you come up like you're told, or I'll brain you with your own rifle and drag you up by your hair."

Henry's eyes flashed hot. Keltin readied himself to strike his companion full in the face with his free hand if Henry tried to attack him. But the fire in Henry's eyes slowly smoldered, and finally went out. He slumped in Keltin's grip like an exhausted child.

"Please, Keltin," he said softly, "don't force me up there. I'd rather die down here than be trapped up in that tiny attic."

Henry began to quietly sob. Keltin let go of his shirt and let him fall back on his pillows. He looked down at the fierce hunter silently weeping and finally realized what he had been too exhausted and burdened to see.

"You're afraid."

Henry held his face in his hands.

"Yes." His voice was small, vulnerable. "I can't go up there. Please, please, I beg you. Let me die down here."

Keltin turned away, listening as the sound of Henry's gentle crying mingled with the grisly sounds of the razorleg gorging itself in the nearby room. What now? Could he really force a man to live when he refused to?

Keltin took a breath. "Henry, at least come with me to the room with the hatch to the attic. You'll be a little farther from the dead beasts downstairs, and we'll be able to get food to you more easily. Come that far with me."

Henry looked up, his eyes uncertain.

"You won't force me into the attic?"

"No."

"And you'll give me my gun?"

"Yes."

Henry took a breath. "All right. Let's go."

"First, I'll deal with the razorleg. Wait here."

One Smasher at the joint between the razorleg's neck and carapace shattered the hard shell and liquefied its heart. Jaylocke came down the stairs as Keltin kicked the dead beast over.

"Took you long enough. I thought I'd have to come down and stick the thing myself." Jaylocke looked past him to the kitchen. "Is Henry coming?"

"He'll come as far as the bottom of the attic ladder, but we need to help him."

Jaylocke gave him a quizzical look but said nothing. Between the two of them they managed to get Henry up the stairs and to the hatch in the ceiling of the master bedroom. As soon as Henry saw the dark hole disappearing up into the top portion of the farmhouse he stopped them.

"This is as far as I go. Leave me here."

"You want to stay down here?" said Jaylocke.

"I can see the top of the stairs from here. I'll keep watch and shoot anything that comes up. You two get on and pull the ladder up after you."

Keltin and Jaylocke eased Henry to the floor just as Jonathan appeared at the top of the ladder.

"Please come up, and hurry. There's another beast coming towards the house."

"What kind?"

"I... I'm not sure."

"Check it out, will you Jaylocke?"

With a nod the wayfarer scurried up the ladder. Keltin considered following him as Henry settled in with his rifle across his lap, his eyes focused on the staircase landing. But no. Keltin knew that he couldn't leave Henry down in the master bedroom, not when he could do something to save his life. One more try. Just once more, and then he was clubbing the stubborn hunter over the head and dragging him up the ladder.

Keltin knelt beside him. "Henry, will you at least tell me why you won't come up?"

Henry's eyes were hard as he watched the top of the stairs. He was silent, and Keltin rose, moving behind Henry as if he were about to climb the ladder. The butt of his rifle was poised over the back of Henry's head when the man finally spoke.

"I kill beasts," he said.

Keltin hesitated.

"That's my livelihood," said Henry. "I kill things of nightmare. I stare down the spawn of hell and shoot it between the eyes. But I'll never die trapped in a hole, even if it's three stories above ground. I'll die in the open, like the grasslands and tundra of my home. I'll die seeing my death as I fire my last shot. I'll not stay up there to die."

Jaylocke appeared at the top of the ladder.

"Keltin, it's another winged strangler. What should we do?"

Keltin lowered his rifle. "Leave it. It shouldn't try coming up here with all that fresh meat downstairs."

Jaylocke nodded and moved away from the ceiling hatch. Keltin turned back to Henry.

"So you won't come up then?"

Henry sighed and looked up at Keltin. "Listen, I know you're trying to do the best you can for me. But you have to understand. I can't go up there. Even if you forced me, I'd be a wreck, and no good to you. At least down here I can kill beasts as they come up the stairs. Please Keltin, don't make me go up there."

Keltin was silent. He considered Henry for a long moment. Looking into the mix of determination and desperation in the man's eyes, Keltin finally came to a decision. Without a word, he turned and climbed the ladder. Jaylocke was waiting for him at the top and helped to raise the ladder and close the hatch. Keltin stared at the closed door set into the attic floor until his eyes adjusted to the gloom and turned to see the place they'd chosen for their final stand.

Most of the space was too low to stand up straight. Dusty beams arched through the tight space and made any movement while upright extremely hazardous. A single, small window was set in the wall where the peaked roof drew to its north-facing apex. The space was filled with old furniture, molding crates and ancient trunks. What room was left was mostly taken up with blankets laid on the wooden floor for them to rest on. Bor've'tai lay in the darkness alongside Martha. Jonathan was keeping watch as Elaine laid out more blankets for the rest of them to sleep on.

"Welcome home," said Jaylocke.

"How much food do we have?"

"Enough for a week, if we stretch it."

Keltin moved to the small window. He waved away Jonathan, who gratefully went to his injured wife's side. Looking out through the dirty glass, Keltin searched what little he could see of the area north of the farmhouse. He saw no sign of the winged strangler that had been sighted earlier, and nothing else seemed to be stirring. Keltin made himself as comfortable as possible at the window as he set about refilling the small boxes of bullets that he kept in his jacket pockets. The familiar chore was over quickly, with each box in every pocket rattling with too much empty space and no more spare rounds left in his pack.

"Mr. Moore?"

Keltin looked up to see Elaine watching him through the gloom of the fading light.

"Is it all right if I light a lamp?"

"I suppose, but just one. We need to save the oil."

There was a brief flare in the darkness and the soft light of the lamp framed Elaine's slender figure. She turned and set the lamp in the center of the floor before moving towards him.

"With Martha hurt, I thought I'd make us something to eat. Should I wake the others for supper?"

"Let them sleep. Cold porridge isn't much of a reason to wake up, and they'll need what rest they can get."

A shrieking call echoed outside. Keltin judged its owner to be somewhere to the south, beyond the barn. The shrill sound didn't seem to affect Elaine as she turned and began measuring out a scoop of meal for their supper. Keltin watched her calmly working and couldn't help being amazed at her fortitude. Elaine seemed to feel his gaze and glanced up at him from the pot she was stirring.

"Is something wrong?"

"No, it's just that I've never known a woman quite like you before."

Elaine blushed and returned her attention to the porridge.

"And have you known many women, Mr. Moore?"

Angela suddenly came to Keltin's mind. He cringed inside as he tried to drive her teasing, painful memory away.

"I suppose not," he said at last.

He tried to say it casually, but something caught in his voice and he turned quickly back to the window to avoid Elaine's curious look. A long moment passed as Keltin wished he could be completely alone. Apart from the other hunters, apart from Elaine, apart from his own memories.

"Mr. Moore?"

"Yes?"

"I was wondering if you might teach me to shoot."

Keltin turned from the window to look at Elaine in puzzlement.

"I thought you already knew how."

"Oh, I've stood watch, and fired the rifle when I thought I might hit something. But I'm a terrible shot, and Jonathan isn't much better. If I'm to be any help, I need to know how. Will you teach me?"

"I'm not much of a teacher."

"Have you ever taught someone before?"

"No." Keltin took a deep breath and nodded. "I suppose I can try."

Setting his own rifle aside, he picked up the gun that Elaine and Jonathan shared. He flipped it open, emptied the chamber of the single Matlik round inside, and clicked it back into place.

Handing it to her, he began making some small adjustments to her grip and posture as he tried to remember the sort of things Uncle Byron used to tell him as a child.

"Easy. Don't be afraid of it. Of all the things there are to be afraid of, your weapon shouldn't be one of them. Remember, it's just a tool, like a broom or a hammer. One's to clean the floor, one's to pound a nail, one's to kill a beast. Try pulling the trigger."

Elaine wrapped her finger around the trigger and pulled it. After a moment of straining the hammer clicked faintly.

"It's always hard to pull," she said as she did it again.

"Try using the tip of your finger, not the middle of it."

The hammer clicked, and clicked again.

"That makes it easier."

"Good. Hold it tight against your shoulder. The tighter you hold it, the less it will hurt when it fires."

"I wish someone had told me that weeks ago."

Keltin smiled. "When it's daylight again we'll go downstairs and have you fire a few rounds at targets from the south-facing window."

"Can we spare the bullets?"

"I still have some practice wax rounds for my rifle. They won't do us any good against beasts, and they'll make it easier for you to see where your shots hit."

"All right. Thank you for the lesson."

"I haven't given you one yet, but you're welcome. We'll practice tomorrow."

Elaine nodded and went back to mixing their cold dinner. Keltin quietly left her to it, grateful for the distraction the short lesson had provided. Afraid that thoughts of Angela would return, he made his way across the attic and gently nudged Jaylocke awake.

"My turn to stand watch?" asked the Weycliff.

"No, but it's getting dark, and I need your help to check on Henry."

Jaylocke gave him a puzzled look but followed him to the trap door and helped lower the ladder. Moving down into the gloom of the second floor of the house, Keltin was careful to listen for any strange movements from downstairs. All was still, and they turned their attention to Henry. He was sleeping, still sitting with his rifle across his lap facing the upstairs landing.

"I'm not surprised he's out," said Jaylocke. "He's still very weak."

"Do you think he'd wake if he moved him?"

"Not if we're careful."

"Good. Then let's get him up the ladder."

"I thought he didn't want to be up there."

"He won't know the difference while he's asleep. We can take him back down when the sun comes up."

"He won't be happy when he wakes up and finds he's been moved."

"Maybe not, but he will wake up, and that's what I care about."

CHAPTER 21 – DESPAIR'S HOPE

"I'm sorry Keltin. I just don't know why he still hasn't woken up."

Jaylocke shook his head, the shadows of the single lamp playing over his features as he looked down at Bor've'tai.

"My Aunt Landria is at a loss as well."

"What about any of your other ancestors? Could any of them have some knowledge of the type of powers at work here?"

"Not that I know off. Besides, they wouldn't speak to me anyway."

Keltin sat back on his heels, staring at the motionless Loopi and wishing that Grel'zi'tael was with them. Beasts he could understand, but this mysterious coma of Bor've'tai's was beyond him. Looking away, he saw the first light of dawn slowly filtering through the attic's single window.

"Well, he's still breathing, so we won't give up on him. Daylight's coming. We'll move Henry back downstairs once it's light enough to see down there."

A crash reverberated up to them from downstairs. Hardly anyone seemed to notice.

"The boils have been at it nearly all night," muttered Jaylocke. "I would've thought even they would need some sleep."

"I know. I had expected the smell of blood to bring them into the house, but not so many, so quickly."

"Could it be the coming winter? The frost outside has been lingering longer every day. Perhaps they're trying to fatten up for the cold season."

"I don't think so. Most of the beasts we've seen in the province would be ill-equipped to weather the snows of northern Krendaria. I suspect they're just desperate for food."

Jaylocke chuckled. "Wouldn't that be something? All this effort, money, and blood spent towards killing the monsters, and they do all the work of slaughtering each other and then freeze to death. What a runny waste."

"Our purpose was always to save the Dhalma crops, not kill off every beast in the province."

"Do you think they've finished the harvest by now?"

"I don't know. I'm no farmer."

There was a slight stirring in the stillness of the attic as Jonathan came into the dim circle of light provided by their sad little lamp.

"Is it my turn to keep watch, sir?" he asked, nodding towards the gray dawn seeping through the window.

Keltin shrugged. "There's little else to do up here. I'm going to take a look downstairs to see what those noisy boils have left of it."

"Could you look for any more food that might still be in the house while you're down there?"

"All right, just let me take a look at Henry first."

Crawling under the low support beams, Keltin moved to where Henry lay stiffly on his back. Drawing close, he could see the man's eyes looking up at him through the gloom.

"You lied to me," he said quietly.

"You were asleep for most of it."

"Why did you do it?"

"You know why, Henry. I'm going to check downstairs and see if it's safe yet to take you down."

"I need to get out of here. Now."

"Fine. Sit tight and I'll be back."

Keltin moved to the hatch in the attic floor where Jaylocke was waiting for him.

"It should be light enough to see down there by now. I'll take a look. If something comes running this way, pull the ladder up like a bolt, understand?"

Jaylocke nodded. "Of course. It should be easy enough for Jonathan to do if he needs to."

"What?"

Jaylocke grinned. "You've made all the heroic leaps into the jaws of hell lately, and I'm feeling left out. I'm coming down with you."

"Don't be a fool Jaylocke, you can't help me down there."

"Of course I can. I'll kill anything that takes more than five pops in the head to help it sleep. There's little space to retreat, so you won't have much time to drop your gun and take up this if you need it in a hurry."

Jaylocke hefted Keltin's Ripper.

"What happened to the sleevak gaff that you were using?"

Jaylocke shrugged. "This thing's better made and would serve better in close quarters. Besides, I can probably use your pointy toy better than you can. So, are we going?"

Keltin hesitated, then gave a wan smile. "Thanks Jaylocke. I still forget sometimes that I'm not hunting alone anymore."

"Not while I'm around you aren't."

Jaylocke slid the hatch open just a few inches and Keltin peered downstairs. There was no sign of movement in the master bedroom or the landing beyond. The farmhouse was deathly silent. Jaylocke went down first, Ripper at the ready. Keltin followed, hunting rifle in his hands, its chamber filled with four Smashers and one precious Capshire Shatter Round. They stalked forward to the top of the stairs and peeked down into the first floor of the farmhouse.

The rooms below were a disaster. Furniture lay in tattered rags and shattered kindling, and several new holes had been opened up in the exterior walls. The reek of death from the half-eaten corpses of beasts assaulted Keltin's nose. An armored leech, blood seeping from a nasty crack in one of its armor plates, was busily chewing the remains of the coiling creeper from the day before. Jaylocke looked over his shoulder to Keltin, his eyes questioning as he nodded towards the beast. Keltin shook his head, and they soundlessly moved downstairs and past the creature to search for any food left in the house.

Scrounging through the kitchen and pantry, they found another bag of beans, some flour, and a few sad little potatoes that had fallen behind an empty crate. They also found some more lamps from around the house and gathered several more pails of water from the pump in the kitchen before finally returning to the top of the stairs and the master bedroom. Climbing the ladder with his arms laden with some of their new provisions, Keltin found Elaine and Jonathan waiting for him at the top.

"Are there any beasts down there?" asked Elaine.

"Just a wounded armored leech. Any sign of movement from outside?"

"Not yet."

"Should we move your companion back downstairs?" asked Jonathan, looking to where Henry lay, his body still rigid as a corpse.

"No, let's have breakfast first and watch the opening for a while."

"Now that we have more than one lamp and some more fuel, I think I can rig a makeshift stove for us," said Jaylocke as he followed Keltin up the ladder. "It won't be pretty or terribly effective, but it should at least get some hot food into us."

"Anything's better than cold green meal," agreed Keltin. "Why don't you get started and we'll all have some breakfast."

"I don't think your friend Henry will be able to eat anything," said Jonathan.

"He can try."

Jaylocke constructed his makeshift stove, and the morning passed quietly as the armored leech and the poor huddled people upstairs ate. Even Henry had a little of their warm, if meager meal.

"Now will you take me down?" he asked as he handed Keltin his empty bowl.

"Yes, I need someone to watch the top of the stairs while I give Miss Elaine a shooting lesson."

They eased Henry down to his vantage point at the foot of the attic ladder before Keltin and Elaine followed him down to the second floor. Keltin checked things downstairs once more before returning to them.

"The only thing down there is that armored leech, and I'm not even sure whether it's asleep or dead. Still, make sure you keep awake when we start firing, Henry."

"Where will you be?"

"In the bedroom facing the barn. We'll be looking and firing out the window, so you'll see anything coming up the stairs before we do."

"I'll keep an eye out."

Keltin nodded and led Elaine to her bedroom at the southern end of the house.

"Shouldn't we close the door?" she asked hesitantly as they entered the room.

"Not with Henry alone out there. I want to be able to get to him in a hurry if he needs us. Now, let's see about getting this window open."

There was no latch, but the window hadn't been opened for months and protested stubbornly as Keltin forced it up. Cold air flowed into the room, and they pulled their coats closer around themselves as they settled next to each other on the window seat. Keltin removed the box of candleshot from his pocket and loaded his hunting rifle with five of the waxy rounds. Clicking the revolving chamber back into place, Keltin turned and looked out at the farmstead grounds. Nothing stirred.

"All right. Let's pick a target. How about that barrel sitting against the barn? That should be a good start for you."

He handed his rifle to Elaine and waited as she took aim.

"Keep it tight against your shoulder."

The rifle roared and left a small, flattened circle of wax on the barrel's weathered surface.

"Did I hit it?"

"You did. Just above the ground there."

Elaine squinted and shook her head.

"That wasn't a very good shot."

"You did hit the barrel."

"But I was aiming for the center."

"You have to adjust for the height of your sights compared to the end of the barrel. Try again."

Elaine fired, and a second waxy mark appeared just to the left of the barrel.

"I didn't hold it tight," she muttered. "It's heavy."

Keltin was about to speak when she fired it again. She emptied the chamber with two more shots and set the rifle aside to judge her marksmanship. Three of her shots had found their mark. Keltin nodded.

"That's a good start. I still have some wax rounds. Shall I load it again?"

Elaine bit her lip as Keltin took the rifle from her and began to load it.

"I thought I was better than that."

"It's all right, you're doing well."

"You could do better."

"I've had years of practice."

"Then why are we still here?"

Keltin stopped in the middle of inserting a round into the chamber.

"What?"

"Why are we still here, Mr. Moore?"

Elaine turned on him, and Keltin was surprised to see her bright eyes flashing as her face flushed an angry red.

"You and your men are supposed to be beast hunters. But what have you done for us? You bring a wounded man here along with a horde of beasts following you. We had survived for weeks before you arrived. Now after just three days this house is a wreck and we're all hiding in the attic waiting to die. If you're such a good hunter, why haven't you saved us?"

Elaine jumped to her feet and started to storm from the room. She had just reached the doorway when she stopped, turned, and sat on her bed.

"I don't have anywhere to go," she said in a low voice.

She began to cry. Keltin was speechless. He stared dumbly at the wax rounds in his rifle's open chamber. After a moment he placed them back in their box and filled the chamber with Smashers and Spinners. Snapping it shut again, he looked at Elaine. Her face was buried in her hands, her long curls swaying slowly with her muffled sobs. Keltin stood and approached the bed. He sat down beside her and reached out a cautious hand for her shoulder. His touch did nothing to stop the tears.

He was still struggling to think of something to say when Elaine thrust herself against him, sobbing against his shoulder while savagely gripping his hunting jacket.

"You were supposed to save us!"

Keltin remained motionless until her fury had played out. She slumped against him, her tears now a soft, tired trickle from her azure eyes.

"Why didn't you save us?"

Her voice was barely more than a sighing whisper, but it tore his soul and left his heart bleeding. She had been through so much. The death of her uncle, the weeks of privation in a besieged farmhouse, the unceasing fear. Then Keltin and his team had arrived, and what should have been a cause for hope became a descent into a yet deeper and fiercer hell. He could tell himself that it wasn't his fault, but that wasn't enough. She was right. He was a beast hunter. He should have done more.

"I'm sorry."

The words were small and frail, but they were all that he could offer. He was about to rise and give her some small measure of privacy, but she held him fast. Keltin thought of Mary, weeping in the darkness, and finally placed his arms around her. She did not resist. He held her, willing his strength to support her, to give the only comfort that he could. Elaine became still and rested her head against him. For a long while, he thought she had fallen asleep and allowed himself to doze in an exhausted haze.

Elaine stiffened. Keltin slowly came to his senses and opened his eyes to look at the slender figure in his arms. She was staring past him out the open window. Turning, he saw a serpent stag approaching the farmhouse. It moved slowly, cautiously, its scaly tendrils dragging across the ground as it felt for the vibrations of anything alive nearby. It had not seen them yet.

Wordlessly, Keltin rose to his feet and reached out a hand to Elaine. She hesitated, then rose and followed him as he led her to the window. He sat her down on the window seat and positioned himself behind her. Retrieving his rifle, he handed it to her.

With gentle patience, he made slight adjustments to her grip and aim, all the while watching the serpent stag drawing slowly closer. When the beast had passed the barn he guided the point of the rifle to the center of the serpent stag's thick chest. He breathed slow and deep in Elaine's ear, encouraging her to control her racing heart. She struggled to gain composure, and began matching him breath for breath. One breath, two. Three. Four.

"Now," he whispered in her ear.

She pulled the trigger. The rifle fired and sent a shock through both their bodies. The serpent stag stumbled and fell, trumpeting a pain-streaked cry as it flailed on the frosty ground. Keltin stood. Elaine handed him the rifle and he fired it a second time over her head. The beast went silent as the echoes of the two shots harmonized in the chill air.

Keltin set his rifle aside and knelt beside Elaine. She turned to him. Her eyes glistened but had a firm resolve behind them. Her hands were shaking slightly, and Keltin took them in his own.

"Don't worry," he said softly. "The first beast is always the hardest one."

CHAPTER 22 – SLIPPING AWAY

"But the number of beasts has grown less and less each day. We've only seen one since yesterday, and you killed that one quickly."

Keltin shook his head. "I'm sorry Jonathan, but trying to leave the farmhouse right now is still too dangerous. Don't forget that the tusked giant is still out there."

"But it's been more than a week since we last saw that monster. We can't stay here forever. It's getting colder, and we're running out of food." He turned to Elaine, his eyes desperate and pleading. "I'm sorry Miss Elaine, I'm not trying to make things any worse by quarreling, but Martha needs a real doctor, and we've been hiding in this attic for days. We have to leave before we either starve to death or freeze."

"And how would we do that?" demanded Keltin. "Between Henry, Martha, and Bor've'tai, we've got three people who can't travel on their own, and any livestock north of Duke Gregson's line was eaten weeks ago. How do you intend to get all of us safely to Carvalen?"

"We may not need to go all the way to Carvalen," said Jaylocke carefully. "If one of us could get down to Baron Rumsfeld's camp, we could talk with some of the dug-in hunters there and bring back some help. The road certainly won't be as dangerous as it was when we last traveled it."

Keltin rubbed his eyes and considered.

"Maybe you're right," he said after a long moment. "We can't stay here forever."

Jaylocke nodded. "And if we don't look for help, nobody will come for us. They wouldn't even know where to look."

"But what about the men you sent back for help when you first arrived?" asked Elaine. Keltin sighed and shook his head. "They're probably dead. Most likely they were killed the same night that they left here."

"But…"

"Nobody's coming to save us," Keltin snapped.

Elaine bit her lip, but didn't reply. There was an uneasy silence until Jaylocke cleared his throat.

"Well, that settles it then. One of us will have to go south for help."

"I suppose so," said Keltin.

"All right then. I'll start putting my things together."

"You? Why you, Jaylocke?"

"You're too valuable here, Keltin. You're the best shot, and you know the most about beasts."

Keltin shook his head. "And that's why I should go. If you want this scheme to have any chance of working, it needs to be me."

"Don't be stubborn about this, Keltin."

"I'm not being stubborn, I'm making sense. You're better in close quarters than I am, and that means more inside this little farmhouse than it would out in the forest. Besides, do you know how to make yourself unseen in snow?"

The first flakes had started falling the day before last and had been continuing off and on ever since. Several inches of stark whiteness now covered the ugliness of the war-torn farmstead grounds and surrounding property. Jaylocke looked out the window at the leaden sky shedding stray flakes of ice and sighed.

"No."

"No," repeated Keltin. "I've hunted in the hill country of

eastern Riltvin, and I know how to move without being seen or heard in the snow. It's slower going, but I should still be able to get to the Baron's base of operations in just a few days, especially if I'm on my own."

Jaylocke gave him a hard stare.

"Rot," he muttered. "Why do you have to make so much sense?"

"It was your fool idea. I just can't think of anything better."

"When will you go?" asked Jonathan.

"No point in lingering. I'll get my things together and go now."

"Do you want to stay for a meal first?" asked Elaine.

"Just make me something for the road. I'll get ready."

Without another word, Keltin turned his back on the others and went to his bedroll and pack. Preparing for the trip took much longer than it should have. Perhaps it was the cold numbing his hands. Perhaps it was the murky haze of too little sleep and impotent frustration clouding his mind. Or maybe he just didn't want to go. He wasn't afraid for himself. A part of Keltin breathed a sigh of relief at the idea of being alone, blessedly alone, for the first time in nearly two months.

No, he thought as he sorted his remaining bullets. Being alone wasn't what bothered him. It was an image, haunting and persistent, of coming back to the farmhouse and finding it barren and cold, filled with nothing but blood and death. A memory of the Heteracks lying dead on the north road returned, and the frozen face of Captain Rok stared accusingly up at him in his mind's eye.

"How many times are you going to count those bullets?"

Keltin turned to find Jaylocke at his side. The wayfarer smiled and Keltin gave a rueful shrug.

"As many times as it takes to actually remember. I'm putting my Shatter Rounds in with my Alpenions. There aren't really enough Reltac Spinners left to justify keeping them in their own box, but I don't want to mix them up with the Smashers."

"Do you want some Matlik rounds to fill it out a bit?"

"No. You're running low as it is, and Henry and Jonathan's rifles only take Matliks. I'll be leaving my revolver with you as well. It'll do you more good than me."

"What about this?" asked Jaylocke, holding up the Ripper. "Do you want to take this?"

"Keep it here. You can give it back to me when I come back with help."

Jaylocke didn't answer as he helped Keltin curl up his bedroll and stow the rest of his gear into his pack. Keltin hefted one of the straps onto his shoulder. It felt far too light. He was only taking enough food for one day's journey. He'd have to push hard to get back to civilization if he wanted another meal after that.

There was nothing left to do, and Keltin said a silent farewell to Bor've'tai before descending the attic ladder. Jaylocke and Elaine followed him.

"I'm going, Henry."

The lanky hunter looked up, his face pale and drawn. He extended a hand that felt disturbingly cold when Keltin shook it.

"Hurry back."

"I will."

Keltin moved to the top of the stairs and peered down. The stench of rotting flesh that permeated the attic was eye-wateringly powerful despite the cold, and he hurried past the dead bodies to emerge into the frigid air outside. Lacy snowflakes settled on his hunting jacket without melting as he turned to Jaylocke and Elaine.

"I will be back."

"We'll be here," said Jaylocke.

He embraced Keltin fiercely for a moment and stepped aside for Elaine to say her goodbyes. She looked up at him, her eyes liquid and deep.

"Be careful."

"I'm always careful."

She started to reply, stopped, and dropped her gaze to the ground. A tear stained her cheek, and she threw herself against

Keltin, wrapping her arms around him in an embrace no less fierce than Jaylocke's. Her touch was warm and soft, and Keltin felt a hollowness throughout his whole body when she pulled away. She hurried back inside, not looking back at him as he turned and began making his way across the farmstead grounds and into the fields to the south.

The maize that had been growing strong and tall weeks ago was brown and dead now, lying on top of itself like rotting corpses. Each plant that had been within running distance from the farmhouse had been picked clean of anything edible, and nothing but the bare stalks remained as a reminder of better times. Keltin pressed on, careful to avoid pockets of hard snow that would crunch under his boots. Soon he was out of the fields and he slowed, straining his exhausted senses to detect the slightest sign of life in the sterile, white world around him.

As the minutes passed into an hour, and then another, he felt the welcome comfort of familiarity. This was what he was meant to do. Stalking between the trees, alone, the fate of innocents on his capable shoulders. He would find the other hunters to the south, he had no doubt of that. If Jaylocke and the others could just hold on, he'd be back with help. It would work.

There were few signs of beasts in the forest. He encountered a few tracks, and once he came upon the half-frozen body of a quilled terror. Studying the carcass, Keltin guessed that it had died several days before. The fact that the body had no signs of damage from something eating off of it was very encouraging. Most likely, it had died from either exposure or hunger. It was a hopeful sign, and Keltin seemed to feel his steps lighten a little as he continued south.

Night came gradually. Keltin dug out a small hole next to the trunk of a large tree and built a rough lean-to to ward off any snow that fell in the night. It was already dark by the time he was done, and he crawled into his simple shelter to eat one of the bland, simple biscuits that Elaine had made using what was left of their flour and a little salt. He tried to sleep with his back against the tree trunk with his rifle across his lap, coming fully awake each time a small pile of snow grew too heavy for its branch and fell to the ground. He welcomed the first pale light of dawn, quickly dismantling his camp and pressing on.

It was perhaps another half hour of traveling before Keltin heard something moving through the brush. He considered continuing without investigating, but the absence of any living beasts in the forest suggested that the sound could be coming from something friendly. Perhaps some of the hunters were pushing forward to make sure the beasts up north had all died. Cautiously, Keltin moved in the direction of the sound. A minute of careful stalking passed, and Keltin caught a glimpse of what he'd heard in the still, cold air.

It was another beast, but this one still had some life in it. He could just make out the head and shoulders of a stork-legged beast through the snow-covered undergrowth. Its head rose and fell with each step as it moved in a roughly north-westerly direction. Keltin had just decided to let it go when a snow-heavy branch broke nearby. The beast's head shot up and turned in his direction.

There was no posturing, no aggressive displays. The stork-legged beast crashed desperately toward him, crushing bushes and careening off trees as it struggled to reach him. Keltin didn't have time for a skillful shot. He fired a Haurizer Smasher into its narrow chest. The beast stumbled but continued on, refusing to fall to the ground until another round hit it squarely at the base of its long neck.

Despite his fatigue, or perhaps because of it, Keltin allowed his curiosity to lead him to where the beast had been stalking. Stepping over a trampled bush, he came upon two sets of beast tracks in the snow. One set belonged to the stork-legged beast. The other set belonged to something big. Something very big.

There was only one beast he'd seen in this province that left a trail like that. The tusked giant had passed this way, heading northwest. The flickering hope that had carried Keltin south died as he stared off in the direction where the tracks disappeared among the trees. It was headed in the direction of the farmhouse. It made simple sense. Keltin should have known. Game was scarce, but there had been food, both living and dead, at the farmhouse when the tusked giant had last been there.

Keltin wasn't sure how long he had been rapidly following the tracks before his fatigued mind finally considered whether he was doing the right thing. Should he go back? Perhaps he should continue on for help. No. The tracks were already half a day old. The level of snow in their sunken surfaces told him that much. Even if Keltin managed to assemble a posse of hunters and rushed back, the tusked giant would be at the farmhouse long before them. The dead beasts around the farmhouse would satisfy it for a while, but after that, hunger would drive it to crack the house open like a gray bear ripping open a rotten log to find more food. There would be no bodies if Keltin tried to get help before returning. He'd find nothing but an empty shell of the farmhouse. Keltin forced his wooden legs to move faster, using the beast's own tracks to hasten his way through the loose snow. Step after step, he raced back to the north, praying that he would somehow get there in time.

CHAPTER 23 – THE FINAL HUNT

It hurt to breath. Frigid air seared Keltin's lungs and throat with each ragged breath. His eyes struggled to focus on the winding tracks before him. Running was impossible, and stealth was long forgotten. Just to continue, to press onward, back to the farmhouse, that was all that Keltin could hope for.

Night was falling when he saw the first signs of the familiar rotting fields through the trees ahead. He leaned against a tree and gasped for breath, his vision blurring with each pulse of his throbbing heart and the stitch in his side threatening to tear him in half. With trembling hands he pulled out the box containing his Alpenions and Capshire Shatter Rounds. He loaded his rifle's chamber, alternating the precious ammunition types and returning the box to his pocket. Prepared, he pushed through the trees and on to the farmstead grounds.

The tusked giant was there. It sat in front of the farmhouse, hunched like a monstrous ape trying to open a locked box of provisions. With its back to Keltin, the beast took no notice of the hunter carefully moving behind it to the cover of the barn. Peeking around the building's corner, Keltin could see that the beast had already torn out a large hole in the wall of the farmhouse and was noisily eating the fetid remains of the dead beasts inside. He wished that he could see some sign of the others in the attic, but its window faced the other direction, and there was no cover to move around to the farmhouse's north side.

Keltin struggled to control his breathing and tried to study the tusked giant through the diming light and the blur of his own tired eyes. The beast was thinner than he remembered, though it still bore the scars of the several attacks that had been made upon it during the campaign. Keltin searched for some serious injury that he might take advantage of, but found none.

The beast thrust a massive paw into the farmhouse again, and Keltin knew he'd have to do something soon. Even if the beast ate every dead body in the downstairs of the farmhouse, there was little meat left on the rotting carcasses. Keltin was just lucky that the beast had not yet noticed the house's living occupants. At least, he prayed that the monster hadn't noticed them.

Keltin forced his tired mind to calculate the giant's best kill point. He considered firing under the beast's outstretched arm for a heart shot. A Reltac Spinner could likely pierce the layers of muscle, but wouldn't do much damage once inside. A Shatter Round or acid bullet might, but neither round could penetrate deep enough. A hindshot would have similar problems. The thickening darkness and the beast's protective tusks would make any kind of shot to its head tricky at best. Keltin searched the farmstead grounds for anything that might give him a better angle on the massive creature.

The hayloft. From the barn's hayloft Keltin would be able to look down at the beast and see the back of its exposed neck. A whole chamber of Alpenions and Shatter Rounds fired into the beast's neck could be enough to sever its spinal cord. Even if it didn't break the cord entirely, it might be enough to partially paralyze the giant, giving Keltin the opportunity to try for a different killing shot.

Unfortunately, there was only one entrance into the barn. Its massive double doors sat facing the farmhouse and the beast's back. Keltin would have to sneak around the corner and into the barn through its open doors, torn apart long ago by beasts seeking the trapped livestock inside.

Keltin watched the beast, waiting for his chance. The giant reached into the farmhouse again, this time inserting its head and most of one shoulder into the gaping hole. Keltin moved with all the stealth and speed he could muster, taking what seemed like an eternity to cross the few yards to the yawning opening and into the safety of darkness inside. Spinning, he saw that he had not been detected by the beast as it continued to root around inside the shuddering building.

Stumbling in the darkness, Keltin searched in the deepening gloom for some way up into the hayloft. Something caught his boot and he tumbled forward into a rotting pile of hay. Silently cursing his luck, he turned to free his foot and realized that he'd stepped between the rungs of a fallen ladder. He quickly righted the ladder and climbed to find more moldering hay and the closed door of the loading hatch set above the barn's open portal.

Keltin was struggling to find the latch for the upper door when a gunshot shattered the night air. A second shot was followed by a sound like a hurricane destroying a home. Keltin found the latch and yanked it up, thrusting open the screeching doors just as a pain-filled scream came from the farmhouse.

The tusked giant was nearly halfway inside the house and trying to force its other shoulder to break through the outer wall. Another scream came from the farmhouse, different from the first. A woman's scream. Keltin fired into the beast's back, hitting it between the shoulder blades in an attempt to draw it back out for a better shot. He fired twice more before the beast finally pulled back with something caught between its paw and mouth. A body.

The beast bit down on its prey, exposing for a moment the back of its neck. Keltin fired twice into the space. The tusked giant shuddered and made a low sound of pain and anger. Turning, its dark, luminous eyes found Keltin. With a sound like a steer being strangled, it lurched at the barn, dropping its forgotten meal in an attempt to kill its new attacker. Keltin fell back into the rotting hay and saved himself from a quick, crushing death as the beast's massive arm shot through the open door. Rolling again, Keltin raised his rifle to fire. *Click*.

Desperately, he dug in his pockets as he tried to keep his footing in the shuddering barn. He found temporary safety in the back of the loft, just far enough away from the beast's reaching arms. His hands were shaking as he struggled to open the chamber of his rifle and push the stubborn ammunition into the cylinders. He'd just gotten the first bullet in place when the arm disappeared above him, and a great form blackened out the lessening light from the barn's double doors.

The beast could not walk into the barn upright. It crawled forward into the suddenly tight space. Keltin had nowhere left to run. The beast looked up at him and rose to its back legs, able to nearly look the hunter eye to eye. With a roar the beast reached for him.

A flurry of gunshots sounded from outside the barn. Keltin barely heard them as he leapt from the hayloft down into a pile of hay that proved too small to completely break his fall. The impact drove him hard to his hands and knees, sending shocks of pain up through his arms and thighs. He fell on his side, unable to hold in a cry of pain. He braced himself for an immediate, killing blow from the tusked giant above him.

An undulating battle cry filled the barn. Keltin looked up to see the silhouette of a figure in the doorway behind the beast, holding his Ripper in both hands. The figure leapt forward and buried the spike of the deadly weapon into the back of one of the beast's knees. The creature screamed and stumbled, flailing wildly as it slammed against the far wall of the barn. The Ripper was torn from the figure's hands, but he ignored it and peered into the darkness.

"Keltin!" It was Jaylocke. "Are you there?!"

Keltin tried to answer, but his voice was lost in another bellow from the creature as it turned, driving the wicked ax blade of the still embedded Ripper into the flesh of its lower leg. The beast stumbled and screamed as Jaylocke backed away, unable to retrieve his weapon. Keltin looked up at the tusked giant as it turned away from him. It was wounded, terribly, but it still had not received a killing blow. It turned on Jaylocke, and Keltin saw that another figure now stood behind the wayfarer in the barn's doorway, firing more bullets into the monster's solid torso. The giant staggered towards them.

Rolling to his back, Keltin risked flexing his aching fingers. They moved. He dug in the hay for his rifle. Its chamber was still open, with just one bullet lying inside. Clicking it shut, Keltin raced to the ladder, forcing his agonized body up to the hayloft. The Ripper in the beast's leg slowed its advance towards the two figures in the doorway, and Keltin sprinted to stand above the beast with his back to the hatch door. With the last lights of day behind him, he saw for a brief moment the beast's face, contorted with feral rage as it looked up at him. Keltin saw the face, the nose, mouth, tusks, eyes. Left eye. Just right of the center. One breath. Fire.

The beast's scream was like the tearing of steel as the belferin acid attacked its optic nerve. The sound of its suffering was deafening. Keltin barely had time to jump to the side before the beast fell forward, destroying the front of the barn with its great weight. The building lurched and tore from its supports, sliding downward in a deafening crash around the agonizing monster. Keltin struggled for purchase on the slanting floor, checking his sliding fall until he finally lost his balance completely and landed on the beast's broad back.

Without pausing to think, he moved to his Ripper and twisted it free of the creature's leg. Moving past its shoulders, he brought the ax head down on the beast's neck. The blade bounced away from the rigid surface. Changing his grip, Keltin leapt up and drove the full weight of his body against the haft of the weapon, driving its point between two of the vertebra in the tusked giant's neck. The impact shuddered up into his body and he fell with a cry. He was trying to roll away from the great monster beside him when he realized that the bellowing beast had suddenly fallen silent.

Looking up, he saw the Ripper wedged deep into the creature's neck. The tusked giant did not move. Keltin tried to rise, but pain drove him back down to the ground. Oily colors swam before his eyes and he could hear the faint sounds of voices from somewhere in the night. Hands touched him, but a comfortable darkness was descending swiftly upon him. He welcomed the oblivion, leaving pain, exhaustion, and the dead beast all behind him.

* * *

Keltin woke up to pain and something else. Something he hadn't felt in weeks. Was it… warmth? He struggled for a long time to gain control of his body, at last managing to open his eyes. Color and light swirled together and he shut them quickly again. From somewhere nearby he heard a soft voice.

"Jaylocke, I think he's coming awake."

There was the sound of hurried footsteps and Keltin could feel someone's breath on his face.

"Keltin. Can you hear me?"

Opening his eyes again, Keltin saw a blur above him that might have been Jaylocke.

"Yes," he answered weakly, "but you've looked better."

The blur grinned. "Maybe, but I'm looking better than you are right now."

Keltin blinked until his friend came into focus. Jaylocke was kneeling beside him inside a small tent. Thought slowly returned to Keltin's sluggish mind, and he realized he was on his sleeping mat with quilts from the farmhouse covering every inch of him except his face. He tried to rise and decided against it with a groan.

"I feel like I'm one big bruise," he muttered.

"Close enough. Still, I suppose that's what you get for dancing with a tusked giant."

"Is it dead?"

Jaylocke nodded. "Very. A Ripper wedged in the back of your neck will do that."

There was a soft rustling of fabric and Jaylocke was joined by Elaine at Keltin's side.

"Are you all right?" she asked gently, kneeling next to him to place a soft hand on his cheek.

"I'm not sure."

Keltin tried to move and felt little shocks of pain from a half-dozen places at once.

"I came down hard when I fell from the top of the barn."

"You sprained both your wrists and twisted an ankle," said Jaylocke. "You didn't break anything though. You were very lucky."

"I don't feel very lucky, but I'll take you at your word. Are you two all right?"

Jaylocke shrugged. "I've had worse after bumbling a tumble pass."

"It never really got close enough to hurt me," said Elaine. "But I don't know if I'll ever stop having nightmares about it. I was nearly mad with fear when that thing started coming into the house."

"Don't let her fool you," said Jaylocke. "When we realized that you were in the barn fighting that thing, she led the way outside and ended up emptying both her own rifle and your revolver into that creature's hide before it was finally over."

Elaine gave a small, rueful smile. "I'm afraid it didn't do much good."

"You're wrong," said Keltin. "I wouldn't be here if you both hadn't come." He suddenly remembered something. "I saw the beast pulling someone out of the farmhouse."

Jaylocke sighed. "That was Henry. We tried to get him up into the attic, but he wouldn't come. At least the beast killed him quickly."

"And Jonathan?"

"He's fine. He's with his wife."

Keltin shook his head. "Then we're only worse off than we were before. We've still got to try to make it south to get help from the others."

Jaylocke's grin returned. "Some good news there, actually."

He moved aside and Garthen stepped into Keltin's field of vision. "Hello Captain, you look terrible."

Keltin stared up at his fellow hunter in shock. "But… how…"

Garthen chuckled. "You're not the only skilled hunter that the good duke hired for his campaign. I made it back to Baron Rumsfeld and reported your position to him. We couldn't mount a rescue attempt until the beasts started to thin, but when the snow began falling, we decided it was time to take the risk. I came along since I knew the way, though we probably could have just followed the sound of the gunshots."

"You might have come a little sooner, you know."

"I'm sorry about that, Captain. Truly I am. We had our hands full trying to protect the workers bringing the harvest in, and there's been a fair share of chaos further to the south."

"More beasts?"

"No, revolution."

Keltin sighed and laid his head back on his pillow. "So, it happened then."

"I'm afraid so. We were able to bring in enough of a harvest to stave off an all-out famine, but the wheels of rebellion had already been turning for quite a while. The nobility of Carvalen are gone. The queen was executed in the street by the revolutionaries, as have any members of Parliament that weren't able to escape the city in time."

Keltin closed his eyes.

"We've failed," he said softly.

"We were hired to hunt beasts, not protect the nobility," said Jaylocke. "Our campaign held off the beasts long enough to bring in enough food to keep the people of this nation alive until the spring. Even Duke Gregson couldn't have asked for more than that."

"Is the duke dead as well?"

"Last I heard, he's disappeared," said Garthen. "The story going around is that he managed to escape along with King Lewis and that he's in hiding somewhere with the infant monarch. We can all forget about getting paid for this madness. It's all become a complete, runny mess, but at least we've come through with our heads."

Keltin felt a lingering drowsiness begin to grow within him as he struggled to understand everything he was being told.

"What about Baron Rumsfeld?" he asked.

"He's here, actually. He came with the expedition to save you, though I think it was a convenient excuse to make his escape towards the northern border. It would certainly explain why he insisted on bringing his family and possessions along."

Keltin nodded and struggled to keep his eyes open. "I'll want to speak with him before he continues on."

"I'm sure you will," said Jaylocke. "But why don't you get some rest first? Grel'zi'tael says that you'll still need some mending before you are ready to travel."

"Grel'zi'tael is here?"

Jaylocke grinned. "Who do you think's been taking care of you? Get some rest Keltin. Your friends will all be here when you wake up, and Mama Bellin has promised a grand meal for you when you wake up again, short rations or no."

Keltin was about to ask if all the Weycliff were there too, but the question faded away as soft, sweet sleep fell upon him once more.

CHAPTER 24 – END OF THE CAMPAIGN

"I'm tired of lying down," muttered Bor've'tai.

"Can you get up?" Grel'zi'tael asked gently.

The Loopi strained feebly for a moment then collapsed back to his sleeping mat.

"No."

"Then what good does being tired of lying down do you?"

"I'm just glad to see you awake after all this time," said Keltin.

"As am I," said Shar'le'vah softly. "You were so far gone when we first arrived. If grandfather hadn't been with us…"

"It was a close thing," said Grel'zi'tael. "A very close thing."

Bor've'tai said nothing as his eyes stared somewhere beyond those gathered around him. Keltin watched his friend and worried whether any permanent damage may have resulted from his close exposure to the warp beast. Bor've'tai seemed awake and alert, but there was a distance in his eyes that had not been there before. Still, Keltin was sure that Grel'zi'tael was doing all that he could for him and tried his best to emulate the Sky Talker's calm demeanor. At least Bor've'tai was alive.

"Where will you go?" Keltin asked the Sky Talker after a

moment. "Back to Malpin?"

"No, it is no safer in our homeland than it was when we left. I think we will travel to the west."

"To Riltvin?"

"Perhaps. We may continue across the North Sea to Erania. I have heard that many Loopi have made a new home for themselves there."

"Well, you'd all be welcome to travel with me. I'll be cutting across country to make directly for the northern hill country. I'm familiar with the territory, and I thought it best to avoid Carvalen entirely."

"Thank you for your offer, but I think we will remain in Krendaria a bit longer. Bor've'tai will not be able to travel fully for some time, so we will make the journey in small stages."

"What will you do for food?"

"We will survive. We are not without means to provide for ourselves in seemingly barren surroundings. Do not fear for us. We shall continue west by and by."

The sound of footfalls crunching in the snow signaled the approach of one of Baron Rumsfeld's hired guards.

"Mr. Moore, the Baron wants to speak with you."

"All right, I'll be right there." Keltin turned back to Bor've'tai. Placing a gentle hand on the Loopi's shoulder, he drew his friend's attention to him.

"I'll come by again later," he said.

Bor've'tai nodded slowly. Keltin struggled for more words.

"Thank you. You're a good friend to me."

For a moment, Bor've'tai's eyes focused clearly on him.

"As are you," he said before closing his eyes and resting his head back on his rush mat.

Shar'le'vah placed a hand on his gently rising and falling chest as she shared a brave smile with Keltin. Bidding a silent goodbye to Grel'zi'tael and Val'ta'lir, Keltin rose and followed the waiting guard to where the Baron and his family had set up their temporary camp somewhat apart from the former members of the campaign. He recognized several of Rumsfeld's men standing guard around the family carriage and the two wagons filled with their belongings. He half-expected to see Sergeant Bracksten among them, but that was impossible. The imposing sergeant had been the final casualty of the campaign, killed by a lingering fever brought on by an infected bite he'd received from a dying armored leech.

Keltin found Rumsfeld sitting beside his quiet wife and three unhappy looking children. Elaine was with them as well, quietly talking with the Baroness. She gave him a warm smile in greeting before answering a question that the Baroness had asked her. Rumsfeld set aside an empty bowl and rose to his feet.

"Mr. Moore, it's good to see you up and about."

"Thank you. It's good to see you too, despite all that's happened in the capital."

Rumsfeld nodded and gestured for Keltin to join him for a walk. The Baron waited until his family was out of hearing before speaking again.

"It was a close thing," he said. "We received word of the revolution from the farmers and field workers as they came north to recover what they could of their crops. I left the guarding of the harvest to Bracksten and rushed home with my private guards. I got back to Carvalen just as the burning began. I imagine that some parts of the city are still smoking. I barely had time to get my family out, and only managed to save a few of our possessions."

"I'm sorry that we couldn't do more to help you and your countrymen."

The Baron shrugged. "It's true that Krendaria will likely never be the same, but its people will survive the winter. We can all take some comfort in that, at least."

They came to the edge of the desolate farmstead grounds. Keltin looked at the pitiful remains of what had briefly been his home and prison. The farmhouse had collapsed upon itself the day before, as if it had finally let go of its weak hold on life. Perhaps some enterprising soul would restore it, or perhaps it would be demolished and rebuilt. Keltin only hoped it would not remain as it was. The bitter husk of a home. A landmark to the atrocities that had happened here.

"It's very good of you to take Elaine into your protection on your way to Malpin," he said after a moment.

"It's no trouble. I believe my wife needed the companionship. This has all been very hard on her, and having a strong young woman like Miss Elaine along will steady her nerves. And what of you? Where will you go?"

"Home."

"I expect you'll be glad to see it again after all this time."

"Yes. It's likely my room will be rented out to a new tenant by the time I return, but I can always find another. It's my mother and sister that I'm really concerned about. I haven't been able to send any money to them for some time." He shook his head. "Well, I'm alive to send more another day. That's what matters."

"Truly."

The Baron took one more look at the farmhouse before turning back.

"Well, there's no point in staying here. I'll give the order to break camp to my men and servants when we get back. If you wish to say goodbye to Miss Elaine, you should probably do it now."

"I will, thank you."

"Thank *you*, Captain." Rumsfeld gave him a slight smile as they began walking back to camp. "We probably won't see each other again, Mr. Moore, and I wanted to tell you something. I know we haven't always agreed or seen things eye-to-eye, but you have always been a true, dependable man. If I ever seemed to push you or rely on you too much during this campaign, it's because I did. From the day your fool of a corporal died, I followed you as much as you followed me, though I could never let the men know it. You knew how to hunt beasts, and I didn't. Thank you for showing me how to keep my men alive."

Keltin was too startled to answer. He struggled to find words but the Baron waved him off.

"Go speak with Miss Elaine. As I said, we're leaving soon."

Rumsfeld turned and walked away towards one of his wagons. Keltin watched him go a moment, then turned to the campfire. Elaine saw him and excused herself from the Baron's wife. Stopping for a moment at a wagon, she withdrew something from one of her bags and brought it to him. She gave Keltin an apologetic smile as she handed him his grandfather's pistol.

"I'm afraid there aren't many shots left for it," she said.

"I'll manage."

"You're going home then?"

"Yes, there's nothing more for me here."

"I suppose not." Elaine hesitated a moment before continuing. "Mr. Moore…"

"Keltin."

"…Keltin, I'm sorry for the way I treated you the day that you gave me a shooting lesson. It was unfair of me, and you were so patient. Thank you. Thank you for saving me. I owe my life to you."

Keltin didn't know what to say. He struggled for a moment, but Elaine smiled and spoke again.

"I suppose you'll be going home to Riltvin then?"

"Yes, I need to get home and get word to my mother and sister. I know they'll be worried when news of the revolution reaches them."

"I understand. I was hoping that we might be able to correspond once we've both gotten settled."

"I'd like that."

"Good."

Elaine gave him a slip of paper with the location of a post office in Kerrtow, and Keltin hastily scratched out the address of Mr. Jastin's courier office in Gillentown in a small notebook that she carried. He was just handing the book back to her when one of the Baron's men approached Elaine.

"We're about ready to leave, Miss."

"Thank you."

She turned and embraced Keltin fiercely.

"Promise me that you'll write as soon as you're able," she

whispered in his ear.

"I promise."

He felt the feathery touch of a kiss on his cheek and then she was gone, quickly disappearing into the Baron's waiting carriage. The driver shook the reins and started the small caravan moving. Keltin watched them roll away until the last wagon had disappeared among the snow laden trees.

"I half-expected you to go with her."

Keltin turned to see Jaylocke watching him from where he leaned against a nearby tree.

"She was just saying goodbye."

"I saw. Would that we all received such nice partings from good friends."

"And what about you? Where's Ameldi?"

"She's with Evik and the others. We've just had a family council, and I wanted to speak with you about it."

"With me?"

"Yes."

Jaylocke's expression turned somber.

"Keltin, I've come to consider you a good friend in the brief time that I've known you. I wanted to thank you for all the times that you've saved my hide."

"You've saved me plenty of times as well, you know."

"Oh don't worry, I know." Jaylocke grinned a moment before growing serious again. "But I want you to know how much I appreciate the way you've stuck with me even as I grew less... useful to you."

"You mean the way that it's becoming harder to draw on the help of your ancestors?"

Jaylocke nodded. "I can't deny it any longer. I've nearly lost my connection with my forebears completely. It's my own fault. I've been too lax, too complacent. The family has discussed it, and they've agreed that it's time that I finally begin atoning for my mistakes."

"How are you supposed to do that?"

"Remember what I told you about each member of the family learning a unique skill to add to the family knowledge?

It's been decided that it's time for me to learn a trade, for the good of the family, and to heal my connection with my ancestors."

"What trade will you learn?"

"Beast hunting."

"You've already done a fair bit of that."

"No, not really. I've been fighting monsters, yes, and I've done a fair share of supporting the real hunters. But I need to learn how to be a true hunter, how to track, how to stalk, how to shoot." He looked off into the woods in the direction of the ruined farmhouse. "It's not just for my family, either. I want to learn this for myself. I've seen the good that you beast hunters can do, and the desperate need for your trade. I want to learn how to hunt beasts, and I want to learn from the best."

Jaylocke took a breath and turned back to Keltin. "Will you take me on as an apprentice, Keltin? I have no skills to draw on but my own now, but I'm a swift study and a dedicated student when I want to be, and I desperately want to be. I'll follow your lead, go wherever you tell me to, do whatever you say I should. I put my education and life in your hands, if you'll take me."

Keltin was stunned. He tried to think through all the consequences of what Jaylocke was proposing. He'd never even considered taking on an apprentice before. Jaylocke waited patiently as he tried to put his thoughts together.

"Jaylocke, I'm flattered, but I don't know if beast hunting is really the best choice for you. You've seen how dangerous it can be. Besides, being a hunter isn't like being a blacksmith or a tanner. There's no guild or master's license for you to earn. How would you even know when you're done?"

"Many of the skills learned by my people are not formal trades. Weycliff tradition only states that the task is complete when I have enough knowledge and experience to teach another. When you feel that I know enough to instruct another in all the ways of beast hunting, my task will be finished."

"But what about Ameldi? Who knows how long it will take to learn everything there is to know about beast hunting? Do you really want to be separated from her for so long?"

Jaylocke took a deep breath. "Keltin, you must understand. Ameldi and I care deeply for each other, but until I do this, the traditions of our family state that we cannot marry. Without my own trade, I am still considered a child by my people, and unable to take a wife. If I ever want a future with her, then I must do this, now. Will you take me?"

Keltin sighed and tried to think. He thought of hunting alone. He thought of the peace and the solitude he'd found by himself in the hills of Riltvin. It had been his whole life until now. Then again, now he knew what it was like to not be alone. To be able to sleep at night, knowing that he could trust another to watch over him. To work together with others, saving lives and doing more good than he could have ever done by himself. Keltin looked at Jaylocke, and gave him a slow grin.

"On one condition."

"Name it."

"If you ever make me green meal for breakfast, I'll make you act the part of beast bait for a week."

Jaylocke returned the grin.

"I can live with that."

They shook on it, and Keltin wondered just what he was getting himself into, but found himself looking forward to it.

"Shall we go tell the others?" asked Jaylocke.

Keltin nodded and they set off together for the Weycliff wagon circle. They had just spied the painted canvas of the wagons through the trees when Maynid intercepted them.

"Have you spoken then?" he asked.

Jaylocke nodded. "It's all agreed. We'll be heading out as soon as Keltin says."

The youth gave him a broad smile. "Evik and Ameldi will be happy to hear it. Maybe you can teach me how to hunt beasts when you get back."

"It could be some time before I'm done Maynid. You may want to pick something else rather than waiting. I can tell you from experience, it's not worth putting off."

The youth shrugged and turned to Keltin.

"I was supposed to give you this," he said, offering him a lumpy sack from off his shoulder.

Keltin took it uncertainly. "What is it?"

"I don't know. The Baron wanted you to have it. He said it was rattling all the way up from Carvalen and he wanted to get rid of it."

Keltin opened the bag and gasped. A set of candlesticks rested atop what looked like a complete dining set, all of it silver. Jaylocke looked over his shoulder and gave a low whistle.

"If it were me, I think I could have endured the rattling," he murmured.

Keltin looked uncertainly at Maynid. "But… why?"

The youth gave him an equally confused look. "I don't know, he didn't say. He called me over and gave me the bag as I was starting to do the lunch wash-up. It was odd though. He insisted that I finish my washing before I brought the bag to you. "

Jaylocke chuckled. "Gave himself enough time for a clean getaway. Crafty to the last."

Keltin could only nod. He examined the contents of the bag for a few moments more, then closed it up.

"Maynid, could you run and fetch Grel'zi'tael and the other hunters? I think it'd be best if we were all gathered together to divide the Baron's parting gift among us."

The youth nodded and dashed away. Jaylocke patted Keltin's shoulder.

"You're a good man, Keltin Moore. You didn't have to share the Baron's gift."

"It's the right thing to do, Jaylocke."

"I agree. Maybe that's the reason why the Baron gave it to you."

"Maybe. But let's divide it up quickly. I'd like to still have some daylight left before we leave."

"Where are we off to?"

Keltin smiled. "Home, Jaylocke. We're going home."

ABOUT THE AUTHOR

Lindsay Schopfer is the author of *The Adventures of Keltin Moore*, a series of steampunk-flavored fantasy novels about a professional monster hunter. He also wrote the sci-fi survivalist novel *Lost Under Two Moons* and the fantasy short story collection *Magic, Mystery and Mirth*. His short fiction has appeared in *Merely This and Nothing More: Poe Goes Punk* from Writerpunk Press and *Unnatural Dragons* from Clockwork Dragon. When he isn't writing, Lindsay is an online instructor for Adventures In Writing, where he helps writers learn about and improve their craft. His workshops and panels have been featured in a variety of Cons and writing conferences across the Pacific Northwest and beyond. He is also a volunteer mentor for Educurious, a Gates Foundation-funded program designed to connect high school students with professional writers.

www.lindsayschopfer.com

Made in the USA
Lexington, KY
24 March 2017